TAOS LIGHTNING

Center Point
Large Print

Also by Johnny D. Boggs and available from Center Point Large Print:

And There I'll Be a Soldier
Top Soldier
Return to Red River
Wreaths of Glory
The Raven's Honor
Poison Spring

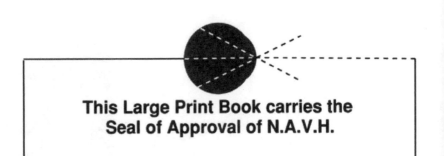

**This Large Print Book carries the
Seal of Approval of N.A.V.H.**

TAOS LIGHTNING

Johnny D. Boggs

CENTER POINT LARGE PRINT
THORNDIKE, MAINE

WESTERN
BOG

This Circle Ⓥ Western is published by
Center Point Large Print in the year 2018 in
co-operation with Golden West Literary Agency.

Copyright © 2018 by Johnny D. Boggs.

First Edition
June 2018

Printed in the United States of America
on permanent paper.
Set in 16-point Times New Roman type.

ISBN: 978-1-68324-827-9

Library of Congress Cataloging-in-Publication Data

Names: Boggs, Johnny D., author.
Title: Taos lightning : Circle V western / Johnny D. Boggs.
Description: First edition. | Thorndike, Maine :
    Center Point Large Print, 2018.
Identifiers: LCCN 2018006758 | ISBN 9781683248279
    (hardcover : alk. paper)
Subjects: LCSH: Large type books. | GSAFD: Western stories.
Classification: LCC PS3552.O4375 T36 2018 | DDC 813/.54—dc23
LC record available at https://lccn.loc.gov/2018006758

For the horses that have tossed me:
Dolly, Jack, Chuck, and Honey

CHAPTER ONE

Even before I'm screaming, I'm running, seeing everything, while praying that I'm dreaming. But this ain't no dream. Pa slams against a post in this big barn, he spins around, and he falls real hard on a bucket of oats. The barn's full of folks, and strangers are racing toward Pa, who rolls off that bucket and lands on the floor.

Now, Pa ain't moving.

I ain't either. On account I slide to a stop when I see something that nobody else here needs to find, so I kick it underneath some hay. Then I hurry over to Pa, only I can't see him.

The horse that just kicked Pa is snorting and pulling against the rope, but this odd-looking black man has gotten inside the stall—don't know how he managed that, or why any sane person would even attempt such a thing, not the way that stallion's kicking—but that fellow ain't cussing the horse at all. Not like I'd be doing. Not like Pa would, neither. By thunder, I can't hear too good on account it seems that everybody in this building's shouting. That's on top of the rain, which has been pelting the roof since daybreak. Yet it sure sounds like the black fellow's singing to that half tame horse.

I want to kill that ornery stallion, but Pa's my first concern.

"Let me through," I say, but folks here in Texas don't listen to no kid. Every ink-slinger and stable-cleaner and trainer and jockey and even a couple of girls have gathered around Pa. "Let me through!" Mad now, I shove my way through shoulders, plant an elbow in one fat gent's ribs, even crawl under a pair of bowed legs. Pa's always joking that a raven's feather weighs more than I do, and that I can hide by turning sideways.

Back on my feet, I bark: "That's my pa!" Somebody must hear, because the wool and denim britches and the yellow slickers part. I slip through.

Seeing Pa at last, I feel like that fool stallion just kicked *me* in the gut.

I've seen my share of horse wrecks, but nothing this bad. A bone's poking through Pa's shirt sleeve, and blood's pooling around him. Pa ain't dead, his eyes keep blinking, but he ain't saying nothing, and this tall dude in a fancy black coat is wrapping a bandanna above that busted bone in Pa's right arm.

"He's in shock," somebody whispers.

"Is he dying?" . . . *"What happened?"* . . . *"Did you see that?"* . . . *"Goodness gracious!"* . . . *"This ain't no sight for a girl, little lady. Best move away."*

I hear these comments. I hear the rain. Don't

hear that black guy singing; the stallion must not be kicking no more.

The man in that black coat looks up at me. He's an old dude, with the starkest blue eyes I ever seen. His voice is pure Texas: "Are you this man's son?"

I wet my lips, try to speak, but can't do nothing more than nod.

"Come here."

Must've obeyed, though I don't remember moving, 'cause I'm kneeling in hay and spilled oats. Pa hit that bucket hard, and my pa, who's rail-thin like me, ain't no match for a bucket of any kind. The man in the black coat is a doc, and he's working his fingers over Pa's ribs now that he's got the bleeding under control.

He says something, but I just stare at him.

"What's your name?" the sawbones drawls again. This time I hear him.

"Evan," I tell him at last. "Evan Kendrick."

"Evan, I am Patrick Jack. And your father's name?"

I have to think about that. The doc, he don't make fun of me or even ask me again. Just waits. At length, I tell him: "Ed. Edward Kendrick."

"Where you from, Evan?"

"New Mexico," I tell him. "Between Las Vegas and Fort Union."

"Are you riding, or is he?" The doc nods at Pa.

He means riding in the race. This race that got

9

Pa all worked up and why we've come better than eight hundred miles to Galveston. So Pa can ride a horse almost two thousand more miles.

"He is," I say.

"He *was*," the doctor corrects.

"The hell I ain't." Well, Pa ain't in shock no more. He's trying to sit up and blaspheming at the doctor and me. The tall doc leans over and forces Pa back onto the carpet of hay, dust, and horse apples.

"Mister Kendrick." The doc don't even raise his tone. He's calm and steady, but his quiet voice sounds firm. "Don't move. You have at least three broken ribs, and you don't want one of those puncturing your lung, sir. Possibly even your heart. And your arm . . . well . . . just lie still."

Pa ain't never been one to listen to nobody but hisself, but he has worn hisself out. His head sinks back.

"We need to get him to Saint Mary's," the doc tells some folks behind me. His calm eyes find me again. "Is your mother here, Evan?"

That numbs me. My fingers clench. I can't answer. Only shake my head.

"Brothers? An assistant?"

"I . . ." I catch my breath. "Reckon I'm his assistant." That must be why Pa brung me all this way.

"No family here? No friends?"

"We ain't never been out of New Mexico till now," I say. "Least, I ain't."

"All right." When the doc stands, golly, it strikes me just how tall he is. He ain't scrawny like me and Pa, but solid. Must be six-foot-four. "He is registered in the race, isn't he?" the doc asks.

"Yeah." I tell him, but I'm thinking: *I mean, I hope he is. I filled out the entry form for him. He said he was going to mail it, but Pa says lots of things that ain't exactly gospel, even when he's sober.* Them thoughts I keep to myself. Because that bone's still sticking out of Pa's arm, and I ain't savvy enough to doctor that kind of wound.

"I'm racing," Pa tells the doc, and offers some of his choicest cuss words to confirm that statement, but the doc don't look Pa's way again.

"Damned bad luck," the doc says, staring toward the stall where, I reckon, that black fellow's still tending to that chuckle-headed stallion.

"Yeah." My mouth tastes like gall as I'm looking down at pa. "Bad luck."

"Fifty, sixty, maybe seventy horses in this barn," I whisper to Pa, but he can't hear nothing. "And you walk behind *ours*."

CHAPTER TWO

This is what brung us out of New Mexico Territory all the way to Galveston Island, south of Houston in the Gulf of Mexico.

<u>THE</u>
GREATEST HORSE RACE
IN THE HISTORY
<u>OF THE WORLD</u>
$3,000 TO THE VICTOR!
All Riders! All Breeds of Horses!
<u>1,800 MILES</u>
10 HOURS A DAY MAXIMUM
A test of endurance of rider and horse
Entry fee $10
Apply to
Richard K. Fox,
National Police Gazette,
Gazette Publishing House,
Franklin Square,
New York City
<u>Details to be provided</u>
<u>upon receipt of funds for entry fee</u>

I fold up the little advertisement that has been fingered over so much, it's almost impossible to read after traveling eight hundred miles in Pa's trousers pocket.

Where Pa got the ten bucks to enter this horse race, I got no notion. By thunder, I don't know how he found the two nickels to pick up the *Illustrated Day's Doings and Sporting World*, which was published by the same folks who put out the *National Police Gazette*. Then again, knowing Pa the way I do, he likely stole the magazine.

It's dark now. Must be past two in the morn, and that stallion kicked Pa sometime shortly before noon. I'm sitting with him in this room at St. Mary's Hospital. It's a big building, three stories high. You don't see no building this tall in New Mexico that ain't a church, I can tell you that. This is a Catholic hospital, but all the nuns I've been dodging for several hours ain't like the sisters I've seen back home. Well, they dress the same, but they don't talk in Mexican or English. French, maybe, but can't be certain sure. The rain appears to have stopped, but from what I've heard, whilst hiding in closets and in other rooms and wandering the halls and stairwells, folks around here are expecting a real frog-strangler of a storm. Golly, I've seen more rain this whole day than I've seen in two years along the Río Sappello.

"Evan."

The voice, hardly a whisper, don't even sound like Pa's. Startles me so much I'm about to blow out the candle, since I ain't supposed to be in Pa's room.

Pushing myself off this little stool by the table, I swallow down my fear as I approach the bed.

Pa has tossed off the quilt, and the candle's flame provides enough light that I can see him scratching, just scratching, and that's enough to break my heart. Because he's scratching the bed sheet, but I guess he thinks he's working on his right arm.

Only . . . there ain't no right arm no more, at least, not below Pa's elbow. Just a bunch of bandages that, from the looks, will need changing directly.

Pa turns his head toward me.

The pill-rollers and the nuns have given Pa plenty of laudanum, but I see the pain in his face and know them drugs has worn off. Pa's sober. And he's serious.

"I ain't ridin' in that race, am I, Son?"

I give him a smile, though I ain't sure he sees it. My head shakes. "No, sir," I tell him. I try to think of something else to say, but at the same time I'm also listening hard for the sound of some approaching doctor or nurse. Not that I'd have anywhere to hide. Ain't no window I could jump out of, which I couldn't do anyway 'cause we're on the third floor.

"Danged arm itches something fierce," Pa says, and I have to look away. I've been telling myself that I won't cry, but that's a right hard promise to live up to.

"Evan," Pa says.

Steeling myself, I turn back and look down on my daddy.

"You gots to take my place, boy," Pa says.

I just stare at him.

"You hear me?"

Oh, I hear him all right, but I'm trying to think where he got the whiskey. That's as fool a notion as Pa has had since he found that advertisement and brought home the copy of the *Illustrated Day's Doings and Sporting World* and started working harder on that ornery mustang that has caused my most recent heartache.

"I can't . . ." I don't finish. Pa won't let me.

"You know horses as good as me, boy. 'Sides, you rode that piece of glue-bait alongside me and that rank stallion all the way here. If them miles and that saddle and that mare's back-jarring gait didn't toughen you up for this race, ain't nothing ever going to."

"Pa . . ."

"You got to race, boy. If you don't, I will."

I see fire in his eyes, but it ain't the candle's reflection. It's that fire roaring up in his belly. It makes him sound like something straight out of a penny dreadful. I try to reason with my father.

"Pa, all we're out right now is . . ." And I'm staring at the bandage where Pa's right arm ends. I have to pause, gather my thoughts, and suck in a bunch of the hospital's stinking, damp air. I swallow down bile. I study the light that creeps through the bottom of the doorway. I make myself keep talking.

"All we're out right now is ten dollars . . . and six weeks on the trail here. When you're up and ready in a few days, we'll ride back home."

Pa don't say nothing. I think maybe he's gone back to sleep, but his eyes are open, and his hard gaze is locked on me. But it's different now. It's real dark, even in the candlelight, but it appears that Pa's crying. His lips move a number of times before he summons up the words.

"Evan . . . if you don't make that ride . . . if you don't win that race . . . we ain't got no home to go back to."

I keep looking at Pa, but he turns away. The words echo in my head.

Evan . . . if you don't make that ride . . . if you don't win that race . . . we ain't got no home to go back to . . . we ain't got no home to go back to . . . we ain't got no home to go back to.

Like some bad dream.

I feel like I'm the one that's been kicked in the gut by that fool stallion. Blood rushes to my head. I circle around the bed and look down on the little figure that is my father.

"What did you do?" I ask. But I know the answer.

He turns over again, I move back around, and this time I lean in close. I space my words carefully. "What . . . did . . . you . . . do?"

"I bet Chudacoff," Pa answers.

Chudacoff. I feel sicker than a dog. Chudacoff owns the store and saloon in what passes for a town near our place.

"You bet what?"

He sighs. At length, he says: "Our place."

Which I already figured.

"How drunk were you?"

Ain't a nice thing to say. I don't mean it to be. I stare down on this bony cuss with beard stubble. He's puny, he's sick, he's got three busted ribs. Worser, he's got a stump where his right arm ought to be. It's all I can do not to reach down and wring this walking whiskey vat's neck. Instead, I turn around and fire off a few choice words I've learned from Pa.

I know why Ma left. I shake my head, thinking: *Why, Ma, didn't you take me with you?*

"Taos Lightning can win, Evan," Pa's saying. "I know horses, boy. That stallion's got what it takes. But you got to ride him. I . . . can't."

"He's a mustang, Pa!" I'm screaming. "Fourteen hands . . . maybe. Eight hundred pounds . . . maybe. And seven years old, I'd guess . . . by his teeth." All the while I'm remembering how I've had to carry Pa home after he had passed out. How I've had to mop up his vomit. How I had to throw a blanket on him while he was sleeping off a bender. How I had to fend for myself, cook my own breakfast, make myself go to the schoolhouse whenever I could sneak off.

"And nothing but heart, desire, and endurance," Pa says, sounding half sober. "I know he can win this race, Evan."

"You *know?* Pa, you're the one that told me that a horse ain't good for nothing. Any horse. Horses are stupid. You ride one to death, you get another and do the same. One horse ain't no better than another. All of them belong at some glue factory. That's what you've told me."

"But . . ."

"Did you look around that mansion of a barn we were in when that stallion . . . our stallion . . . that idiotic numbskull, Taos Lightning, tore off your arm? By thunder, I thought maybe he had knocked some sense into you!"

The door opens. Light shines in from the hallway, hurting my eyes. I hear voices, prayers being said, and footsteps. But I don't care.

"Did you see the horses in that barn? Horses we'd have to beat? Quarter-horses. Morgans. Thoroughbreds. Arabs. Andalusians. That horse . . . *our* mustang . . . doesn't have a chance. Eighteen hundred miles?"

A hand clasps my right shoulder. I jerk away.

"You told me you'd never bet on any horse in any race because anything can happen. How could you've been so foolish? Betting . . ."

The hand's back on my shoulder, tighter this time, but it ain't there for long.

"Betting Chudacoff? Betting our place? My home? You never answered me, Pa. How drunk were you?" I'm moving in closer to him, but this time more than one hand grabs me. Off balance, I'm pulled away, stumble back against the wall so hard a crucifix falls to the floor.

Others are in the room, and someone's praying in that strange tongue, which I reckon's French. I want to get to Pa. I aim to strangle him.

"Get out of here," the doctor says.

'Course I can't savvy nothing that the nun's praying, but I sure hear what everybody else is yelling.

"You shouldn't be in here." . . . "How did this boy get in here anyhow?" . . . "I don't know, Doctor." . . . "Sister Elaine, bring laudanum." . . . "Leave my boy alone. He's got every right . . ." . . . "Fletcher, fresh bandages. Now!" . . . "Rest easy, Mister Kendrick. Rest easy." . . . "Move, boy. Move or you'll be a patient here, too. . . . "Go . . . go now . . . or we shall call the police!" . . . "Amen."

I'm shoved through the door. Two burly men and a nun twice my size follow me to the staircase, down the well, and make sure I'm out of the hospital. Head down, I walk away, through puddles and streams flowing down the streets.

20

CHAPTER THREE

Don't ask me how I found the stables again. I'm across the street, just staring. The big door is closed, and four large men stand in front of it. These dudes look a lot meaner than the two city policemen who told me to get off the streets. But it ain't like I got anywhere else to go in Galveston. Pa never got us a hotel room. Maybe he figured to sleep in the stall with Taos Lightning. No, that ain't what Pa would have planned. Ain't it at all. Maybe I'd be sleeping in the stall with that ornery mustang, but Pa? He'd be in the nearest grog shop.

Quit stalling. Move, I tell myself. Then I'm walking ahead in my water-logged boots. Dawn can't be far away, but it's likely warmer and drier inside Edgar's Lone Star Stables.

The burly men pitch their smokes, grinding their heels on the butts, though the water would've put out the cigarettes the second they touched the cobblestones. One of the men waves one of those Chicago nightsticks at me.

"What's your business here, boy?"

"I'm in the race," I say.

The one with the thick mustache laughs.

"And your name?" asks the one with the nightstick. He sounds Irish.

"Evan Kendrick," I tell him.

"Kendrick," says the smallest of the guards, though he ain't small at all. "Isn't he the one who got his arm mangled?"

"Yeah," I say.

"Your arm looks fit as a fiddle," the Irishman says. He hasn't lowered that nightstick.

I turn my face away from him, recalling Pa's stump of an arm. Finally, somehow, I find enough breath and voice to tell these fools that the man with his arm torn up is my father.

For a while, they don't say a word.

Finally, the smallest one says: "Let him in, O'Rourke."

"What if . . . ?" the Irishman counters.

"Look at him, Jimmy. He's not big or old enough to hurt a fly. And a Shetland pony would be too much horse for him."

No one laughs. I don't have to bite my tongue. I left all my anger back on the third floor of St. Mary's Hospital.

The one who hasn't said a word shifts and slides open the door.

I step into the warmth and the scents that once soothed me—horses and hay. The door shuts. I let out a long sigh.

I'm reminded of the stables and corrals at Fort Union. That's where me and Pa would take most of the mustangs we rounded up. We'd break them ourselves . . . though they were all pretty green when we sold them to the Army. For a spell, that had been a right good business. But finding horses got harder and harder, and Pa couldn't sit any of those we did catch long enough to pass even the sergeant's muster. Besides, years back, Fort Union had been a major post, always bustling with men and horses, but lately, with most Indians dead or defeated, and the Army getting smaller and smaller, well, the market for half broke mustangs all but dried up and blowed away.

Inside this massive barn, guards keep an eye on me, but none says a word. I move down the aisle and spy a few men sleeping in stalls. Others are already awake. Coffee's cooking somewhere.

Finally, I stop. I see the bucket that smashed Pa's ribs has been moved. The quirt Pa had been using hangs on a nail outside the stall. Taos Lightning is inside, sleeping. He looks so blessed peaceful and contented.

Which he sure as blazes ain't.

Grabbing the handle of the quirt, I feel that anger rising in me, that hatred, and I want to whip that mustang for all he's worth. Which ain't much. Instead, I suck in a deep breath, hold it, and finally let it out. I hang the quirt back on the nail.

"I'm glad that you don't fancy that quirt," a voice says behind me.

It's that lean, wiry black cuss. The one who had

somehow managed to get hisself into the stall, grab the rope, and sing some song that calmed Taos Lightning.

I can see him clearly now as lanterns get turned up. Horses are awakening, peeing, doing their business. Doors and windows open. It must be daybreak.

"Thanks," I tell the man who's blacker than the ace of spades. That causes him to take a step back, like he ain't never been thanked before. "For helping calm him down." I jerk my thumb back at the mustang.

He sizes me up. I let him, because it gives me a chance to stare right back at him. I admit I ain't never seen many coloreds out in New Mexico, but this fellow, he don't look nothing at all like those I have seen.

His hair is close-cropped, and he has beard stubble down his cheeks and across his chin. A long earring dangles from his left lobe, and he wears something that's a cross between a blanket and shirt, with not much in the way of sleeves. A sash, decorated with pins and things, crosses over his right shoulder and disappears around his left hip. His pants are buckskin. On his feet are moccasins. And pinned in the center of the crown of that big hat he wears are the crossed swords I've seen on the hats of the troopers at Fort Union.

"Hey!"

We both turn. If this black gent looks strange to me, the newcomer causes me to open my mouth.

"How's your pa?"

I ain't seen many Negros in my life, but I have seen girls. This one, though, is mighty different. She wears pants and boots, and she must've been sleeping in the barn, too, because hay is stuck here and there in her unmentionables that she's brazenly displaying above her waist. She's wiping her face with a bandanna, and then she's pulling this calico shirt over her person. She tugs out the tied knot of the bandanna so that it sticks out from the unbuttoned part of her shirt. She grabs a hat that was leaning on a corner post, shakes out her yellow hair, and pulls that hat—it's filthier than mine—low and tight on her head.

"I asked you how is your pa," she repeats.

I shrug.

"He gonna be able to race?" she asks.

My head shakes.

"That's bad news." It's the black man who says this, and I make myself look away from the girl.

"Good news, you mean," the girl says. "For you, I mean. One less horse and rider you have to beat."

"You, too, Miss Arena," the black man says.

"Nah." The girl walks over to me. "I had him beat already." She stops and peers into the stall where Taos Lightning laps up water like a parched hound. "The old man, I mean. The

25

horse . . ."—she looks back at me—"I don't know."

She reaches behind her and pulls something from the back pocket of her pants. Then she's holding the bottle out to me.

"It's yours," she tells me. "Your pa's, I mean. I saw you kick it when all the commotion commenced. Lot of it spilled. I didn't drink none of it . . . well, no more than a swallow. I swear. And that mustang didn't give your pa no chance to cork it."

It's the bottle of forty-rod. Ain't but a few fingers left.

"Didn't give your pa no chance to use that quirt on him, neither," says the black man, causing my hands to ball into fists, and I step toward him, but the girl stops me.

"You want this bracer, boy, or not?"

I make myself look back at her. "No," I tell her.

"Do you mind?" She holds up the bottle. There's a gleam in her eye. I shake my head, and she lifts the bottle to her lips, tilts back her head, and me and the Negro watch the whiskey disappear.

"Ahhhh," she's saying as she looks at the bottle, now empty, and tosses it into a wheelbarrow that is partly filled with horse apples and trash. Her eyes—they're blue—ain't even watering none, and whatever Pa could afford in a city like Galveston would've gone down like coal oil seasoned with rattlesnake heads.

"You gonna drink yourself to death, Miss Arena," the black man tells her.

"I'll still outlive you, Dindie Remo."

I've had enough of this crazy-outfitted black dude and this girl who dresses and drinks like a man. I move to the stall and look at the ornery mustang.

But the two can't take no hint. The girl shows up on my left. I smell the whiskey on her breath. The black man steps to my right. He stinks of sweat and horseflesh and other odors I can't rightly make out.

"What's his name?" the girl called Arena asks.

I don't feel like answering, but I do. "Taos Lightning."

The girl cackles, and hiccups. Pa's whiskey, she's learning, ain't for the faint-hearted. Must've gone straight to her head, not that she ever had no brains to begin with.

"So he's fast as lightning, is he? Taos? That some kind of Roman god?"

I shake my head. This girl's dumber than me.

"No," I tell her.

The black man—Dimdee or Dindie or Dandy or whatever that girl called him—starts to say something, but he stops, purses his lips, and looks at the horse. *My* horse.

"It was what they called whiskey. Mountain

men. Up in Taos." I don't know why I'm talking to these folks, giving them a lesson.

"North of Santa Fe," says the black man, who knows more than the girl.

"Uhn-huh." And I could let it go at that, but now my mouth won't stop. "In New Mexico Territory. That's where I . . . we . . . come from. Anyway, that's where Taos Lightning got its name. Taos, I guess 'cause that's where they brewed it. Lightning . . . I reckon . . . because if you took a swallow, you'd feel like you got struck by lightning."

"Uhn-huh," the black man says. "Like forty-rod. Take a sip, and you run forty rods."

"So your pa named the horse that," the girl says, "because he can run like lightning. Maybe farther than forty rods, though."

"No." I don't want to say what I'm about to say, but can't stop myself. "That mustang's the color of Taos Lightning. And that's one thing my pa would know."

Staring at the mustang, my mustang, Taos Lightning don't look so ornery now. Wearing a sleepy look, ears flopped to either side, he just stands there, waiting to be fed. I wouldn't have called him pretty. To me, he ain't nothing more than another rangy little mustang, worth ten dollars, about four times less than a good saddle.

Taos Lightning's what most folks would call a liver chestnut, and Pa says that any chestnut horse has got one hot temper. Bays and browns are horses you can depend on, he says, at least as well as you can depend on any dumb animal. Which makes me wonder why Pa would enter a liver chestnut in an eighteen-hundred-mile race.

A thin stripe runs down Taos Lightning's face, and he has four short socks. Which reminds me of something else Pa's always reminding me: *Don't ever buy no horse with four white feet.*

By thunder, I'm thinking with bitterness for about the millionth time, *how drunk was you, Pa, to enter this horse in this race?*

Taos Lightning needs a good brushing, and I should've cleaned his hoofs yesterday, but Pa's busted arm and that black-coated doc and them nuns and folks at the hospital pretty much kept my day filled.

The stallion is lean. His legs are hard. So are his feet. Ain't much more to say about Taos Lightning. Except this: He ain't got a chance to win this race.

"Good hoss," the black stranger's saying. "Mighty good."

"He's a beaut'," the girl adds.

I turn and stare at him, then the girl. I'm trying to see if they're joshing me, but if they are, they're good at hiding the joke they're playing.

I say: "My name's Evan Kendrick."

The big man turns, nods. "Dindie Remo." We shake hands.

"I'm Arena Lancaster," the girl says. "Nice to meet you, Evan Kendrick." She does this little curtsey thing, and I figure she is playing me for a fool. Till she asks: "You had breakfast?"

I shake my head.

Dindie Remo says: "They's supposed to be feeding us at the hotel across the street." He frowns. "Not sure if they mean me, though. My kind."

"You're in this race," Arena Lancaster says. "I guess that means they got to feed you, too."

He don't look so confident, but something else is on my mind.

"What makes you think Taos Lightning's something special?" I ask.

Remo looks down on me. His eyes practically burn through me. "Horse like that, Evan Kendrick," Remo tells me, "will carry you anywhere you want to go. As long as you treat him right."

I try to comprehend that. But Dindie Remo, he ain't done. He adds: " 'Course, you wouldn't know about that. A quirt leaves a mark on a horse."

My muscles stiffen, and I come close to balling my fists. Arena Lancaster must have sensed what I was feeling, and she says that it's too early in the morning for fisticuffs and that she's hungry and it might be the only free breakfast we get.

The black man don't move, just stares down at

me, and it strikes me that Dindie Remo is right. I've lost track of all the times Pa laid that quirt on Taos Lightning's back.

"I'm hungry, fellows." Blonde-haired Arena sounds impatient.

"I need to give Taos Lightning his breakfast." I can't quite believe I'm hearing these words come out of my mouth, but there they are. "And clean his hoofs."

The girl stamps one of her boots, but I'm already walking into the stall.

Dindie Remo says: "You'd best grain and water that pretty little palomino of yours, Miss Arena."

"Yeah, and I suppose you already fed and watered . . . maybe even groomed that piece of glue-bait you ride, Dindie Remo," she barks right back at him.

The big man chuckles. "Yes, ma'am. Indeed I have. But don't y'all worry. I'll wait whilst you finish your chores."

CHAPTER FOUR

Remo's standing, puffing on a corncob pipe, when I leave Taos Lightning. He removes the pipe, and nods his approval. I don't exactly know where the girl's stall is, but I figure if we ain't moving for that restaurant now, she must still be working on her horse.

"You know horses," Remo says before returning the pipe between his teeth.

I shrug.

That pretty much ends our conversation, because I've never been one to talk much to strangers. Especially when I have to start the talking. So I shift my weight while looking around for the girl. And I see all kinds of riders. All kinds of horses. Some men in sack suits busy themselves by talking to folks and scribbling in notepads. Newspaper reporters, I warrant. Another fellow, wearing a straw hat with a flat brim, is sketching a picture of this man wearing a big cowboy hat and sitting in the saddle on a bay cow pony.

Staring again at Dindie Remo and his pipe, I make myself say: "Mind if I ask you a question?"

The pipe comes out of his mouth, and Remo studies me. "Ask. Might not answer. But you can ask."

I think about forgetting it, but something about the way he looks at you makes you want to know him. "What . . . ?" I stop. It's a danged silly question. "What kind of name is Dindie Remo?"

He grins. "It's the kind of name that my ma and pa laid on me." He must have smoked out his pipe, because he turns it over and taps it against a post top. "Negro-Seminole." After feeling the bowl with his thumb, he slips the pipe into a pocket.

I don't know exactly what a Negro-Seminole is, or means, but that girl, Arena Lancaster, runs up to us.

"Good," she says. "You didn't leave me. Come on. I'm practically starved."

Much to Arena's displeasure, we don't hurry out of the big barn. We stop at stalls to admire some horses, eye the riders. Others we barely give a glance. Some are impossible even to peek at because ink-scribblers, businessmen, or fancy folks block our view.

We see Kentucky thoroughbreds and Irish hunters. One rider, a little bitty man who makes me look like a lumberjack, says his horse is a cross-country runner from France. I'll have to take his word on that.

A big man with silver-white hair and dressed in his Sunday-go-to-meetings is saying that his horse has the best blood of any animal in this entire barn. The horse, Robb Arthur, was sired by Slender Stanley, whose sire was none other than Braggadocio, and that means something to anyone who knows horses. And the dam was from Denton County's legendary Mayflower. I reckon I don't know a thing about horses, because I've never heard of Robb Arthur, Slender Stanley, or Braggadocio. The only Mayflower I'm aware of is the boat that hauled Pilgrims across the Atlantic. Never heard of Denton County, neither. As we walk away, the silver-haired man starts talking to a newspaper man about his rider. How he has won match races and prized purses and weighs one hundred thirty pounds and knows when to use the whip and when to give the horse all the rein he wants.

Ahead, two cowboys are leaning against a stall, wearing big Texas hats and giant rowels on their spurs. One is smoking a cigarette while the other chews tobacco, and both are laughing.

"Hey, Sultan!" the one with the cigarette says to whoever is in the stall, and then he pokes the tobacco-chewer's arm.

"That ain't no sultan," the other Texan says, "it's Sinbad."

"Nah," says the first. "Sinbad was a sailor."

"That's his boat."

They laugh again.

When we're in range of seeing the man in the stall, who ignores them and keeps his attention on the horse, I understand what the Texans are doing. They're funning this guy because of how he dresses. I've only seen the kind of clothes he wears in storybooks and maybe a *Frank Leslie's* or a *Harper's*. What you'd see in one of those *Arabian Nights* kind of stories. A white sheet like a veil over the man's head, a black band around his head, tying it on. And a fancy robe—this one navy blue with some gold trim. He has a dark mustache and beard.

I give this dark-skinned Arab nothing more than a glance. It's the horse that catches my fancy for the second time. I'd seen the big gray the day before, after me and Pa had arrived at the barn, when I was searching for the privy. The rider, or owner, or whoever he is, hadn't been in the stall then. I just saw the horse.

Fifteen hands, with a peaked neck and shoulders that sweep down and are long. His back's short, his girth deep. I love how an Arabian horse carries his tail, arched high like he knows he's beautiful and powerful and that no horse can ever be his equal. This big gray sure puts Taos Lightning to shame.

"Hey." The tobacco-chewer has spotted us. He elbows his pard, who turns and laughs as he sees us. Actually, it turns out that both of them are laughing at Dindie Remo.

"Which one you think is darker?" the smoker cowboy says after he grinds out his cigarette on the barn floor with a boot heel. "The darky or the Arab sheik?"

The other one spits tobacco juice, and says: "You entered this race, Remo?"

I guess Dindie Remo nods, but I'm too busy staring at them two Texas blowhards.

"Do the boys at Fort Clark know you've done stole one of their Army mounts?" the chewer asks.

"I'm done scouting for the Army, boys," Dindie Remo answers.

"So now you think you're man enough to ride all the way to . . ." the tobacco-chewer stops, pauses, then shrugs and says, "wherever it is we're supposed to be riding to?"

"I guess you'll see," Remo says in nothing close to being called a friendly voice.

"You mean you'll see," the tobacco-chewer says.

The other cowboy adds: "That's right. You'll see the dust from our horses."

"You mean mine!" says the tobacco-chewer, who takes a good-natured punch in the shoulder from his pard. They start to walk off, but the first one, who had been smoking and not chewing, stops and turns.

"Why don't you come with us, darlin'?" He's speaking to Arena Lancaster.

"No. But thanks," she says.

I can tell Miss Arena ain't too friendly with these Texans, neither.

"You wasn't so haughty last night, darlin'," the taller one says. "Then again, we had rye last night."

"We can get some more," the tobacco-chewer says.

"I'll stick with my friends," she answers.

"Friends!" the smoking cowboy says. He smiles, but his voice and eyes show he's agitated.

Me, I'm thinking what does she mean by *friends?* I just met the girl and the Negro-Seminole. I wouldn't call them friends. By thunder, I just learned their names.

"A half-colored, half-Injun buck?" says the tobacco-chewer, shaking his head, before he looks at me. "And this . . . runt . . . who don't weigh more'n a toothpick?"

"My choice," Arena Lancaster tells them.

The tobacco-chewer shrugs. The other cowboy grins, and, in a voice that's colder than the February wind back home, says: "Just the same, darlin', you'll come back to our stalls tonight. We'll have some rye for you."

They turn around, letting their bowed legs carry them toward the open door of the barn.

CHAPTER FIVE

The Arab keeps working on his horse. Dindie Remo just stands there, but I can see the anger in his eyes, and Remo ain't a fellow I ever want mad at me.

"Y'all go on," Arena Lancaster says. "I ain't hungry no more."

"You got to eat." The words don't come out easy from the big Negro-Seminole.

She shakes her head.

Remo clears his throat. "All right, you might not be hungry, Miss Arena." Then he gestures at me. "He might not be, either, but I am. And I need you both to come with me."

"Huh?" That don't make a lick of sense to me. Not only that, I am hungry. Especially if it's free. That's one thing Pa was good at during our travels from northern New Mexico Territory all the way down to Galveston, Texas. He'd learn which saloons handed out free sandwiches or peanuts or maybe just pickles or crackers, and we'd go there, and he'd order us both nickel drafts and he'd drink both beers and eat a bit and make sure I got my fill before we left. With Pa up in that hospital, I'm sort of at the mercy of . . . well . . . right now, Dindie Remo. And Arena Lancaster.

"They might not cotton to serving a man of color," Arena Lancaster explains to me as if I'm the dumbest boy she's ever laid eyes on. Likely, I am. "And he sure ain't gonna win no medals if he strides into that hotel with me."

"Had me a hard-enough time getting into this race," Remo says.

Which reminds me of something I should've thought about before. I let an oath slip out, but Miss Arena ain't offended. She actually giggles.

"I need to find someone who's in charge of this race," I say. That's when I see the doctor in his fancy black coat. I run across the big barn as Dindie Remo complains that he ain't never going to find even a cup of coffee.

The tall, silver-haired sawbones disappears behind a stall about two rows over from where we'd run into the Arab and those two hard-rock Texans. I weave around some folks, dodge a Mexican boy hauling a bucket of water somewhere, almost knock a reporter into an empty stall, and finally get to the place where that doc is.

"Wind galls," the doc says as he turns to face this whip-thin dude in a bowler hat and congress gaiters.

The dude removes his bowler, starts turning the silly little hat over and over in his slim fingers. "I figure he's just sore. Caught a stone in his shoe. That's all there is, right, Doc?"

The doc's head shakes. "How far did you ride this horse to get here?" he asks.

"Fort Stockton," the man says. "He's all right, ain't he?"

"You could've caught a train from Stockton to Houston, mister."

"Trains cost money, Doc."

"So do horses. Those fetlocks are swollen like balloons. You rode him too hard, too long."

"But . . ."

Not even raising his voice, just stating the facts with a quiet forcefulness, the doc explains: "This isn't a stone in a shoe, mister. Wind galls aren't like a sore tendon, a little bruise or bump. And those fetlocks are the worst I've seen in years."

"Doc . . ."—the man stops twisting his hat—"I gots to win this race."

"You won't win it, mister. Not with a horse suffering from wind galls. You won't even get out of Texas on that horse. All you'll get is a lame horse. Lamed forever."

"It's my horse."

"But it's my decision."

The man drops the hat. He reaches for something tucked underneath his shoulder. I figure it to be a pocket pistol or Derringer, but the doc stops him with a look.

"Horses," he says, "are required to pass my muster. Yours doesn't. You want to make something more out of this, go ahead. Make your play. That horse will be better off without you for his master."

The man leaves whatever he was reaching for alone. Instead, he squats, picks up his bowler, and plants it on his head. "We'll see about that, mister. Lucky Baldwin's a friend of mine. So is Richard Fox."

"You'll find both having breakfast at the Tremont. Tell them I sent you," the doc says.

Well, that fellow makes a beeline right past me. I'm trying to think about what I need to tell this doctor. Taking one last look at the horse, the doc packs up his black satchel, and heads out of the stall. He stops at me and nods politely.

"How's your father?" he asks, his tone soft and polite.

I try to think of an answer. It strikes me that I never saw this doctor at that hospital. Fact is, the only place I've ever seen him is at this here barn. And then, as though he's a mind-reader, he tells me why.

"I'm a veterinarian," he says. "Doctor Patrick Jack. Texan by birth, but a graduate of the Veterinary College of Philadelphia in 'Fifty-Seven. And you are . . . Ethan was it?"

"Evan," I tell him. "Evan Kendrick."

"That's right. And your father?"

I sigh.

"They had to amputate his arm?" he asks.

I can only nod.

"It's for the best, Evan. How is he?"

I'm thinking to myself: *Pa still can hold a whiskey bottle with his left hand. That's all that matters to him.* "He came through," I tell him.

"I served in the War of the Rebellion, lad. Many a man maimed for life learned that the loss of a limb need not mean the loss of career, of life, of dignity."

I ain't here for no sermon, so I say: "Pa says I need to replace him in this here race."

Dr. Jack studies me, looks up at the entrance to the stall, then walks away. I turn and follow him, thinking I might have to follow him all the way to his horse-doctoring office, but he stops. That's when I see Miss Arena and Dindie Remo.

Doc removes his hat, and gives Miss Arena a little bow. He nods politely at the Negro-Seminole. "You two with him?" Doc Jack juts his jaw toward me.

Remo lets out a little chuckle. "I don't think that kid's with anybody, Doc."

"And the horse?"

Dindie Remo shrugs. "Got spirit. And sand."

"Balderdash," Arena Lancaster chimes in. "Puny little thing. You seen that Arabian that foreign dude's got? Or that beautiful black that Spaniard's riding?"

Doc don't answer. He just shoots a glance my way, and stares again at Dindie Remo and Miss Arena. "Have y'all had breakfast yet?" he asks.

Them two shake their heads.

"Care to join me?" Doc says. He looks my way. "You, too, Master Kendrick."

"Doc . . . ," Dindie Remo says, smiling something fierce. "You speak the language of my tribe."

Turns out that the doc has had dealings with Miss Arena and the Negro-Seminole. I'm learning all of this whilst devouring biscuits covered with sausage gravy, scrambled eggs, and bacon piled high on tin plates, and I'm washing all that down with gallons of coffee. Oh, I don't think the folks at the hotel care too much at having either Miss Arena or Dindie Remo or even me eating at a table by the big plate-glass window that shows us to every man, woman, and dog coming down the boardwalk. But nobody in this establishment has gumption enough to argue with Dr. Patrick Jack.

As my belly's starting to bloat, Doc Jack guides us out of the hotel's dining room, across the street, and back to that big old barn. Doc tells Miss Arena and Remo good bye, and then he's taking me across the street and down boardwalk after boardwalk. I figure we must be going to see Pa at St. Mary's Hospital, but, instead, we slip into this bank building and climb the stairs up to an office. I read the name stenciled into the double glass doors. It's Doc Jack's place.

"How old are you, Evan?" Doc asks once

we've settled inside his office. It ain't the office I expect some horse doctor to have. It's plush. Fancy. And upstairs above a bank. It'd be hard to get a sick horse up here. But I figure there's more to this doctor than just telling folks about wind galls. I recollect overhearing in the big barn that the name Jack means something in Texas, and has since before the days of the Alamo.

"I'm going on . . . ," I begin.

Doc raises his hand, and I stop before I can tell him that I'm going on eighteen, which ain't no shameless falsehood. I will be eighteen. In two and a half years.

"We Texans like to brag, Evan," Doc Jack says. "But we also know when to speak the truth." He's got this look that says he's a man that you just don't lie to.

"I turned fifteen in April," I tell him.

"Evan," he tells me, "Arena Lancaster got in this race because her entry form said Arena Lancaster. She's eighteen. A hard, grown-up eighteen. But from her application, no one knew that she was of the fairer sex. Once we found out, the committee had a meeting. Lucky Baldwin, the promoter, didn't like it. Most of his backers stood with him. They argued that it would be a disgrace to allow a woman in a race like this. Actually, a mere girl not out of her teens, riding astride a horse. Not sidesaddle. Riding with men. Sleeping, unchaperoned, with cowboys and other wastrels. But Mister Fox, publisher of the *National Police Gazette*, reminded them about who reads his publications. Fox will print anything that will sell his magazines, and if churches and mayors and governors complain, he'll sell even more. And risqué images of a girl in bloomers riding astride a horse won't hurt sales either."

I tell myself to remember this word, *risqué,* and learn what it means, though I got a good notion, having seen Miss Arena in her unmentionables.

"Dindie Remo was an easier sell. After all, this is Eighteen and Eighty-Six. President Lincoln and our Congress saw to that. And Mister Fox again liked the idea of how it might boost the circulation of his publications."

He paused and headed over to get a decanter, from which he fills a real small, shining glass with liquor that's not the color of Taos Lightning's hide. He finally continues: "But yours is a different matter, I fear."

I don't give him no chance to fear anything else.

CHAPTER SIX

By thunder, I'm begging Doc Jack, but I don't feel no shame. I tell him about all that Pa has bet. I tell him that if I don't win this race, I ain't got nothing to my name. No home, nothing.

"On a mustang that won't top eight hundred fifty pounds with you and the saddle?" the vet says.

It's not a mean thing to say, at least, not the way this sawbones puts it. He's just spitting out facts.

"Pa," I tell the tall doc, "he says that a mustang is the most noblest breed of horse there is. Taos Lightning might not be sired by Slender Stanley, and his ma's veins might not be flowing with the blood of Mayflower, but he comes from a line straight down from the first Spanish explorers who set foot in this land. Maybe his sire was Coronado's horse. Maybe his ma come from the line that begat De Vergas's stallion." I stop. Can't believe I'm spouting such flapdoodle.

Doc Jack grins for a moment, sips his drink, and guides me to the far corner of his office, the one near the window that looks across the Gulf of Mexico. We ain't looking out the window, though, but at this giant globe in the corner.

"It's one thing to look at this race on a map," Doc tells me. "It's another to see it on a globe."

47

This beautiful ball's so big, it's amazing. The doc gives the world a little spin just above the wooden center brace. He stops the globe's spin and jabs a finger at this splotch of red and tan and brown near a bit of blue. "This is Galveston," Doc Jack says, before he sends the world a-spinning again. When he stops the big ball's movement, he points again to Galveston. His finger follows not a trail or path, but something of a suggestion. He taps another spot of green and yellow. "And this is where you're bound for. New England. That's all I can say for now. Eighteen hundred miles, Master Kendrick, if the map-makers are right. More if you get lost. Maybe two thousand. Who knows? To be run in six weeks? Eight. Nobody really knows because no one has ever attempted such a race on this continent."

He spins the globe again, and steps away. He studies me. "Are you sure you want to do this, Evan Kendrick?"

No, I ain't certain of nothing, I think to myself. *I don't want to run this race. I don't want to ride a mean-spirited widow-maker who'd rather buck me off than carry me from Galveston to New England.*

"I don't have a choice, Doc," I tell him.

His head starts shaking. "Every rider has a choice," Doc Jack says. "Unless I say he doesn't. Riders have choices. The horses they command . . . well, they don't always have a say in the matter.

I won't have you running a horse to death, not even that mustang of yours who's worth no more than fifteen dollars . . . and that's if the liveryman shoes him, grooms him, and throws in bridle and saddle." Doc's eyes bore through me one more time. "Is that your plan, Evan Kendrick," Doc asks, "to run this mustang to his death?"

I shake my head. I ain't lying. I ain't meaning to speak ill against my pa, but I know what I've got to do, and what I've got to do is win that prize money. That'll put a lot of stew on my table mornings and nights. It means I'll have a table, a home for me and Pa.

"A dead mustang means I don't win that three thousand dollars," I tell the vet. "And I've got to win this race."

For a long minute, Doc Jack just stands there staring at me. He puts his fingertips together, don't say nothing, just looks me in the eye.

"I see," he says at length, and I'm mighty glad he sees something, because I don't see a thing. There's no future. I don't have a chance at winning this race. But, by grab, I gots to try.

Finally, the doc nods slightly. "I'll put in a word for you with Mister Fox and Mister Baldwin. Fox will likely want you to run. You're a boy, with an invalided father, trying to win a race against all odds. He'll like that. That might sell extra copies of his publications. But the bottom line, the final decision, will be determined by Mister Fox *and*

Mister Baldwin. It's their money. We'll see what the committee says."

I just nod.

"What's the most you've ever ridden in one day?" Doc asks.

A shrug serves as my answer. I really have no clue. Finally, I say: "Forty miles, maybe. It could've been a mile or two more."

"All right then. You should hear something tomorrow. No later than noon."

I just bite my lip.

"I'll find you if the committee requests an interview," Doc Jack informs me. "You might have to plead your case. Where are you staying?"

I have no answer.

"With your father?" he asks.

I don't reckon the nuns and the surgeons and pill-rollers really want me back in St. Mary's again, so I shake my head slightly.

"You're sleeping in the stall?" Doc Jack asks.

This time, I answer with a quick nod.

"And remind me of the name of your horse," Doc commands.

"Taos," I tell him. "Taos Lightning."

He finds a pen and scrap of paper and scribbles down my horse's name.

CHAPTER SEVEN

It's morning, and here I am inside that grand hotel, across the street from that big barn. Only I ain't in the dining room, but on the top floor, waiting outside a room and feeling like the loneliest kid on earth.

There ain't no chair to sit on, so I been standing here for twenty minutes. Finally, the door opens, and Doc Patrick Jack sticks his head into the hallway. He don't say a word, just nods, and pulls the door all the way open.

My legs work. I take a deep breath, breathe out, and step into the room.

Doc closes the door behind me and takes the lead. I follow. This ain't the kind of hotel room I expected to see. Pa and me usually paid for a stall in some livery on our travels to Texas, or maybe we spent the night in a wagon yard, but often times we just slept in the open. In this room, there ain't no bed, no wash basin, but I see two more doors, one on either side of the dark paneled walls. In the middle of the room are four men sitting in chairs. Then Doc takes his place in the last chair on my left, leaving me standing. The four other dudes are staring hard at me.

I guess nobody ever told the guy in the middle, who dons a gray hat, that it's bad manners to wear a hat indoors. Me, I'm wringing my battered old hat in my hands, like that dude did his bowler before Doc Jack told him he couldn't race his horse on account of those swollen fetlocks. Thinking of that makes me lower my hat to my side.

Anyway, this guy with the hat sports big ears and a handlebar mustache. He's twisting one end of the mustache with his left hand, while the fingers on his right tap some papers before him. His coat and vest are checkered. His shirt is collarless. He stops twisting and tapping and says: "A good day to you, Evan Kendrick."

The accent's pure Irish, like he was one of the soldier boys Pa and me dealt with up at Fort Union. "My name is Richard Kyle Fox, publisher of the *National Police Gazette* and other magazines, and organizer of this race." His head tilts toward the guy sitting next to him.

Turns out, that's Lucky Baldwin. He's dressed in black, with a black cravat and white shirt. His hair is receding but he sure ain't bald. He sports a well-groomed mustache and beard, both starting to gray, and his eyes are too close together. In the barn I heard talk that Baldwin made his money in California during the gold rush, but not by panning for gold. Mr. Baldwin don't say a word, just nods after Mr. Fox introduces him.

The third guy, who don't even look up from the

Galveston *Daily News* he's reading, is introduced as Charles J. Wetherhill. The fourth man, I've seen talking to folks and writing in his notepad in the barn, which is what he's doing now, although I can't figure out what he'd be writing. Seems to me he already knows everyone in this room but me. His name is Adam Franklin. He stops writing and hands me a copy of the *National Police Gazette*. The pages are pink. The picture on the cover is of a woman. She's running from someone, down some steps, and her dark hair's blowing and her skirt is raised and you can see her limbs. I try not to stare, make myself lower the magazine.

So here I stand, hat in my left hand, and the *National Police Gazette* in my right. I feel like an idiot.

Of course I know Doc, but Mr. Fox introduces him anyhow.

"All right," Mr. Fox says. "So you want to replace your father in this grand race? Is that right, Kendrick?"

"Yes, sir."

"This boy didn't enter the race," says Wetherhill, who still hasn't looked up from his newspaper. "We haven't allowed any replacements."

"Ah," says Doc Jack, "but have you seen Kendrick's entry form?" He takes it off a small sheaf of papers and slides it down the table. The newspaperman glances at it, then pushes it to Mr. Fox. The form don't go no farther.

"E. Kendrick." Mr. Fox laughs and shakes his head. "What is your father's name, lad?"

"Edward."

"That's rich. Edward. Evan. E. Kendrick. I say we can't say for certain that Edward Kendrick did not mean for Evan Kendrick to run in this glorious event to challenge man and beast."

"And a girl," the newspaper reporter adds.

"He can't enter," says Wetherhill.

"Oh, come off it, Charles!" Mr. Fox squawks, and slams his balled fist on the papers before him. "You don't want anyone in this race except your beloved Texans. You didn't want the Negro-Seminole scout. You certainly didn't want that intriguing little wench. You didn't want the Arab or the Spaniard." The Irishman whirls to Doc and asks: "What's the boy to ride?"

"A mustang," Doc Jack answers.

"A mustang." Mr. Fox shakes his head and laughs. "Surely, Charles, you don't think a mustang can beat your cowboys on their cow ponies."

"He paid his entry fee?" Lucky Baldwin asks.

"Of course," the newspaperman says. "He wouldn't be here if he had not. Wouldn't have known where to come and when."

"And his name is on the list," Doc Jack says.

" 'E. Kendrick, Mora County, Territory of New Mexico.' "

That's what it says, all right. I remember we were at home. Pa never learned his letters, so I had to write it out for him. He was drunk at the time, in a hurry, telling me that he had to get this off to Chudacoff's store, which is the nearest place to post a letter. Though I ain't certain, I guess that's why I just wrote 'E' and not Pa's rightful name.

"Then why are we even having this conversation?" Mr. Fox asks.

"How old's the boy?" Wetherhill finally lowers his newspaper. His face is bronze, his nose Roman, his eyes cold. He has a thick gray mustache that droops down past his chin. He's staring straight at me.

"Fifteen." I don't lie.

"A kid."

Now it's Doc Jack who laughs. "Charles, you've told me you were on your own, fighting Comanches and Mexicans, when you were twelve."

"I thought it was eleven," Mr. Baldwin says.

Wetherhill clears his throat. "You think this is some joke, but you know we've already gotten complaints from that American Humane Society and that society to prevent cruelty to all dumb critters. Some newspapers have argued that this horse race is nothing but abuse. Bad publicity."

"Charles," Fox says, "even bad publicity is publicity, and any publicity is grand."

"The fools protest the mistreatment of animals and children," Wetherhill seethes. "And after what happened at Haymarket a few months back, radicals are going to all extremes. Anarchists are everywhere."

"Not the American Humane Society," Baldwin says. "Or the Society for the Prevention of Cruelty to Animals."

"Maybe not, but there are sick people who are inspired by radicals. Isn't this why we're keeping our route a secret?"

All of this is news to me. I don't know a thing about Haymarket or no Humane Society. I've never heard of radicals. I don't even know what an anarchist is.

Wetherhill picks up his newspaper and says from behind the printed page: "I vote no."

But the other four say aye. Mr. Fox wishes me luck.

"What's your pony's name, Kendrick?" he asks.

I tell him.

"Taos Lightning. That might sell some magazines. Franklin, go with Kendrick to the barn. See what this Taos Lightning looks like. Maybe have Haskell make some drawings. But tell him not to spend too much time on a mustang from New Mexico. I want to see plenty of drawings of that spunky young petticoat."

I'm out the door even though Mr. Fox is still talking.

Back in the hallway, Doc Jack closes the door behind us. I stare at him. Can't find the words to thank him.

Again, Doc seems to read my mind.

"Don't thank me, Evan. I think perhaps I should have sided with Charles. I didn't do you any favors. Fact is, I might have signed the death warrant for your horse. And you."

CHAPTER EIGHT

Adam Franklin, that writer fellow, follows me to the barn, asking all sorts of questions on the way. I answer most of them, till he asks about my father. Franklin wants to know where my pa is, how he's doing, what does my mother think about all these goings-on. He really doesn't give me a chance to answer before he's on to the next question. My head starts to hurt, but, finally, I'm back at my stall, and I'm looking at that liver chestnut I'll be riding. Doc Jack's words keep bouncing around in my head.

Before long, Adam Franklin introduces me to a young artist named Willie Haskell, who asks if he can do some sketches of me and Taos Lightning. I just shrug, and this Haskell starts drawing in his pad while I get to my chores.

I find a carrot and slowly come up to the mustang. Suspicious, Taos Lightning's ears prick up alertly, and his nostrils flare. Can't blame him none. Pa never once showed that horse any kindness. Deep down, I know I've never done the mustang no favors, neither.

"Good," Haskell says. "Can you hold the carrot like that for a minute?"

He thinks I'm doing this for his picture. Taos Lightning don't know what to think.

"I need you, boy," I whisper.

"Why don't you give 'im a long nine cigar, kid?"

The voice belongs to one of them two loud-mouthed Texas cowboys.

"I let mine drink rye, but he'll only take Old Overholt," the voice of the other.

I drop the carrot, and turn. The Texans laugh, punch one another's shoulders, and tell the artist that he if he wants to draw a picture of the winning horse, he should come over to their stalls. Then the two cowhands start joshing about which of their two horses will actually win the race. Before long, they ain't joshing, but arguing.

But before fisticuffs can break out, an official-looking man appears. He has to holler several times before the Texans and others shut up.

"Thank you," the man says, and takes a step forward before announcing loudly: "All riders are to report to the front of the barn in fifteen minutes. This is a mandatory meeting where you will be given the rules and your cards. The race will begin tomorrow."

It's like a slap across my face.

Until now, I don't reckon it ever struck me that I'd actually be riding a horse from here to New England. My stomach turns over. I lean against the stall just to keep myself from falling down.

The Texans hurry away. Willie Haskell folds up his sketchbook and stows away his pencils, and then makes a beeline for the front of the barn. Franklin is already up there, probably asking all sorts of questions.

For a moment, I consider walking out of this place, getting my horse in the corral two blocks over, and heading home.

Fifteen minutes later, we're all at the front of the barn. A man, who says his name is Baxter, is talking, using one of those speaking horns so everyone can hear. Haskell's a few rods over, straddling the top bars of an empty stall, working his pencils over his sketching paper. Mr. Fox and Mr. Baldwin stand behind the man who's talking, but I don't spy Dr. Jack.

"We have fifty-six entries," the man says through his horn. "When your name is called, you will come up to Sebastian here on my left, your right, and get a card. This card you must carry with you at all times. At each station, your card will be punched and signed. You must have this card at each checkpoint. This is our record that shows you have checked in at every station. You must rest for at least one hour at each and every one of the way stations. At the home stations, where your horses will be examined by veterinarians, you must rest for at least two hours."

"*Excusez-moi*," this little French fellow asks of the speaker. He has a good-looking white horse with the smallest, worst-looking saddle I've ever seen. "What is the difference between a home station or a way station?"

Baxter ain't one for interruptions. "I'll get to that directly," he says, eying the Frenchie. "Please, save any questions till after we're finished. These rest periods, along with the limit on the number of hours you may ride in a day, should make those idiots with the American Humane Society and the American Society for the Prevention of Cruelty to Animals feel a little better. Maybe."

"And don't forget the bloody Royal Society for the Prevention of Cruelty to Animals!" a guy with an English accent yells.

"We've got one in Dublin, too!" shouts an Irish-sounding man.

"Gentlemen!" Baxter yells, but even with his big horn, he can hardly be heard over the curses and catcalls.

"Leave them out of it!" By thunder, that's Miss Arena's voice. "These groups care about the animals. Most of y'all don't give a whit about anything but the prize."

"Shut up, you little hussy!"

My hackles rise. It's one of those two Texans, and I want to find him, but I can't even figure out where the voice came from.

"If you don't want to ride . . . ," the Texan tries to continue.

"Withdraw your insult, sir." Those words cause

the commotion to end. I can see the man who said that. It's the Spaniard.

Then silence. Finally, the Texan steps forward and says: "Begging the little lady's pardon, I meant no insult. Just want to get this race started, so I can win."

A smattering of laughter follows, and Baxter clears his throat and brings up his big horn again.

"You are limited to riding ten hours a day. The new day starts after midnight. When you choose to start riding again, after your mandatory rest, is completely at your discretion. But you may ride no more than ten hours. So, if you stop at noon, you cannot start riding again until after midnight."

"I can get a right smart of drinkin' done between noon and midnight," someone says, and laughs at his own joke.

There are other rules. A lot of them.

Baxter keeps stressing that after riding ten hours, we must stop—no matter where we are—and wait until the next day.

A slim rider standing in front of me sniggers and tells this nimble foreigner next to him: "I'm glad I bought me an Illinois watch!"

The foreigner and a few others laugh, but I don't. It strikes me now that I don't even own a watch.

"Does that mean *ride?*" someone asks.

"That means," Baxter says, "you do not ride,

you do not gallop, nor trot. And . . ."—he raises his finger and wags it to get his point across—"you do not lead your horse and walk. You stop. S-T-O-P. Wherever you are, you cease for the day. Or risk disqualification."

"What's he gonna do?" a high-pitched fellow says. "Ask my horse?"

Baxter goes on with the rules.

One horse per rider. Lose your horse, the race is over for you. You can't substitute another. Rider gets hurt and can't continue, another rider cannot take over that horse. The race is over for you and your horse.

If we don't make a checkpoint on the day specified in the rules, a race official will remain behind for two more days. If you do not report to the checkpoint during that allotted time, you will be disqualified.

At each checkpoint, Baxter explains, we will be given a map to the next station.

"This map . . ."—Mr. Baldwin, the promoter, holds up a map and waves it over his head as Baxter continues—"shows a path to the next stop. That path is merely a suggestion. You may take any route or blaze any trail that you wish. But you must check in at the next station within the allotted time period. And . . ."—he stops while he takes out a card and raises it for all to see—"you must have your card . . . this card . . . punched."

Each stop, Baxter tells us, will be a distance of between forty and sixty miles.

This causes quite a few gasps.

One gent off to my left says: "Forty miles. Eighteen hundred miles. That's forty-five days."

"You done that cipherin' all in your head?" the man behind him asks.

Laughter among the riders has become scarce. Even the two Texans ain't carrying on.

"At roughly every fourth or fifth stop . . . say two hundred to two hundred fifty miles . . . your horse will be examined by a reliable veterinarian. These are the home stations I previously mentioned. They will be marked on your map. Your horse must pass each examination. You must rest two hours. There will be food, and lodging facilities if you care to sleep. At the home stations, you will be given a new card to be punched. Your originals will be kept with race officials."

Baxter goes on to suggest that alliances, while not required, are highly recommended. "Most of you will be traveling in strange country. Partnerships might prove beneficial. Friendships, even better." Now he lowers the horn and smiles. He shouts without it, and we can all hear him. "Friendships could be beneficial at least until the last day or two of the race. I don't think I've ever had a friend worth three thousand dollars." He laughs. "Then it's everybody for himself. Or herself." He nods off to his left.

Even though I stand on my tiptoes, I can't see Miss Arena Lancaster.

There are more rules and information, which overwhelms me.

"These way stations," Baxter says, "if you will, will vary from each other . . . from a wagon yard or a livery stable, to a family farm or ranch, a hotel perhaps, and, quite often, just a clearing alongside a trail or road. The home stations should be somewhat less rugged, but you won't be staying at the Capital Hotel and you won't be eating at Delmonico's. Your final destination will be a city in New England. That's all you need to know. Are there any questions?"

There are plenty, most being a rehash of what we've already been told.

"The only thing you need to know right now," Baxter says, "is that at seven tomorrow morning, you must be at Old Ferry Point."

"You mean we're taking the ferry?" someone shouts. "What if we want to swim across to Port Bolivar?"

There's laughter until Baxter answers: "That's your choice." He's dead serious.

Other questions get shouted out, and most get answered.

The organizers are trying to avoid protests, or maybe even violence. Secrecy is in order. Whatever happened at Haymarket must've put a scare in some folks.

"Yes, this is quite an enterprise," Baxter tells us, "and Mister Fox and Mister Baldwin should be commended, as certainly much more than three thousand dollars has been spent to organize this grand venture, this great adventure."

"Yes, riders may carry firearms, as long as you don't use one on your competition," Baxter jokes, "but if you get arrested for violating a city's firearms ordinance, that'll be your own tough luck."

"No, we will not transport you back home. Lose your horse, you're out of luck. You got here by yourselves. You'll get home by yourselves."

Someone shouts: "What about that guy who got his arm smashed? You're paying his bills, we've heard. So you'll pay a guy who ain't got the sense not to walk behind a horse, but you won't pay our way home?"

This appears to stump Baxter. Mr. Fox and Mr. Baldwin have a brief talk, and, finally, Mr. Baldwin steps up on a crate, grabs the horn, and says: "Richard Fox nor I paid one dime for that luckless man. Doctor Jack has been footing his bill. We have paid for your meals here . . . not the whiskey, not for your dalliances . . . but your meals. And you will find food and coffee at the stations as you travel. We didn't make you come here. You did that yourself. If you don't like our rules, I'm sure your competitors won't mind seeing you pull out of this race right now."

I don't listen to the next round of questions. Instead I go searching for Doc Jack, but he's nowhere to be found.

When the last question gets answered, Mr. Fox takes his turn on the crate. He calls out the first name. The first card gets handed out. And before I know it, I'm back in the stall, staring at this card, five by seven inches, that ain't got no clues as to where the first station might be. Just a number and the words **Way Station** or **Home Station** and blank lines where I guess some race official will write in the rider's name, the date and time, and punch a hole in the square by the number. We're told that we can fold the card in half, and we are once again reminded to keep it safe.

I think: *Inside the back pocket of my britches? No, that might be hard on this piece of paper, bouncing in a saddle for forty to sixty miles a day. Inside my hat? Definitely not. Throw it in my saddlebags? Do I need saddlebags? That's a lot of extra weight. Do I need a slicker? The clouds outside look threatening. It's the first week of September, which, in New Mexico Territory, means things can turn right chilly. How cold will it be in six weeks in New England? What do I need to take?*

CHAPTER NINE

"Do you own a watch, Evan?" Doc Jack is asking me.

I whirl around, make myself smile, and slowly shake my head. Don't know where Doc Jack come from, but I'm glad to see him.

He steps inside the stall, reaches inside one of the pockets in his black coat hanging on a nail, and pulls out a gold watch. It has an open face. He hands it to me, saying: "I didn't think so. Take this."

I hesitate.

"It's not a family heirloom, son. The truth of the matter is that I won this in a poker game. I don't need an extra watch. I already own six."

A man who owns six watches! No wonder he can afford to have an office above a bank.

I take the watch. It's a Seth Thomas. Nothing fancy, but it's running. "I . . ." I'm staring at the doc. "I'd like to go see my pa."

He nods. "I have a buggy outside. I can take you to the hospital."

I slip the watch into my vest pocket. "You've done enough, Doc. I can't hardly even find the words to thank you. And . . ."—I make myself grin—"walking might be good for me. I'm gonna be sitting down for nigh two thousand miles."

We shake hands. His grip is strong. I start out, but he calls my name.

"What Baxter said a while back," Doc says. "Partnerships. Alliances. You'd do well to find someone. Stick together. As long as you can."

I study on this for a minute or two. I sure ain't going to ask those Texans. The only folks I know even slightly are Miss Arena and Dindie Remo. I don't know if they'd want to partner up with a fifteen-year-old kid.

"I'll think on it, Doc," I tell him.

A young nun leads me up the stairs to the top floor of St. Mary's Hospital. I don't remember her from the night they threw me out, but there were a lot of folks getting me out of Pa's room and it was fairly dark. We don't say nothing. She stops at the door, opens it and, her voice soft with a thick accent, says: "You must leave by four-thirty."

I nod, and she holds the door open for me. For a moment, I hesitate, but then I go into the room. Pa's sleeping. I drag a stool up alongside his bed, and look at that arm stump first. I also see he needs a shave, and that he looks thinner, like he hasn't had much to eat. And, since the lamps are burning, I can see just how pale, how frail, he is.

Finally, his head turns on the pillow, and his eyes flutter open. They lock on me, slowly focusing, and I wonder if he knows it's me.

"Boy," he says, and coughs.

He knows it's me.

"Pa," I tell him, "I'm in the race."

His eyes narrow. He wets his lips, tries to talk, and motions for the bottle on the table. It's laudanum. I see the teaspoon in the saucer next to the bottle, and pick it up.

"No," he says hoarsely. He snaps his fingers on the one hand he's got left. I glance at the bottle, but there ain't more than a couple of spoonfuls left, so I leave the spoon and hand him the bottle. He drinks it down, lets the bottle slip out of his hand and onto the bed, and looks at me again.

"What you mean?" he finally manages.

"They let me in the race," I tell him. "I'm to ride Taos Lightning."

"You?" His laugh is menacing, mocking. "You ain't riding that race, boy. I am. The hell you think you're doing?"

I try to ignore him. I tell him that my mare is still in the livery and that maybe he can ride her back to Mora County, or sell her, and get hisself a train ticket. He keeps right on hissing and cussing, and I think that might be a good thing. Likely, he'd just sell that pony for whiskey.

Pa's so weak I don't think any doctor or nun outside can hear him. He says I'm stealing his horse, that they hang horse thieves. I try to tell myself that this ain't my Pa, that it's the laudanum doing the talking, causing the meanness. But I'm lying to myself, and I know I'm lying. Finally, Pa just wears hisself out, the laudanum does its work, and Pa's sleeping again.

I pick up the empty bottle, put it on the table, and stand over him.

"Pa," I tell him, "I'll do my best. Me and that stallion." I draw in a deep breath, and let it out. "But it ain't for you, Pa. It's because I don't have a choice."

CHAPTER TEN

September 6, 1886.

Feels like turkey buzzards are flapping inside my stomach. All I had for breakfast is coffee, and I'm shocked that one cup has stayed down. I've managed to get the saddle and bridle on Taos Lightning, and I've led him out of the big barn. The stallion ain't happy. I'm miserable.

Rain falls in sheets, pounding so hard it hurts through the India rubber poncho I've pulled over me. The stinging drops thumping my hat sound like thunderclaps. I hear a couple of the race officials complaining that this weather has spoiled a chance for a picture.

I can't see nothing but gray rain. Can hardly make out the folks in front of me.

Someone behind me yells: "Well, boys, y'all might as well concede that three thousand bucks to me. Because I happen to have the only *sea* horse in this here race!"

For some fool reason, they've crammed all fifty-six riders on this barge—ain't no way I'd call it a boat, and it ain't like the ferries Pa and me taken to get across Texas and to this infernal island. It strikes me that Mr. Fox and Mr. Baldwin and everyone else involved in this "endurance" race didn't think things through.

First off, there's the weather. When we got to Galveston, folks were still cleaning up fallen trees and making repairs from a hurricane that passed through sometime in August—and went on to leave the city of Indianola, Texas, in ruins. Everybody's been telling us that this is just a summer storm, but it's dumped more rain on me than I've ever seen.

And this ferry? It ain't nothing more than a big, flat barge—flatter than the island of Galveston—and the rain has slickened the wood, and the winds are making us rock, rock, rock. Riders get jostled enough at a gallop, and all we've done is walk our horses onto the barge, mounted up, and formed several rows of men and beasts.

Horses don't like rocking on unsteady things like ferries and barges.

Riders don't much care to be on a stallion that's standing next to a mare, which is standing next to another stallion.

Taos Lightning rears. There's no room on this floating contraption for rearing. The other stud horse, which I can barely see because my eyes are being slapped with rain, starts showing off, too. It's all I can do to keep my wet seat. Men are cussing, especially the little dude on the mare, which dances this way and that, and apparently don't care a whit for my liver chestnut or for that bay.

Taos Lightning, maybe for spite, bites the dapple on the other side of me.

There's cursing and screaming going on. Apparently, my chucklehead and that other gent's stallion aren't the only ones to find themselves in close proximity to a mare.

Some fool—maybe the ferryboat captain—blows a whistle. Which don't help none at all.

Bucking. Snorting. Stamping. Biting. Rearing.

The boat dips to the side. Lightning streaks across the sky. I almost fall onto the mare's back, because we're right cramped on this boat.

I hear a splash, followed by: "Oh, my God!"

What I want to do is slide out of my saddle, get a good grip on the reins, and try to keep Taos Lightning under control. But there's no room, and with all these horses rearing and hoofs a-slashing, and the boat rocking this way and the other, I don't think I want to be afoot.

"Two hundred yards!" someone roars. "Two hundred yards till land!"

Might as well be two hundred miles.

There's another splash. The rider in front of me leans over and vomits. I mean he hurls up enough juice to fill a well bucket, and that goes right on the fellow next to him, on his chaps and boots and stirrups, but the rain washes most of it off right away.

Once Taos Lightning stops bucking, the stallion on the other side of the mare rears at the same time as we come to a sudden stop as the barge strikes land. The rear of the boat caroms to the north. A bunch of splashes follow, along with screams and curses, of which I'm doing my share. Somehow, I don't lose saddle or reins.

"Off!" someone yells. "Off. Get off. Ride. Ride, boys. It's time to ride."

Yesterday, folks told us to ride off in an orderly procession to allow photographers and artists and writers a chance to document this historic event. The rain must've changed their thinking, or maybe the ferry captain fears he might lose his ship. It don't matter to me. The horses in front of me start leaping onto dry land.

Dry? Not hardly. When Taos Lightning splashes down, the water's up to his hocks. I urge him after the horses ahead of us, but we slog through knee-deep water that eventually shallows down a mite to the stallion's cannons. But, at least, we're off that blasted boat. I pray we don't have no more ferries like that one on this horse race.

Maybe Taos Lightning thinks he still has a chance at that mare, so I give him rein, all I can. I feel the rain slam into my left side and the wind blast me, too. Although we're not rocking anymore, my stomach is about to cut loose.

Before we left the barn this morning, they punched and signed our cards, writ the name of our first way station on it, and give us all maps.

Part of me wants to pull the map out of my

trousers pocket, but I don't want to lose any ground. Besides, I know the map pretty good. There's only one road, if you can call it a road, a single trace that runs pretty much through the center of this strip of land for like twenty miles. Ten more along the coast, then we're supposed to turn north for something like twenty miles to a place that's identified on our official card as: **Way Station No. 1**. After which is written in fancy cursive: ***Marsh. Texas. Chambers Co.***

Fifty miles? In this weather?

It's like riding through soup.

One thing I figure on, though, is that nobody will be taking some short cut to Way Station Number One. The only thing to my right is the Gulf of Mexico, which I can't see. The only thing off to my left is the East Bay, and excepting for that fellow who says he's mounted upon a seahorse, that bay looks way too far for a horse and rider to swim.

So for twenty miles, I figure, I just need to keep riding east.

A pinto passes me on the left, followed just a few seconds later by a couple of dark-colored horses. About the only thing I see is a rain slicker on the middle rider. Next, five or six mud-splattering horses and their riders pass me.

That's all right. In fact, I pull in on the reins some. This ain't no Western match race of maybe a quarter mile. I have eighteen hundred more to go. The only thing I want to do right now is reach that first way station. I hope they'll have coffee and shelter, but considering how this *test of endurance of rider and horse"* has been run so far, I ain't real hopeful.

It's getting dark.

Ain't seen anyone for the past couple of hours, not in front of me, not behind me. The rain's still pounding. Man, I sure hope this ain't no hurricane. I've slowed Taos Lightning to a walk, as this road has turned into a ditch and water's flowing down toward Port Bolivar. That means something, though. We're headed uphill, although an ant hill would be considered a mountain in this miserable country.

I climb out briefly to water that's only up to the stallion's coronet. Looking behind me, I see just rain water and dark skies. I look at the Seth Thomas that Doc Jack gave me, and I sigh. If I'm reading the watch right, the ten-hour limit is coming up fast.

Far as I can tell, I haven't even reached the point marked on the map as High Island, where we should turn north. I'm all for turning north.

I'm all for ignoring the rules. How are the judges supposed to know if we ride ten hours or twenty? There ain't no way they'd have anyone patrolling the route, especially in this soaking, pounding, brutal rain.

What else can I do but laugh? I don't have much time left before I'm supposed to stop my horse and camp for the night. I've got some jerky and oat cakes in my saddlebags. No coffee. My soogan is soaked.

"At least we won't go thirsty," I say, and lean over and give Taos Lightning's neck a wet pat.

I sit up in the saddle. That's the first time I ever gave that stallion a gentle pat, a bit of encouragement. He sure deserves it. He has practically swum this whole day.

I'm looking up at lightning flashes across the sky to the east. And I see something. Can't make it out, but it looks like folks. In a castle? I must be dreaming.

Thunder rolls. I stand in the stirrups, straining to see through the rain and the coming dark. There's another flash of lightning, longer this time, followed by a series of four, five streaks.

No, it ain't no castle, but there's definitely a person, maybe two, on this little dome.

Maybe it's judges, who want to see if I'll ride past the ten-hour limit. Could be strangers. Most likely it's some other riders caught in the same predicament as me. All of this is just guessing, naturally, but I'm sure of one thing.

"Come on, Taos Lightning," I say, and tap his sides gently. He snorts and moves on.

I wave my hat, in hopes they can see me. I call out a *"Hallooooo"* and say I'm coming in, hoping they can hear me above the wind and rain. I pray they ain't road agents.

Whoever they are, they're on higher ground than I am. And high ground is where me and Taos Lightning want to be.

"It's that fool kid!" The voice, oddly familiar, reaches my ears. "And that mustang."

"Dindie Remo," I say to myself.

It's him, all right. He's wearing a slicker, and water's pouring off the brim of his big hat, but when he comes up close, I find myself smiling. The girl, Arena Lancaster, comes up to Remo's side. She holds a blanket over her head.

"Best light down," she says, and nods off to her left. "We got the horses picketed over yonder."

I swing to the damp ground, and spot what must be a half-dozen mounts on a picket line a few rods over. Remo and the girl ain't the only ones here.

"Where are we?" I ask.

"High Island," Remo answers.

I can hardly believe it. High Island ain't no island, and it sure ain't high. Not even forty feet above the gulf, but at least I'm not slogging through water up to my boot tops.

Remo grabs the reins and leads Taos Lightning to the other mounts, which, I'm right glad to see, are all geldings. I lug my saddle back to this makeshift shelter they've put up, and step under the lean-to, the roof made of the riders' soogans, blankets, slickers, and at least one duster. I pull off my poncho, and use it to cover the saddle. Not that it'll do much good, soaked as that slickfork is, but maybe it'll help. Then I squeeze in beside Miss Arena and some fellow in jodhpurs and a bowler hat.

"They say Laffite once hung around here," says this one dude, who is leaning against a pole that helps hold up our roof.

"Who's Laffite?" I ask.

"Pirate" is the only answer I get.

High Island ain't nothing but a salt dome, but the dude who knows about Laffite also says that Indians and even white settlers would come here during hurricanes to keep from drowning.

"I hear Laffite even buried treasure here," he adds.

"I'm all for findin' it," says another rider, one wearing a big Texas hat—but he ain't neither of them two Texas blow-hards with their big mouths, short ponies, and bad manners.

"Gots to be better than this fool stunt," comments another racer.

"How far have we come?" Miss Arena asks.

"Thirty miles," Remo says.

"Thirty miles!" Miss Arena sounds like her heart just shattered in thirty thousand pieces. "We'll never catch up. We haven't even made the first checkpoint."

"Rest easy, little lady," the Texan says, as he

pulls out the makings to roll a cigarette. I figure his paper and his tobacco must be too wet to smoke, but he's working on it, using only one hand to sprinkle Bull Durham into his paper.

"Ask me," the soggy bowler hat wearer says, "we've done right well. Thirty miles in ten hours?"

What he says makes sense, and I add: "And in this turd float."

That gets Miss Arena to laughing, which I try to ignore. I wish I'd kept my big mouth shut.

The laughter fades, but the rain don't, and Miss Arena asks the dude in the bowler hat: "Why'd you enter this race?"

"I own the fastest horse in Natchitoches," he says. "Maybe all of Louisiana. Like to see how he'd do against other horses. Now what puts a bony girl with corn-silk hair on a palomino gelding for eighteen hundred miles?"

"Never seen New England," she answers, and turns the question to the big black Seminole. "What about you, Remo?"

"Something to do," he answers.

Come morning, I push my still-soggy hat off my eyes. I stink like wet horsehide. Bones and muscles aching, I lift my head off the saddlebags I used for a pillow and try to find the sun.

Wherever it is, the clouds are hiding it, but at least it ain't raining.

Suddenly, I realize that I'm looking through what had been our roof. Only most of the ceiling's gone. Bedrolls and slickers are missing, too.

Thinking everyone has left me, I bolt to my feet, only to find Miss Arena rolling up her soogan. Dindie Remo is saddling his blue roan at the picket line. That little claybank, ridden by Bowler Hat, is starting down High Island. Everybody else is gone.

"Cheery-ho!" Bowler Hat calls out as he leans in his saddle and moves down the dome. "I'll see you gents . . . and you, too, ma'am . . . in Boston. New Haven. Providence. Wherever."

When he has disappeared from my sight, I grab the horn and give the slickfork a jerk. It's almost like that saddle pulls back, because it don't hardly budge, and I find myself on my knees again.

Miss Arena Lancaster is laughing so hard, she's crying, which gets my ears turning red. I come up to my feet, and this time I have myself braced real good when I lift the saddle. I carry that heavy, wet rig to Taos Lightning.

"Is it all right to ride a wet horse?" Miss Arena calls out as I drop the slickfork by Taos Lightning.

I stare at her as if she's the most clueless girl I've ever seen.

"Horses sweat," I tell her.

"And saddles slip," Dindie Remo says.

He's rubbing down that blue roan with a bandanna that appears fairly dry.

I'm about to toss my blanket on, but it strikes me that there's some truth, maybe, to what that Negro-Seminole just said. So I rub down Taos Lightning's back before the water-logged blanket goes on, followed by the soggy saddle. Once I have the cinch tightened to my liking, I look over the saddle and down from High Island.

"By thunder . . ." I point.

Miss Arena stops saddling her palomino, and Remo finishes lashing his bedroll behind the cantle.

We all stare down at the road. Something like four to six specks are moving down the road. Behind them, we can see the outlines of other riders.

"Golly," Miss Arena says, "we ain't last."

Dindie Remo swings into his saddle. "We ain't first, neither," he says. He starts down the hill, but stops to look back at me and the girl.

"Y'all good?"

"Good," I answer as I step into the wet saddle and pull my hat down low. "See you in New England, Remo."

He grins. "I'll settle for the first way station, Kendrick." After tipping his hat at the girl, he moves the gelding down the dome.

I'm amazed. I didn't think that fellow would remember my name.

CHAPTER ELEVEN

Way Station No. 1: Marsh. Texas.

Yeah, that's where I am, all right. There ain't nothing around here but marshes, weeds, and a tent about as big as a cathedral, with a massive red guidon popping in the wind and a white **1** emblazoned on the silk.

The fellow in the yellow slicker punches my card and writes the name of our next way station. It's in some town called Orange, which is still in Texas.

Looking over this big patch of Texas, I try to figure out what the big to-do is about this state—and I've seen a lot of it, riding down from New Mexico. Ask me . . . there ain't nothing really worth looking at.

At the first station, there are pots and pots of coffee, and quite a few horses. Two farriers wait by a fire, but nobody's taking them up on offers to shoe any horses.

Some of those fellows who had been down the road when I left High Island have passed me, only I don't see them here. I make myself drink coffee, and hand Miss Arena a cup, when she moves over to the fire pit and table. The coffee's hot. It's black. It's bitter. And stronger than anything Pa ever brewed.

There are biscuits and tortillas, but I'm not sure I need any food in my stomach after all the trotting I've been doing. Feels like my guts got bruised from bouncing up and down.

At least it ain't raining. There's no sun to speak of, except a few rays poking out from dark clouds. But the wind has dried my clothes.

The man in the green tie gives me a map.

Next, he punches Miss Arena's card, scribbles the name of our next stop, and hands her a map, too. Only he unfolds hers to show her that this is the map, as though she's completely ignorant.

"How many are ahead of us?" she asks.

He shrugs.

"Behind us?"

Green Tie might show her a map, but he sure ain't offering no more information. Reckon he ain't supposed to.

"Dindie Remo come through already?" I ask.

That gets me another shrug.

"The big Negro-Seminole?" I know he won't answer, and he don't, just walks off to punch and write on another rider's card.

I pull my Seth Thomas from my vest pocket, look at the hands, and start winding the stem.

"What time is it?" Miss Arena asks.

I stare at her, and then shake my head. "I ain't rightly sure," I answer.

"You just looked at your watch, confound you!" She slams her cup of coffee on the table.

I drop my watch in my pocket. "Well . . . ," I start, but feel like an idiot, because other riders, those coming, those leaving, start staring at me.

"Fool can't tell time," says one.

I take out the Seth Thomas again and show Miss Arena the watch's open face.

"We got ten hours to ride," I explain. "Learned enough in school that I know the little hand tells the hour, so, when I get on this horse, I set both hands at the twelve. That way, when the little hand gets to the ten, I know it's time to stop riding."

Her face reveals her utter amazement as I return the Seth Thomas to my pocket.

Since we've ridden twenty miles since sun-up, I figure we'll never make the second station today. After we and, more importantly, our horses have rested the mandatory hour, Green Tie tells us how much longer we can ride today.

"We best start riding," I tell Miss Arena, and move to Taos Lightning, tighten the cinch, check the bit, and climb into the saddle. My legs feel raw. My back aches.

I stick the card, wrapped safely in wax paper, in one of my saddlebags, and open the map. Miss Arena pulls her palomino up alongside me. She's looking at my map, too.

Another rider bolts out from underneath the

giant tent. There's another rider ahead of us.

Before I can ask her what she's doing, she tells me: "They said we'd do well to form an alliance." Her shoulders slump, and she adds: "Please."

She ain't hard to look at. It's just that I've never seen no girl who didn't ride sidesaddle.

Sighing, I point at the map. "They got two paths drawn on this one," I hear myself telling her. I show her, just like that fellow in the green tie done earlier, as if she ain't got sense enough to see what they've drawn out for us.

"One route heads northeast, practically at a straight line, to a place called Beaumont. Then we're supposed to follow this here line, that's not exactly straight, to this place on the Louisiana border called Orange."

"That one looks shorter," she says as she points at the line that runs pretty much straight due east, till it has to veer north past Sabine Lake. Then it moves north and east to Orange. Our next way station is something scribbled down as the **Gateway City Lumber Mill**, which is on the western edge of Orange, Texas.

"Yeah," I agree. "You know anything about this country?"

She shakes her head.

"Well, I don't like this here." I point at the place marked Sabine Lake. Then I point at the big line of blue, long past the halfway point between here and Orange, that leads straight into Sabine Lake.

"Some river," she says.

I fold the map now, stick it in my vest pocket underneath my Seth Thomas so I don't have to go digging in my saddlebag for it.

"Well, as much rain as we've had," I tell her, "I got a feeling it'll be mighty hard for anyone to swim that river . . . maybe any river. And there ain't no ferry marked on this map."

She purses her lips. "You have to cross that very same river after Beaumont, too."

That's a point I already considered. "But Beaumont's north. The rain was coming in off the Gulf of Mexico. And it ain't raining no more. And there's a ferry at Beaumont."

"Are you leaving?" Green Tie asks.

We study him. He's holding a pencil and another pad.

"Reckon so," Miss Arena answers.

She kicks that palomino into a run, and it takes me forty yards before I've caught up with her.

"I can sure pick a pard, can't I?" she yells. Her hat slides off her head, secured by a latigo, and bounces on her back.

I have to admire her grit. Heck, I almost smile myself.

'Course, those maps these officials give us ain't what you'd call perfect. Certainly they're not complete. What has been marked on the second map I've got is **Cat Bayou**, **Sabine River**, **Neches River**, and **Sabine Lake**.

We climb in and out of a lot of gullies and bayous and ditches. The road is washed out in more than one place. We don't even see Beaumont before I make Miss Arena rein up and get down from her gelding.

I point at my Seth Thomas. "It's almost ten. I mean, it ain't ten o'clock, but we've been riding ten hours."

She shakes her head. "Who's going to know we rode ten and a half hours? Or fifteen?"

It's a subject I considered for quite a few miles today. Yesterday, too.

"Did you look at your card after they punched it?" I ask her as I loosen the cinch. When she shrugs, I keep talking. "They didn't just punch it. They noted the time we got there. And that dude in the green tie . . . well, I expect that somewhere he wrote what time we left that first way station. Same probably when we rode out of Galveston. So I think them race folks are keeping a close watch on everybody's traveling times and could figure out if there has been cheating going on . . . especially if we make up five or six hours in one night."

"You really think that?" she asks.

I shrug. "Or maybe Green Tie is in the next gully, just waiting to catch us cheating."

She grunts and curses before beginning to loosen the cinch on her saddle. "Just my luck. Partnering up with a spoil-sport."

We make the best camp possible. The ground is soaked, and I can't find enough dry tinder or fuel to get a fire going, and it's not like we got tin cups for coffee, or even a pot. Don't even have coffee. So we sip from our canteens. She shares some hardtack. I gnaw on some jerky. When I offer her some, she passes.

Darkness overtakes us. Bullbats come out to feast on the bugs. I find some mud to cover my hands, cheeks, and neck to keep mosquitoes off me.

"I suppose," Miss Arena calls out from her spot, "that I'll have to trust you to be a gentleman tonight." She laughs. "I bet Mister Charles J. Wetherhill is having a conniption. Me . . . an unmarried girl, sleeping with no chaperone, with this wild young thing from New Mexico Territory." Her laugh turns into a cackle. "But that'll certainly get both of our likenesses on the cover of Fox's pink-papered magazine."

I'm aching all over. But now I'm picturing that drawing, and I'm thinking about Miss Arena's legs, and maybe she's wearing nothing but that chemise like when I first seen her.

"Why are you in this race?" she asks.

I stop thinking about her. All I really want to do is sleep. But I tell her: "Because my father did

91

something stupid and had to get his arm cut off, so I had to replace him."

"You didn't have to," she says. "You didn't have to do nothing."

"Why are you?" I ask.

"Why am I what?"

"Racing? Where'd you find that palomino?"

She don't answer, and I figure she has fallen asleep. Knowing that's a smart idea, I close my eyes.

When my eyes open, I see only darkness. No stars. The clouds have yet to break. I wonder if the moon's somewhere behind those clouds.

Over yonder in the dark, Miss Arena snores. It sounds a whole lot more pleasant than Pa's snores.

CHAPTER TWELVE

We're at Adams Bayou, Miss Arena and me, on the west side of Orange. At least, that's what the farmer we met before reaching town told us. He even give us some oranges to eat. Wouldn't take a nickel for them. The oranges was so sweet, and I was so starved, I even ate some of the peel. That meal kind of gave me new faith and hope.

But both faith and hope start fading when we see a horse—a zebra dun—floating on the edge of the bayou. The rider, who ain't much older than me or Miss Arena, is on his knees, pulling on the reins, begging, cussing, screaming at the horse—he calls him Edward—to get up.

"Get up, damn you! Get up! We've got to get to the way station, Edward. Get up. For God's sake, get up!"

The rider wears jeans and a checkered shirt, both covered in mud and muck. He has lost one boot, and the stocking on that foot is practically coming off.

I glance at Miss Arena, but finally ease Taos Lightning a little way downstream of the fellow and his drowned horse. The bayou ain't shallow, but it's not that deep. I hold my breath. I feel light-headed. My horse is like most horses and can swim. I can't. That's another reason I opted to take this route rather than ford the river down south.

Taos Lightning swims easily, and the bayou ain't much bigger than an *acequia* back home. Once we climb out and up the bank, I rein in the stallion, and turn around to watch Miss Arena and her palomino swim across.

Up ahead, smoke rises out of chimneys in the town of Orange. I look back at the fellow and his drowned zebra dun, and ride back toward him.

"Mister?" I call out. He just keeps pulling on the reins. "Mister!" No reply. "Mister, you can swing up behind me. I can give you a ride to the next station."

"Edward!" he's still screaming. "Get up, Edward. We're almost there! We've almost made it to New England. Get up, Edward. For God's sake, get up!"

A chill racks my body again. Edward being my pa's name.

Turning, I stare at Miss Arena. Her head shakes. I let out a sigh, tug on the reins, and we ride back to the road.

As we trot into town, we ask a man in a hay wagon for directions to the Gateway City Lumber Mill. They're pretty easy to follow.

At the way station, a fellow, wearing a red and white polka-dot tie, punches my card, writes down what time I got in, and where I'm to ride to next. Then he hands me the map for the next leg.

"There's a fellow back this side of Adams Bayou," I tell him after sticking my card and map in my vest pocket for the time being. "His horse drowned."

The man don't even look up. "That's his tough luck." He finishes with Miss Arena's card, thrusts a map at her, and drops that hole-puncher on the table.

"I just thought . . . ," I start.

He's in no mood. "You want to ride back and bring him in, that's your choice. He knew the risks. I'm just sorry it was his horse that drowned and not him."

I hear something buzzing, as Miss Arena tugs on my sleeve.

"Come on, Evan," she says. "There's nothing we can do. Let's go. I smell gingerbread."

I don't smell anything sweet. What I smell is sawdust. What I hear, I realize, is the sound coming from the lumberyard. Trees being sawed into planks and two-by-fours and whatever. Our horses start to turn skittish.

Which is another strike against Mr. Fox and Mr. Baldwin. Who would put a way station at a lumberyard, especially after what feels like a hundred miles of the most miserable riding ever done?

"I'm hungry," Miss Arena says, "and we've got an hour before we can start to the next station."

We go to the chuck house, fill our bowls with

beans and cornbread, and get some coffee. As I look around, I don't see no other riders eating, and I don't remember seeing no horses outside. I wonder if we're dead last.

"What's the next stop?" I ask, as I shovel food into my mouth, not tasting a thing. It's just something I have to do.

Miss Arena's studying the map. "All it says is Bull Bayou Plantation, Imperial Calcasieu Parish, Louisiana."

"Rivers?"

She swallows coffee, looks again at the map, and shrugs. "Calcasieu River . . . I've no idea if I pronounced that even close . . . and then, a good bit down the road, something called English Bayou."

"Ferries?"

"One's marked for the river. Nothing on the bayou." She dunks her cornbread in the beans, and puts the bread in her mouth, chewing, mouth open, and she blurts out: "You're mighty concerned about rivers. Can't you swim, Evan Kendrick?"

My face hardens. "You got a short memory, girl."

Well, I reckon both of us start picturing that poor gent we'd come across, and his drowned horse. How will that fellow get home? Where does he hail from? What made him enter this race? And how does a person feel once his dreams end after not even three whole days?

Now, I'm regretting those words I spoke to Miss Arena, 'cause she slides her chair away from the table. She picks up her map, folds it, sticks it inside her blouse, and pulls on the hat she had set on the table beside her bowl and cup.

"See you in New England, boy," she says. "I'm dissolving our partnership."

I don't catch up to Miss Arena before Bull Bayou Plantation way station. Don't even see her in Lafayette, where I ask the guy serving coffee if this town's named after that pirate who buried his treasure on High Island along the Texas coast.

He stares at me, as he chews on his cigar. "Lafayette? A pirate?" Then it hits him like a kick from Taos Lightning's rear hoofs. "You mean Lafitte?" He snorts, and him and the others around don't stop laughing till I take my card and my map and head to the stables.

Of course, I can hardly understand most of what he says. Folks in these parts speak some language that's harder to understand than talking to a Jicarilla Apache back home.

It's different now. Riding alone, I hardly pay any mind to the cypress and the alligators, the giant bugs, and all the noises croaking out of these bayous and swamps. This place stinks. You can't see nothing, can't hardly even see where you're going.

I miss New Mexico. I miss the West. I miss seeing nothing but land, mountains. This is like I'm in a cave or a tunnel. Mostly, I miss riding with someone.

All along the way to Galveston, I'd had Pa. Which oftentimes felt like I was riding alone, as Pa and me didn't talk much. Miss Arena, now, she talked. Maybe she made fun of me, but she never struck me as being mean-spirited.

Riders gallop past me, but I'm holding Taos Lightning steady. Not too fast. Not too slow. I'll put him in a lope, ease off into a trot, and even slow to a walk so he can catch his breath.

Back home, Septembers can get chilly—even get some snow in the high country—but Louisiana feels like a furnace. After all that rain the first day and night of the race, now the sun blisters my hands and my neck. I got soaked by rain out of Galveston. Now, I'm soaked from sweat.

I stink as I ride into West Baton Rouge.

It's the first home station. I guess we've covered two hundred and fifty miles. The man takes my card, hands me a receipt, and gives me a new card and a new map.

"This," he says, "must be signed by the

veterinarian, after he clears your horse. The livery is over there."

"Is it Patrick Jack?" I ask.

"There are several vets." He motions me off.

My horse doctor ain't Doc Jack, but some old miser with his sleeves rolled up and a silver mustache and goatee. He don't hardly give Taos Lightning a gander before he signs the card. I don't think he could've told me if my horse was a stallion, gelding, or mare.

Looking around, I still don't see Doc Jack. Don't see Arena Lancaster, either. I find the cookhouse, and eat some sausage and red beans. The food's got some kick to it, not like New Mexico's chiles, but it is the first grub I think I've actually tasted. If I weren't so tired, sore, and rattled from all those miles, I might have even enjoyed the chow.

Finally, I fold out the map, and there it is—big, and blue and black, and frightening. And this is just a small piece of paper.

Mississippi River

There's some writing off to the side of this card, but I'm studying the map.

Ferry across the river into Baton Rouge. There are some hotels marked. I guess if we don't want to sleep on the ground, or in our saddles, and we got the money . . . Then it's pretty much a straight line to our next way station, which is marked as Hammond. I'm noting the blue lines, meaning rivers, because the rivers in this country ain't nothing like the rivers back home.

A river in New Mexico would be called a ditch in Louisiana.

Amite River. I frown. There ain't no ferry marked. Gray's Creek. Again, no ferry. Something I can't make out as the ink's all smudged, but it don't look no bigger than the Amite, and neither's as massive as the Mississippi. Tickfaw. Then what appears to be a long dry spell before the Blood River—again, no ferry—but a crossing marked as being **good**, and a few others before we check in at something called the **Old Shoe Factory** in Hammond.

Next, I go back to that writing on the side of the map. The blood rushes to my head and my ears turn beet red.

I'm back at the desk where the man hands out cards and maps.

He sees me, pulls a pencil from off his ear, and says: "Yes, you've rested two hours. Are you riding out now?"

I show him the map.

"This says we're supposed to take a ferry run by Denmon," I tell him.

"Quarter mile south," he says.

"But it says the ferry leaves at nine in the morning."

"That's right. Earle comes back at seven that evening."

"What time is it now?"

"Don't matter. You wouldn't have caught the ferry if you'd arrived hours ago," he says. He smiles, but that don't hold long because he can see how angry I am. "Are you riding out now?" he asks me again.

Mocking me, I figure. I want to clobber him something good.

"So I have to wait here till morning?"

He don't smile, but I can tell he wants to when he tells me: "You can always swim the Mississippi."

That's the wrong thing for him to say to me.

Then I'm back in the stalls, and I'm saddling up Taos Lightning. Next, I'm riding down toward the ferry landing, and I'm looking across that big river. There's boats of all sorts, and the stacks of steamboats in Baton Rouge proper belch out thick, black smoke. That town's bustling. Here in West Baton Rouge, the place is practically asleep. And will be till Mr. Denmon's back and the ferry's loading up—with me and who knows how many other riders who will have gotten in by then.

Spotting a man of color fishing from the bank, I call out to him: "Excuse me!"

He turns, studies me, and says: "Yes, sir?"

"What time is it?"

He pauses, looks at the sky, then shrugs and says: "Four, four-thirty, I reckons. Maybe five."

I'm back in the saddle, and I'm easing Taos Lightning down the bank. His forehoofs step into the water. I loosen my hold on the reins, and let him drink. I'm staring. Sweating. My heart's pounding. I ain't never seen nothing this big. A barge comes down the middle of that river, and I can hardly make out the crew working the big boat's decks, they look so small.

That's when I sink down in the saddle, and gather up the reins, thank the Negro again, and climb back up the bank.

As I ride back to the stalls, I see the man at the desk checking in another rider. The goateed old coot who calls hisself a veterinarian is examining another horse. I ride down to the end of the stables and stalls, and rein up.

"Hello, Evan," Doc Patrick Jack says.

CHAPTER THIRTEEN

I've been hoping to see Doc Jack, and I know I should be glad now, but, well, if I don't get across the big river today, I'll be pushing Taos Lightning mighty hard just to keep from losing more ground. Already, I've fallen pretty far off the pace. If I get too far behind, they'll close up the way stations. I'll be out of the race.

And homeless.

Still, I manage a smile, and lean down to shake the tall man's hand.

"You've made good time," Doc says.

"Not good enough," I tell him.

"Better than I thought," he says. "What are you doing here?"

"Missed the ferry," I tell him.

He lights his pipe.

"Did you see Dindie Remo?" I ask.

"No, but there are three veterinarians here. A lot of horses have come through, so I might have missed him."

That ain't exactly what I want to hear.

Back at the desk, one of the riders is giving the man with the cards and maps a hard time. I guess he just realized he'll have to wait a day more, too. Or swim the river, which I don't have the guts to try.

"How about Arena . . . Miss Arena Lancaster?"
I ask Doc Jack.

"I did see her. She barely made the ferry this morning." He laughs. "She actually galloped down the bank and jumped her horse four feet onto the ferry. A drawing of that jump . . ."—he shakes his head like he's recalling it—"will definitely wind up on the cover of Mister Fox's *Illustrated Day's Doings and Sporting World*."

I would have loved to have seen that jump. I can almost picture myself racing alongside her, and both of us doing that leap onto the ferry.

"You all right, Evan?" Doc asks.

My shoulders and head raise. I give him a half-hearted grin. "Just falling farther and farther behind."

Doc cocks his head. "So why are you waiting here?"

I shake my head. "I've seen one horse drowned already, Doc, and that bayou where it drowned wasn't nowhere near the size of that thing." I point toward the river behind me.

"Evan . . . ," he says in that commanding but soft-spoken drawl.

I study him when he doesn't continue. Then I explain: "The map says the ferry leaves only at nine in the morning."

"And what," Doc says, "is the map?"

"It's the route we're . . ."

I sit up straight. I'm thinking and remembering,

and I'm doing both real clearly. I'm recalling the rules as they were explained to us. *This map has a path to the next stop. That path is merely a suggestion. You may take any route or blaze any trail that you wish.*

An oath slips out of my mouth.

Doc grins before asking: "Have you ridden ten hours today?"

I shake my head.

Doc Jack smiles and says: "I was thinking about going into Baton Rouge for supper. A mile north . . . if that far . . . Old Man Bastarache has a skiff he uses to ferry passengers across the river. If he's not there now, he'll be returning shortly. That man keeps long hours. Dime for a passenger. Two bits for a horse."

He pulls two quarters from his pocket, flips them to me, and, somehow, I manage to catch both.

"Doc . . . ," I say, not knowing how to thank him.

"You just be careful, Evan," he says. "And find yourself a partner. This race is too tough, too dangerous to try to go it alone. Your horse all right?"

"Doc Thatcher cleared him."

"That's not what I asked."

"He's fine. I haven't given him his head."

He nods. "You might think about letting him run," he says. "There are a lot of riders ahead of you."

I ask him: "How'd you get here so quickly, Doc?"

He grins as he looks up.

"Son, I traveled by train. You might try it someday. It's a lot easier on your hindquarters than a saddle."

Laughing, I turn Taos Lightning around and start to spur him, but Doc calls out to me. I look back, he's pointing at the man with the maps and hole-puncher, and he reminds me: "You have to tell Howarth that you're riding out, son, so he can mark your time. Rules are rules."

The abandoned old shoe factory in Hammond. A railroad yard in McComb. Now I'm riding down a road between cotton fields in Hinds County, Mississippi. 'Course, this time of year, there's no cotton. It looks like a couple of field hands are resting in the shade of the one big tree up ahead. Maybe they can give me directions to the next station, or just let me know that I'm on the right route.

I slow Taos Lightning to a walk, and, as we near the trees, I realize that there ain't a couple of hands cooling off, but just one man.

Taos Lightning starts fighting the reins. He ain't done that since we started this race, excepting that time he felt frisky beside that mare on the barge. He don't want to move. Even bucks a couple of jumps. When he stops, I leave the stirrups and jump off, keeping a tight grip on the reins.

"What's the matter with you?" I'm tempted to pop his nose with leather. Instead, I walk ahead, pulling him. Eventually, he gives in. Maybe he's tired. By thunder, I am. And he has been carrying me for a long, long way. A walk would do our legs some good.

As I get nearer the tree, I know why my stallion balked. I should've paid mind, maybe cut across the barren field.

My throat goes dry. I want to turn away, just can't.

The man's black. And for a moment, I fear it's Dindie Remo. But this fellow, he's too short for Dindie. His hair's white. He ain't got no shoes. His shirt's been ripped off. His pants are more like rags than clothes. Not the wild duds Dindie wears. The fellow's hands have been bound behind his back. And as the wind picks up, and his body turns with the breeze, I can see the lashes on him, the flies buzzing around him.

Now he's facing me again. Only he can't see nothing.

The tree's a big oak. Squirrels are running about, gathering acorns, jumping between limbs and branches. They don't pay no mind to the man swinging beneath the big limb. His face is all swollen, and the rope around his neck's stained with blood. It looks like he bit off his tongue.

And his eyes. They don't blink. But it seems like they are staring at me.

I make myself look away. Studying the ground, I make out the tracks of a dozen or so horses. It's just something to do so I don't have to look at the poor man. But it don't seem like it ought to take twelve men to string up one old man.

There's nothing you can do for him, nothing at all, I tell myself. *Just keep going. Don't think about it.*

I know Taos Lightning is glad to be past the man once I step into the saddle because before I can sit, the stallion's loping down the field road.

We don't stop till we come to a crossroads.

I'm looking at the map, when a twig snaps in the woods off to my left. A horse whinnies, and Taos Lightning's ears prick. I start wishing I carried a revolver, or something other than the knife that's in my saddlebags.

"It's all right," this fellow says as he comes out of the woods.

I feel like I'm about to fall out of my saddle. Likely would have, especially since Taos Lightning is twisting and snorting.

"Evan?"

It's a voice I recognize, and once I've got a tight grip on the reins and have the chuckle-headed liver chestnut under control, I'm staring at Dindie Remo and Arena Lancaster.

"What in Sam Hill are y'all doing hiding in the woods?" I bark. It strikes me that they're playing some joke on me, wanting to see if they can make me get tossed from the saddle. I'm trying to get my breathing under control as I slide out of the saddle.

"You saw . . . what was back there?" Dindie Remo asks, as I realize he is trying to pretend that he ain't scared.

I wait before I answer. There's some things I'd like to just erase from my memory. That poor colored man hanging from that oak limb . . . that's first on my list right now. Might always be first.

"Yeah," I tell him.

"We can't go riding in this country alone," Arena says.

I look at her.

White girl. Man of color. Slaves got freed better than twenty years ago, but some things ain't changed, I guess. The old man I left alongside that field's proof enough of that. But I sure ain't happy to see Miss Arena.

"Seems I recall you dissolving our partnership," I tell her.

"Listen," Remo says, "I found Miss Arena by that man hanging back yonder. Got her this far, then we seen some riders. So we took to hiding. I ain't proud of it. Ain't happy I left that old man just swinging there from that tree. But I had this girl to think about. You figure it out. You want to ride on with Miss Arena . . . you do that. I'll go it alone."

"You ain't going it alone, Dindie," I assure him. Then: "You ain't either, Miss Arena."

I swing into the saddle, though I don't reckon *swing* is the right word . . . not as stiff as I feel. But I'm sitting. That's all that counts.

They bring their horses out of the woods. Suddenly, I can't believe I'm staring at those two folks.

"How'd this happen?" I ask.

Remo gives me a stern look. He must think I mean the lynching.

"You were way ahead of me," I tell him. I nod at Miss Arena. "And you had to be some hours in front of me. That was only when I reached Baton Rouge. Y'all ain't been hiding in those woods for ten, twelve hours."

"Don't think we were ever that far ahead of you, Evan," Remo says. "And you've got a good horse underneath you. You just don't know it."

"You kept him steady," Miss Arena said. "Holding him back. You know how many horses and riders have dropped out of this race already?"

I ain't thought to ask nobody at none of the stations.

"Nineteen," Remo says as he climbs aboard his blue roan. "Least, that's what the man at McComb said."

CHAPTER FOURTEEN

After we go through the signing-in process at the next station at a plantation's barn five miles up the road, we find ourselves eating grits, ham, and eggs, washing them down with our choice of cold buttermilk, coffee, or tea.

Dindie Remo is talking as I try to figure out why folks eat grits. I ain't sure what grits are. The ham and eggs taste fine, though.

"What started the war betwixt you two?" Remo asks, as he scoops up his third helping. Must not have no problem with grits.

Thinking back, I can't recollect what I said that upset Miss Arena so, or what she said that riled me. Wasn't nothing important, near as I can remember. Maybe we was both just hurting, because all I can recall is that drowned horse and the grief-struck rider.

Remo shakes his big head. "Y'all was probably just sore and cross from riding. It happens. Like as not, it'll happen again before we get to New England. But I think we should form a new alliance. The three of us. Till . . . oh, Massachusetts or some place like that."

Feels good to be riding with someone again.

But the day's getting late, and my watch says

the ten-hour riding limit is fast approaching. We camp alongside the road, but I can already see smoke from a campfire a few miles ahead of us. I figure it to be another rider.

We're gaining ground.

There's times when I wish she wasn't a partner. Miss Arena, I mean.

It's morning. She's already up and giving her horse a good rubbing, and I'm walking into the woods, looking for a place to do my morning business. And when you spend ten hours a day in a saddle, mostly at trots and lopes, your stomach and innards bouncing all the time, your morning business ain't pretty.

So, figuring that I'm deep into the woods, I spy a fallen, rotting log that'll serve me. I'm reaching over it to grasp a branch to help me climb over, when a rush of air whips right past my arm. All I see is a flash of blackness. And down I go, atop the log, and I see what that flash was.

Well, I scream like a schoolgirl, and I'm rolling off that log as this snake pops at me again. Then I'm on the safe side of the log, only the log ends right where I've fallen. And I get a good look at that snake. It's big. I mean it's fat and long and evil and ugly. And it's crawling right at me. Like it's chasing me. *Charging.*

Never seen nothing like it. Ain't got no pistol or nothing, so all I find myself doing is backing away like a crab on my feet and hands. I try to get up, but . . . well, I'm too scared. Those eyes on that snake . . . they's like diamonds.

Just when I think I've got enough sand to stand and do something, a stick jams that snake's head down, pushes it deep into the pine needles, rotten leaves, and twigs. Then Miss Arena is leaning over, and she sticks a knife right through that snake's head.

Dindie Remo catches up to us. He sees me, sees the snake, sees Miss Arena. He's holding a revolver. I didn't even know he packed one till now, but he lowers the hammer and shoves the long-barreled weapon into his waistband.

"Cottonmouth," Miss Arena says.

"Big one," Remo agrees. "He bite you?"

Teeth rattling, I shake my head. I point and cuss. "He charged me," I say.

"Ain't they got snakes in New Mexico, Evan?" Miss Arena asks, as she cuts off the snake's head.

"Yeah," I say. "Rattlers. They can kill dogs, horses, cattle . . . even killed one neighbor. But, at least, them snakes give you a warning before they strike. And most times they'll run from you." I can't stop myself from shaking.

Remo studies what's left of the snake. "Four foot," he admires. "But, Kendrick, I've seen bigger."

"You all right?" Miss Arena asks me, as

she tosses away the stick. She leaves the cottonmouth's head and the rest of that monster on the ground.

"Best get going," Remo says.

"Ain't you gonna thank me, Evan?" Miss Arena asks.

I stare.

"I did just save your life. That big, bad serpent might've eaten you for breakfast."

The mud is turning thick. Must've been some good rain showers up here before we arrived. Down in Texas, the ground was so sandy, so dry, it sucked up a good portion of the rain—once it stopped raining, that is. But here? The reddish-brown globs stick to our horses' feet like tar. It's about as hard to clean off.

We ease past one rider who's whipping his horse left and right with his reins. It's a bay, and she's all lathered with sweat as she's snorting, straining, and sinking into the mud up to her knees. We've gotten off the road, using the leaves and grass to protect us a little bit. Besides, the road's sunken, and the banks ain't quite as muddy. The rider on the mare hasn't noticed that. His eyes are as wild as the bay's. His hair's plastered across his red cheeks, and his shirt is dark with sweat.

"Twenty," Miss Arena says once we're past him.

"Don't get cocky, ma'am," Remo says. "There but for the grace of God . . ."

I don't get what they mean till fifty yards later. Twenty riders are out. That leaves thirty-six. And we're just coming into the crossroads on the map, the Delta Presbyterian Church grounds and cemetery—the next home station, where we are to get new cards and another map.

No grits get served here. Looks like a bunch of Chinese have settled in this country. I thought you only found Celestials working on railroads or in laundries. The preacher here tells us that a few showed up maybe fifteen, eighteen years back. Mr. Wong—he points to this tiny little fellow with a pigtail—owns a restaurant in town. Good food, he tells us.

Other than the rice, I don't know what I'm eating, but it's filling. Mr. Wong points to a pile of sticks in the middle of the table that I guess is what we're supposed to use instead of spoons and forks. But my fingers work fine.

"You notice something interesting?" Remo asks.

I look at him after I've slurped the juice and rice and vegetables out of the bowl, which I set on the bench table as I wipe my mouth with my shirt sleeve. Out of the corner of my eye, I glance at Miss Arena. The look on her face says she don't know what to think.

Well, maybe I ain't got manners. But I was starved.

"What?" I ask Remo.

"Look around you," he says. Me and Miss Arena start looking around the eating area. "What do you see?"

"Bunch of riders," I tell him, which reminds me that we have to have our horses checked out, so I remind them as I wonder if Doc Jack is at this checkpoint.

"A *bunch* of riders," Miss Arena agrees.

Grinning, Dindie Remo lowers his cup of tea.

I look toward the stalls where the vets are, but I don't see Doc Jack. I see a line of men waiting to get their horses.

Then I'm standing, staring, but I ain't looking for Patrick Jack.

"I don't see them two Texans," I say.

"The Spaniard's not here, either," Miss Arena says. "Or that Frenchman and his English saddle."

"But there's the Arab," Remo says.

Sure enough, and the sheik, or whatever he is, still wears his robes and cloth headdress instead of a hat. I watch as he saddles that beautiful horse of his.

"Maybe the Texans and the Spaniard's behind us," I say hopefully.

"I wouldn't count on that," Remo says.

The Arab's swinging onto his horse, kicking the stallion's ribs, and then he's flying through the cemetery, leaping his horse over the fence, before heading out to the road that leads to . . . ?

I look at the map for the next stop. "Winona," I say out loud, even though nobody asked me. Then: "We head pretty much north and east from here. Nothing but some creeks marked on the map. No big rivers."

Miss Arena wipes her mouth and stands. "You can swim, can't you, Evan?"

I sigh and slowly shake my head. To change the subject, I say: "I wonder if we can catch that Arab before the next station."

"Don't try that, my friend," Remo warns. "Run your own race. We haven't reached the halfway point."

"You want to take some eggrolls"—Remo points to a bowl—"for supper tonight?"

Miss Arena grins. "He don't have to. He can just lick his dinner off his shirt sleeve."

Doc Jack ain't part of the crew to check horses, but the vet who says Taos Lightning's good to go assures me that Doc Jack will likely be at Memphis. He don't know that he just broke a rule. He's just told me that Memphis will be one of the home stations where they'll check our horses again. Three, four stops from here, I'm guessing.

They house us in an old warehouse in Winona, right in the center of town. We get to eat fried chicken and biscuits. Afterward, we all bunk on crates. The place smells of tobacco, dust, and sweat, which mingles with the odors of horses and leather.

Every joint in my body aches. I'm afraid to look at the insides of my legs. Feels like there's hardly no skin left.

"You know what the man told me?" Arena Lancaster asks from her private bunk. The folks in Winona, Mississippi, have put her in a small office in this big, drafty building. Remo and I are sleeping close to the door to watch out for her. The locals helping out won't hear of having a young girl sleeping with fifteen men, especially, I heard one say, since one of them ain't a Christian and is, in fact, an Arab. A prune-faced widow who smelled like mothballs added: "There's that big colored boy, too."

"What man?" Remo says in answer to Miss Arena's question.

"The mayor, I reckon. The one who give the speech before we ate."

"You think he's the mayor?" Remo asks.

I've closed my eyes as the two get nowhere fast in their conversation.

"What the Sam Hill did he say?" I finally snap at them. "All I want to do is sleep."

"He said we get a bath in Memphis," Miss Arena says.

I sleep hard. Feel like I could sleep for a week, but a burning in my eyes makes me open them. The warehouse is pretty dark, but I can see a light flickering. I can hear horses are starting to stamp, snort, and whinny. I tell myself I must be dreaming.

Somebody coughs as I start to crawl out of my bedroll. Out of the corner of my eye, I see Dindie Remo shoot up into a sitting position, and his revolver comes up with him.

"What the . . . ?" he says.

Then I'm leaping to my feet, cussing, when I ought to be praying.

Others are coming awake now. More coughing.

"Fire!" somebody yells.

I'm busting inside that office, finding Miss Arena, pulling on her arm. "Miss Arena," I say. "Get up. The building's burning."

"Quit it," she says.

Then Dindie Remo is standing next to me. He ain't got the patience I do. He kicks her foot.

Her eyes open angrily.

"We got to get out of here!" Remo orders.

There's only sixteen of us riders in the warehouse, plus our horses. Might be a few race officials, but I figure they got themselves rooms in a Winona hotel or boarding house.

"Open it!" a fellow is yelling, pointing at the

twin front doors as we come out of the office with Miss Arena. "Now!"

I leave my boots behind as I run toward the makeshift stalls the locals have put up inside this old building. The Arab's ahead of me. He opens one of the stalls, then moves to the next one. He's heading right for the fire.

I'm on the other side of the aisle of stalls now. I reach the first stall. There's a dun pounding inside, screaming. Through the smoke I can see the terror in her eyes. I knock down the poles, and jump out of the mare's way. She's heading toward the big doors that somebody's gotten open. Some fool tries to catch the mare, only to fall flat on his chest, barely avoiding getting his skull smashed in by a hoof.

Another man is yelling over the roar of flames: "No! No! No! There's enough men freeing horses. Saddles. Get the saddles! Saddles, tack, everything. Make a bucket brigade! You . . ."

I don't hear no more.

I'm at the next stall, pulling away the first bar. This stall holds a black that looks like a thoroughbred. I pull at the second bar, but it's stuck.

A man in long-handle underwear shoves me aside. "What do you think you're doing?" he bellows. "Trying to win the race for yourself?"

The thoroughbred rears, kicks, screams. The

man—who must be addled—starts to put the bar I removed back in place.

I shove him, guessing the black is his horse. "You want to burn to death?" I yell at him. "You want to kill your horse?" I grab at the pole. The horse rams the top bar.

The man lets go, balls his left fist, swings at me. Ducking underneath the fist, I slip on the straw and hay, and fall to my knees. The man's clasping his hands over his head. He's about to bring both down on me, but I grip the pole he has dropped and swing it up. It catches him right between his legs. He grunts as he collapses, and by then two other men are grabbing him. One hauls him away toward the door. The other helps with the remaining pole. I want to go with the man headed toward the door.

But I can't.

Opening the doors seems to have caused a draft in this rickety old tinderbox. Flames shoot up. Heat and smoke blast my face. But I run to the next stall, get it open. Now I'm dodging horses and men, and I start coughing real bad. My eyes begin to sting even worse. I can hardly see.

But I can hear. Hear something I'll never get out of my mind.

The fire has reached one of the stalls and a horse is being burned alive.

"Taos . . ." I whisper.

No, not him. Somehow, I make out my stallion.

Taos Lighting is ramming against the bars of his stall, down two from where I am.

Riders work both sides of the warehouse. Panicked horses rush out as soon as they are freed. One, a black or dark bay or brown—can't rightly tell from all the smoke—slams someone on the other side of me, sending him bouncing off a center pole. Two men hurry to him. Pick him up. Carry him away.

At the end of the building, the roof caves in, sending showers of sparks flying amid the thick, bitter smoke and savage bursts of orange flames.

I can hardly see, but I'm letting out what I believe is Miss Arena's gelding. Might be her palomino. Might be a dun. I struggle to put a halter around him, but he busts me in the shoulder, and I spin and drop to my knees again. The horse bolts for the door. I come up, and just manage to duck out of Taos Lightning's path, which sends me to the floor again. Pushing myself up, I feel sparks landing on my shirt. Miss Arena's lying on her back. A horse must have knocked her down. Someone jumps over her, runs past me.

I try to breathe, but it hurts too much. I crawl underneath the black, choking smoke, and reach Miss Arena.

"Arena?" My voice sounds raw.

Her forehead's bleeding, but her eyelids are fluttering.

"Where's Dindie?" she mutters.

Don't even try to answer. It hurt like blazes just to say her name. Ahead of me, the flames are dancing tauntingly, starting to spread across the floor that smells of pinesap, devouring the hay and straw and anything in its path.

Grabbing Miss Arena's shoulders, I pull her up. "I can . . ."—she coughs—". . . walk."

But we're running out of time. I toss her over my shoulder, somehow get to my feet, and stagger through the smoke, holding my breath, straining, sweating, praying that I'm going the right way.

On Main Street it's chaos, but at least I can take in fresh air.

Setting Miss Arena down by a water trough, I wash my eyes. Can't see clearly, but I see enough. The hotel's burning. So's the café, the mercantile, the post office. I can hear the cries and screams of the folks over the roaring flames. Bells ring from the church steeples, except for the church that's been swept up by fire. Folks in their nightclothes have pulled a red and copper steam engine up alongside the hotel. Both townfolk and riders are holding the hoses as they pump water onto the fire. But it don't look like they're putting anything out.

A farm wagon comes up. Even after setting the brake, the driver has a hard time keeping the mules under control. He yells: "Throw saddles and gear in the back. Hurry. Hurry!"

I see one of the race officials sitting next to the driver. Neither one of them wears shoes, and it strikes me that I'm barefoot, too. I look back at the warehouse, but I sure ain't going in there for no stinking old boots.

We fill that wagon up with everything us riders saved. The wagon pulls away just as another arrives, but this one's just a buckboard. We fill that one, too.

"Meet at first light at the railroad depot!" the official yells. "If it hasn't been consumed by flames."

"Come on, Kendrick." A hand grabs my shoulder, gives it a squeeze.

Turning, I feel my heart leap. It's Dindie Remo.

"Let's lend a hand," he says.

"What about the race?" one of the riders asks. "Where's my horse?"

"Forget your horse, mister," another fellow says. "Forget this stupid race."

I follow Remo to the trough where Miss Arena is sitting, holding a cloth to her forehead. I fill a bucket of water, pass it to the Arab in front of me, who passes it on to one of the townfolk. Then Miss Arena joins in and hands Dindie Remo another bucket, and he passes it to me, and I give it to the Arab, who gives it to a Texan who don't act like a jackass.

This seems to go on for eternity. And then it's over.

• • •

Soot blackens my face, my hands. My lungs burn with each breath.

A wagon loaded with kegs of beer has pulled up to the depot where all the riders were to meet up. The driver says we can drink as much as we can hold. He ain't got no saloon no more, but he wants to thank all of us, even the Arab, for doing our part to save their town.

Which, from the looks of Winona, Mississippi, ain't much. Most of the homes and all but one of the churches, which was in the center of town, have survived. But I don't reckon more than a dozen buildings on the main street remain standing. Even the icehouse is gone.

No one takes the brewer up on his offer, but he taps one of the kegs and pours hisself a foamy beer.

Going through the wagons that hold our things, I find my saddle, my saddlebags, my bridle. Soogan is gone. No hat. No boots, which ain't good since I lost one of my socks at some point during the fire. I check one of the saddlebags and find my card. The map's still in my vest pocket, along with the watch Doc Jack give me. Luckily, last night I had been too tired to take off my vest, or put my watch inside the crown of my hat, which was my usual habit.

"Where's my saddle?" says the rider who tried to stop me from saving his horse. "Everyone's saddle's here but mine. I knew you jackals would do this to me. I knew it. You probably set the fire to . . ."

The Frenchie in jodhpurs walks up and punches him right in the mouth. No one laughs. No one is shocked. The addled fellow touches his busted lip, but he don't say nothing more.

"We have thirteen horses in the corral by the livery on the west edge of town," the race boss tells us.

Thirteen? Sixteen had been inside the warehouse and I know one didn't get out in time and is buried amongst the burned-out débris of the warehouse. But it's a miracle they caught up thirteen of our mounts.

"I'm missing stuff," says a pockmarked fellow with a big mustache. "My card and map were in the pommel bag."

The race boss sighs, and the gent next to him reaches inside his coat and pulls out a map and hands it to the pockmarked man. "You can use my map. We'll give you a new card at the next home station, providing you make the way station along the route, the Sardis train depot near the Little Tallahatchie River."

"If your horse ain't one of the missin'," a fellow with a Texas accent says.

"We have several Negroes and our own stable hands scouring the woods for the missing horses," the race boss says.

"One didn't make it out of the warehouse," Miss Arena says.

A silence descends among the men.

"I lost my boots, my pants, my shirt, my leggings, and my hat," says the man in his union suit, which is covered in small burn holes. He spits tobacco juice, and adds: "You expect me to ride like this?"

"We will outfit everyone in Sardis," the second man says. "This I promise you."

"Why not here?" demands a red-mustached man in denim trousers, with no shirt, only a bandanna around his neck and another wrapped around his smoke-smudged head.

"Look around you, man!" the race boss says angrily. "These people have lost practically their entire town. You've lost clothes."

"And a race," the crazy one with the busted lip says, adding: "Along with three thousand dollars. And the honor of winning."

I almost feel sorry for the fool.

"The map says Sardis is a lot farther than fifty miles," says another.

"I dare say it's closer to seventy," says the race boss.

Shaking our heads, us riders start cussing and moaning.

"The longest," says the man next to the race boss, "of the entire race, I do believe, or close to it."

"You can quit," the race boss announces. "Or you can ride. The ten-hour limit is suspended for the time being for you riders till you reach the home station in Memphis."

"So what'll it be, boys . . . and ma'am? Ride? Or quit?"

What choice do we have? We ride. Well, all except three of us. On our way out of Winona, we try not to stare at the women, children, men . . . their faces ravaged and uncomprehending, eyes reddened by smoke, and tears. Tucked-tailed dogs whine. The bells of the churches start ringing as the injured and dead are helped out or collected in wagons.

CHAPTER FIFTEEN

Remo has gone on ahead. Miss Arena and me, we're on a woods road, and can't see nothing for all the pines. I reckon just about every rider has passed us by now, except the three we left in Winona, and if the horses of two of them are found, it won't take those riders long to catch me.

Or Miss Arena.

"You saved my life in that warehouse," Miss Arena says. "I won't forget that."

My bare foot slips out of the stirrup again. I cuss as I put it back in. The bottom of my foot is getting rubbed raw. My other foot, with the dirty, stinking sock, don't feel much better. And without a hat, my head bakes in the sun. I'll be glad when the sun slips behind the trees.

"You forgot about that cottonmouth," I tell her. "So we're even."

"I'd rather die from poison than get burned alive," she says.

I keep recalling the screams of the horses.

There's lots of things I've seen and heard during this race. My list of things I never want to see or hear again keeps getting bigger.

"You want my hat?" Miss Arena asks.

I shake my head.

"Want some water?" she asks.

That I do, but I decline. I shift in the saddle, try to find some position somewhat tolerable, but we're moving at a trot, and my backbone feels like it's about to poke up through the top of my head. I've ridden some horses with an easy trot, but not many. Taos Lightning ain't one of the exceptions.

"I got some whiskey," she says. "Want a snort?"

"No."

"It'll cut through the dust and the smoke you swallowed."

I turn and stare at her real hard.

"Don't you like to talk?" she asks.

"Not especially," I answer.

"Dindie said he'd wait for us a couple of hours in Sardis," she says. "But if we don't see him there, we'll most likely see him in Memphis. You ever been to Memphis?"

She won't shut up. Walking, trotting, or loping, she don't hardly stop talking all that day. We decide to stop for a bit. I loosen my saddle. Hers, too. Once Taos Lightning has cooled off, I ask if I can borrow her hat.

"You don't need it now, Evan," she says, but she removes the hat and hands it to me. "Sun's low."

Taking my canteen, I pour water into the hat's crown, and bring it to the stallion. He practically inhales the water.

"That's my hat, not a pail or a trough," she

snaps at me as she reaches for it. Since I'm in an ornery mood, for some reason, I pull it from her grasp. Her eyes fire up, and though she's trying to look angry, I can see she's full of humor. She reaches out again. I wave the hat, and right then Taos Lightning bites out a hunk of the brim.

"You!!!" While my stallion chews contentedly, she charges and crashes into my chest. Down we go, but the ground's right soft here. She's laughing. So am I, and we roll over a couple of times. At length, she has the hat, and she's sitting on my stomach, studying the gouge in its brim.

I try to move, but she drops the hat and leans down. Her hands grab my shoulders. "I ain't letting you up till you promise to get me a new hat. In Sardis. Maybe Memphis." Her hair's brushing against my face. I can smell smoke in her hair, as I stare into her eyes.

They change. Soften. They're so clear and blue and beautiful. She has freckles on her nose. It's a cute nose. There's a gap between her two front teeth, not a big one, just a tiny sliver. Her breath don't stink of whiskey or smoke.

Before I can make that promise or do anything else, she rolls off me, picks up her hat, and heads to her horse. She lets the gelding drink water from the crown.

I get some salt from my saddlebags, and give a bit to Taos Lightning. Then I hand some to Miss Arena. She thanks me without looking.

"What's your horse's name?" I ask.

Without looking, she answers. "Horse-Horse."

"Horse-Horse?"

She almost smiles. She don't look my way, and she might be smiling at the feeling the palomino's tongue makes on her hand as he licks the salt.

"There was a little girl," she says, still staring at her gelding. "Four, five maybe. Down near Pleasanton. Little town down around San Antone. That's where I got him." She reaches up, and rubs the gelding's neck with a circular motion. The way Pa, when he was sober, told me always to rub a horse.

"This little girl . . . she started crying when she realized her pa was going to give away Horse-Horse. She begged enough to break a heart, if I had had a heart. But her pa'd already give me the bill of sale, and I'd paid him . . . paid him real well. So I knelt by the little girl, and I promised to treat this horse right. Love him. Cherish him. I told her that I needed this horse. This horse could take me places. Take me far away."

Miss Arena then puts the hat she'd been holding on her head. She brings her right hand up and brushes at her cheeks, then turns so I can't see nothing but her back.

"The little girl," she says, "turned away from me, sobbing hard, and she said . . . 'Can't you take me with you?' And that did break my heart which I thought I didn't have."

All day, Miss Arena has been talking, but I can't tell you hardly a thing she said. But now she is talking. Really talking. Things I reckon I'll always remember.

"The little girl's pa . . . he was a widower . . . on a hardscrabble place. He started to scold her, but I turned and showed him my meanest look. And he knew he got a good deal. Got more than the horse was worth.

"I tried to tell the little girl I couldn't take her, that Horse-Horse couldn't carry us both, and that I was sorry. She just ran to the little dogtrot cabin. But she stopped at the door and yelled back at me . . . 'Just don't ever call him anything but his name. Horse-Horse.' "

I want to go up to her and comfort her, put my hand on her shoulder. But I don't move.

Both horses have lowered their heads and are eating grass.

"It's dark," Miss Arena says. "We spending the night here?"

"No." My voice sounds distant. "No, Miss Arena. . . ."

She spins around, so fast, so unexpectedly that her horse shies away, but she reaches out quickly and grabs the reins. I'm going for the reins to Taos Lightning, who's still nothing better than half broke.

"Please, Evan, please. Don't call me *miss*. I ain't no miss, no mama, nor ma'am. Call me

Arena. I don't call you Mister Kendrick. My name's Arena. All right?"

My head bobs.

She sighs. "How long are we staying?"

"Full moon tonight," I tell her. "Or close to it. When the moon rises, we'll ride."

We just stand there, not saying anything, looking at each other, too scared, too uncertain to move. Finally we tend to our horses, then wait till the moon begins to climb.

Again, we ride.

Arena don't talk now. Oddly enough, I miss her voice, her stories, even the flapdoodle. There's nothing to hear but the clopping of hoofs and the wind rustling through the trees. It's a strange sound, the wind. I keep looking up expecting to feel raindrops. But it's only the Mississippi wind.

I reach for her. She pulls away. I lunge.

My eyes shoot open, and I'm grabbing for the horn. Taos Lightning does a stutter step, but I don't lose the reins. More importantly, I don't fall out of the saddle onto this road.

Arena laughs.

Slowly, my head clears. I see we're out of the woods, riding through a cleared field. I look over to Arena on the palomino.

I shake my head.

"Have a nice nap?" she asks.

I don't answer. I've been asleep in the saddle. Can't recall ever doing that before, but then I've never ridden . . . gosh, I don't want to even consider the miles. Or the days.

"You look sweet when you're asleep."

My eyes find Arena again. Her partly eaten hat bounces on her back. Grinning, she shifts in her saddle. I guess those bad memories, dark thoughts, are gone. She's cheerful again. Maybe she'll start talking. That might keep me awake.

"Is it morning already?" It's bright enough.

"No, silly." She points overhead.

"Golly." I'm looking up. "That's some moon."

CHAPTER SIXTEEN

We cross the Little Tallahatchie River. No bridge, no ferry, but the river's fairly shallow, with a rocky bottom. I squeeze horn and reins, and slide into the dark water. I lose my last sock . . . ain't no big loss. Wasn't enough left to darn anyway.

You got to say one thing about the race officials. They live up to their word.

In front of the depot for the Louisville, New Orleans & Texas Railroad, a big canvas tent has been set up. Inside are tables and shelves stacked with all sorts of plunder. Even saddles and tack.

"Come on, son. Ma'am." A man in a green-checked sack suit rushes off the station platform, snapping his fingers. A couple of young Negroes step out to take our horses.

Legs, feet, and backside burning, I slide from the saddle and step on a sharp rock. I swear, but the fellow and Arena pretend they don't hear.

The place is buzzing with activity.

A man stops us, starts to reach inside his coat pocket, but then just smiles. "No, no, no," he says. "That's plumb silly of me. I'll give you the map after you've outfitted yourselves."

Then a plump, middle-aged woman's walks up to us. She carries peaches—real peaches, not canned peaches—and apples in a basket. "You poor children. You poor, poor children. What an awful thing to have experienced." She gives us each a peach.

As we continue to walk, we're pulled into this circle of people. In the middle there's a preacher, a big, big man who ought to try a diet of fruit, rather than what he must be feeding hisself. He's leading a prayer. Now, I ain't got nothing against praying, but this fellow goes on way too long for me. And soon Arena and me lose interest. We are, I want to remind him, running in a long horse race, and we're nowhere near in the lead. But not wanting God mad at me, I keep my head bowed until I just can't stand it.

Once we make our escape from that circle of devouts, several women rush up to Arena, making a motherly fuss over her as they lead her toward the wood-framed mercantile.

As Arena disappears inside the store, I'm pretty much pushed inside the big tent. I don't rightly know where to begin. Never seen so much plunder to be had, and before I know it, folks are coming up to me, offering this and that—some things I need, some I don't. I wonder if they've been treating all of us riders this way. Well, it ain't their money. Ain't mine, neither.

A boy not much older than me arrives with a bunch of hats. I try a few, but nothing fits.

"By George," he says as he tosses aside another hat, "you have one big head, sir. If you don't mind my saying. What's the biggest hat we have, Thaddeus?" he asks the skinny, buck-toothed man with him.

Turns out, the biggest hat they find is a derby— flat topped, extra fine felt. Worth two dollars and two bits. Out of Bloomingdale's, they say. It fits, but I hand it back. When I tell them I ain't wearing no derby, they protest.

"It'll get blowed off once I put my horse into a gallop," I complain.

They skedaddle to see what else they can find.

The boots that I'm offered by a man called Cliff fit pretty good, though I'll likely have to soak them in water till they shape to my feet better. The socks feel heavenly, especially after the rubbing the bottoms of my feet took from those stirrups.

"Those pants must go," says Cliff.

I start to protest, but when I look down at my britches, I see just how covered in dirt and grime they are. They'll never come clean.

"Off. Off. Off," Cliff orders me, snapping his fingers each time he says *off.*

I try not to laugh. I bet Sardis, Mississippi, never had nothing like this happen here before.

Cliff don't laugh, though, once my pants are off. I'm sure glad Arena Lancaster ain't here to see my limbs. I wish that Cliff weren't, neither.

"Goodness gracious. You need a doctor, young man."

I grab the new duck britches, start pulling them on. "No. I'm fine," I tell him, fearing he'll see the panic in my eyes. I try not to look at the sores on my legs. My cotton drawers have been ripped off way above my knees, and what's left ain't fit to wear. Saddles wear on a man's limbs something fierce.

"Fetch some undergarments," Cliff tells the older man who enters the tent.

"No!" I protest.

"Why don't you wear a union suit?" Cliff asks. "Or chaps?"

"Extra weight," I tell him.

"My goodness. I never would've thought . . ."

The old gent brings me some long-handles, but I ain't about to pull off my under britches in front of him. I want to get my gear, find a hat that fits, and get out of Sardis, Mississippi.

Before we get into an argument, a sweet little woman old enough to have known George Washington brings in some tea. I drink the cold concoction. It's real cold, with ice. And it's been sweetened with sugar. And it's just what I need to get me to Memphis.

Standing outside my tent, refreshed inside and out, I am offered a new saddle. I get the suspicion that these merchants are looking to run up as big a bill as they can to give to Mr. Fox and Mr. Baldwin. I make it clear to the balding man that I don't need a saddle. I guess they don't understand that we're in a race and the last thing you want to be doing is breaking in a new saddle. Don't think Taos Lightning would want me to be doing that, neither. I do take the new saddle blanket, though. Mine is fraying and smells like smoke.

I pull the new vest Cliff gave me over my new collarless shirt. Then I put my pocket watch in a vest pocket. I top it all off with a bandanna.

"Will either of these fit, sir?" The gent with the hats has brung over three more to try on.

I don't even think about reaching for the one that's made out of plaid material. The straw one don't fit. The beaver hat, though not a perfect fit, ain't a bad hat.

"Excellent," says the fellow.

I know why. I see the price tag on this hat. Three dollars and fifty cents.

Finally finished trying things on, I'm anxious to get back to the race, even though I didn't get to rest. As I look around, I see that the field hands have Taos Lightning saddled, and so is Horse-Horse. I walk over to the horses.

"Thanks." I take the reins to my horse, and am about to swing into the saddle when I remember something mighty important.

I climb up on the platform of the depot and find the gent in the green-checked suit. He's staring down the road.

"Sir?"

He looks at me, smiles, nods.

"The map . . . to Memphis?"

"Oh, for heaven's sake." He hands me the map, and looks back down the road. "Are others coming?"

"Two," I say. "If their horses have been found. That's all that should be behind us. That were in Winona during the fire."

"A tragedy. A terrible tragedy. Anarchists."

I blink. "Anarchists?"

"That's what one of the riders told me. A member of one of those societies out to protect the horses. Horses over men. What rubbish. What a waste!"

I slip the map into my vest pocket for the time being.

"I'd take a horse over some men," I tell him. Back in Winona nobody never said nothing about an anarchist or some horse lover starting that fire. But I forget all about what that fellow just told me on account Miss Arena has just stepped around the corner.

She smiles up at me as one of the Negro lads hands her the reins to Horse-Horse.

"Thanks for all your hospitality," I tell the gent, tip my hat to the old woman who brung me the sugary tea, and thank the colored guys again.

Arena is already in the saddle, and she kicks her palomino into a lope.

I catch up with her. This time, I do the talking.

"Nice hat," I say.

She smiles, which makes me happy.

Arena Lancaster still wears her old one, the one Taos Lightning took a bite out of, but she has on new togs, and she looks mighty fine.

CHAPTER SEVENTEEN

Memphis ain't no city for a horse race.

Wagons, carts, horses, mules, donkeys, men, women, children, even two of these things called velocipedes pack the street. There's folks playing banjos and fiddles, harmonicas, drums, brass horns, and things I never seen nor heard before. You can't hardly tell who's playing what song. Women dance on a balcony, and they're hardly wearing anything.

"What are you gawking at, Kendrick?" Arena says, and pulls on the reins to head in a different direction.

I blink, have to make myself look away from that balcony. Staring ahead, I spot Dindie Remo standing in the street. I ride up to him.

"Gosh, Dindie." I hold out my hand. With a wide grin, he takes my hand in both of his.

"Miss Arena with you?"

I hook a thumb to my right.

"Split up. She took the street over yonder. I hope hers ain't as crowded as this one." A thought strikes me. "Hey, is all this foofaraw for us?"

He laughs. "They're celebrating whatever day it is, Evan. They're celebrating being alive and being in Memphis."

"Memphis?" says a pot-bellied black man

wearing a green shirt, yellow britches, and a purple sash. He's got earrings hanging from both ears, and two of his front teeth sparkle with gold. "I thought this was Gomorrah."

"Same thing," Remo says to the man, but the stranger has vanished in the crowd.

I follow Remo's directions to the home station, even though a couple of alleys are almost too narrow for Taos Lightning and me to squeeze through. But we get there.

I find the vets and the check-in dude. Have to tell them my name, where I hail from, my horse's name, and once they confirm that I'm on their list, they make me sign an affidavit that tells them that I am swearing to race brass and God that I indeed was at the warehouse in Winona, Mississippi, when it catched fire.

Y'all want to see where the hair on my right arm got singed off? I think about asking them that, but I bite my bottom lip, and let it go.

The horse-holder hands my stallion's reins to one of the horse doctors. The check-in man tells me that I'll be given a map and my new punch card if Taos Lightning gets a passing grade. He nods at the stairs on the side of a red-brick building. "The bathhouse is up there."

I snort.

"The bath," he tells me, "is mandatory."

That wasn't in none of the rules they give us in Galveston, but I begrudgingly climb the

146

steps, every one of them causing me pain, and enter through the door. The room's like an attic that's lined with nothing but washtubs. I think I recognize some of them boys in the soapy suds from the warehouse in Winona. Don't see the Spaniard, the Arab, or the Frenchie. A fellow in a white coat comes up to me, grabs my arm, and hustles me toward an empty tub.

"What's your name? How old are you? Height? Weight? What kind of horse are you riding? Have you ever suffered from measles, smallpox, heart palpitations, diphtheria . . . ?" He hardly finishes one question before he's on to the next one, and a lot of what he asks, I can't answer. Then he motions to a tub and says: "Take off your clothes and climb in."

"In front of you?"

"I'm a doctor."

He don't look that much older than me.

"If you don't get into that bath, mister, you won't be continuing in this race."

I oblige him, and start to get into the tub, but he says: "The . . ."—he coughs in disgust—"drawers shall be removed . . . Goodness gracious!" The pad off which he read his questions falls to his side. "Your legs."

That tears it. Now everybody's gawking at my legs, and I don't mean just the doctors. One fellow stands up in his tub. Hurriedly, I whip off what's left of my drawers and try to get into the tub, but two of those gents in white coats stop me.

It ain't fun, being stark naked, held by two strangers with two more coming up to you, and one of them dropping to his knees and putting his hands on my chaffed and blistered thighs. The calves ain't so bad because of the boots.

"Son, you can't ride like this."

"The dickens you say!" I bark. "I've ridden from Mora County, New Mexico, to Galveston, Texas, and all the way here."

"If these sores get infected . . ."

"They ain't nothing. Don't even hurt," I say.

The man on his knees stands. He grins. "Is that, so?"

The gents holding my arms let go, and the oldest doctor motions to the tub I was about to climb into.

"Go ahead. If you can sit fifteen minutes in that tub, I'll sign a release."

"By grab, Kendrick, how'd you manage it?"

Dindie Remo and me is in the bunkhouse, or what's supposed to be a bunkhouse but is really another warehouse. This one smells like dead fish rather than cured tobacco. I'm lying on my bedroll. My legs feel like they've been doused with coal oil and somebody just struck a match.

"Salt bath probably did him some good," Doc Jack says as he brings the blanket over my bare legs.

"Bath wasn't nothing," I tell them two. "You making me get my pants off once I got here was ten times worse."

"Why not wear a union suit?" Doc Jack asks. "Or at least chaps?"

My head shakes stubbornly. "Pa said whilst we was riding across Texas that a race like this might come down to an ounce or two."

"Kendrick," Remo says, "you don't hardly weigh more than two ounces yourself."

"No, sir," I tell them. "You know why I got to win this race. I can't chance nothing."

I push myself up, but then Arena Lancaster enters the warehouse and comes over to us. My face turns blood red.

"We're supposed to be riding out of here in ten minutes," she tells me. "We can cover three more hours of riding before we have to call it a day."

"I'm not sure Evan Kendrick's going any farther," says Doc Jack.

The doc's words are like a punch in my gut.

"Taos Lightning?" Arena cries.

Doc shakes his head at Arena, and points at my legs. "Evan," he says, "you have two good legs. You keep this up, you'll be lame for life . . . or you could end up with stumps to get you around."

"I might have an extra pair of long-handles in my saddlebags," Remo says. "But they'll be too big for him."

"Remo." Doc's head shakes again. "This isn't . . ."

"Come on, Doc." Remo raises his voice, and Doc stops, even takes a short step back. "You know what this race means to him. I figured the kid would be out of the race before we left Texas. We're in Tennessee. He's stuck with us. That ain't just due to that mustang he's mounted on, neither."

"Doctor . . ."—Arena's voice is more soothing—"you'll let him go one, won't you? Look at him at the next home station. If he's no better, then you end his race."

"What the Sam Hill are y'all doing?" I practically scream. "You should've been loping out of here two, three hours ago, Dindie." I point a finger at my . . . *friend?* That's right. Dindie Remo's a friend. The thought takes me by surprise.

He shrugs. "That ol' blue roan of mine needs a rest. Long ways to go yet."

"Don't start defending me. I'll . . ."

"Shut up," Arena says, and for some reason—maybe on account of my burning legs—I do. "What do you say, Doc?" she asks.

He studies me.

Shaking his head, he says: "He needs some protection underneath his trousers. And he's not leaving here without either long unmentionables or chaps."

"You'll have a hard time finding a store open now," Remo says.

Which, I believe, is what Doc is thinking, because he says: "Then he can ride out of here in the morning."

That certain sure will put winning this race far out of my reach, unless everybody else drops out or dies. I don't see that happening to those blow-hard Texans, the Arab, the Spaniard, or the Frenchie. And I don't want it to happen to Arena or Remo.

"Well, maybe if I got . . . ," Dindie Remo starts, but Arena laughs.

"Two Evan Kendricks would fit in your drawers, Dindie," she says. "But me? I'm not much bigger than Evan. And back in Mississippi, I got an extra pair of bloomers."

Now my face turns thirty shades of red. "I ain't gonna . . ."

Arena's already running off to find her saddlebags. I start to throw off the blanket and get dressed, but Doc Jack leans over, and his voice—and his eyes—become pure ice.

"Listen to me, young man. I'm not just a horse doctor. I'm a race official, and if you want me to release you, you'll be putting on that young lady's unmentionables. Otherwise, you wait till morning when the dry-goods store opens. So, don't cross me, Evan. I've been more than fair to you."

I sink back onto my bedroll. The coffee in my stomach begins to sour. I want to be back in our ramshackle outfit in New Mexico. I want to die.

Because here comes Arena Lancaster, waving a pair of unmentionables for everybody to see. She drops them on the blanket that covers the lower half of my person.

"Here you go. Try them on."

"Not in front of you!" I bark.

She giggles. "You're no fun, Evan Kendrick." But she hurries away.

That leaves me with Dindie Remo and Doc Jack, and I don't feel like putting on no silly pantaloons in front of them, neither.

"My wife," Doc says, "God rest her soul, went to a bloomer party back in 'Fifty-One. It proved quite the scandal in Nacogdoches." And he hands me some ointment to put on my legs.

CHAPTER EIGHTEEN

The next stop is at a blacksmith's barn in Dancyville, but I don't think all the smithies here live in this town. In fact, it wouldn't surprise me none if the blacksmiths outnumber the townfolk. Having passed one rider leading a lame horse on the road, I figure it'd do me and Taos Lightning good to have the stallion's shoes checked.

I'm waiting when Arena rides Horse-Horse in. She hands the reins to a smithy, gets her card punched and filled out, all the while smiling at me.

"How are your . . . limbs . . . doing?"

All I do is shrug. But the insides of my legs do feel better.

A thin, hard-boned woman comes over and hands both of us cups of steaming-hot coffee. It's too hot to drink, so I study the map they give me when I checked in. Arena looks over my shoulder. So does the woman, who clears her throat, and when Arena and me stare at her, she glances at the smithies.

"Listen, children." Her voice drops into a whisper. "Your next stop is Parker's Crossroads. I lost my youngest boy there in 'Sixty-Two." She adds with pride: "He rid with Forrest."

"I'm sorry . . . ," Arena says, but the woman waves her off.

"Hush up and hear me. That was more'n twenty years ago. Lucas's been with the Lord all this time. I'm talkin' 'bout today. That map. That has you goin' straight into Jackson. But don't ride to Jackson. You give it a wide berth. Both of you." She spits. "It's the Baptists. They done taken over Jackson."

"Baptists?" Arena repeats.

Her head bobs slightly while she fingers the snuff from between her gums, drops it on the floor, and reaches for a can of snuff in her apron pocket to replace what she just removed. "That's right. I ain't got nothin' ag'in' Baptists, but they gots a new preacher and he's full of vinegar. Baptists, they ain't got nothin' ag'in' hoss racin', but this here preacher done preached from the pulpit that this here race ain't got nothin' in it but cowboys, demons of the most wickedest souls, and rapscallions. And I reckon they might be right. I done seen a big darky stop here to get his roan shod. And another darky in the strangest get-up I seen outside pictures put inside some of 'em big Bibles."

I figure she means Dindie Remo and the Arab.

"But you two look like nice young 'uns. You . . ."—she points at me—"even reminds me of my youngest. Lucas was his name . . . or did I say that already? His bullet holes was through his front, so we ain't ashamed of him. He's with the Lord. You stay out of Jackson, children. Them Baptists there'll try to save your souls. And you'll never win this here race."

We ride, me and Arena. Past plantations, places thick with hardwoods, over hills, near ponds, across creeks. We ride through cotton fields, cornfields, the crops long harvested and the acreage sitting fallow till next spring. We ride by dairy farms, hayfields, and the ruins of a tannery. We take the snuff-dipping woman's advice and skirt around Jackson.

We think about the old lady's dead son when we stop at Parker's Crossroads. It's peaceful. You'd never know a battle had been fought here. No graveyard, no headstones, just a few tents, a campfire, and men to punch our cards and hand us the next map.

Four black men, using long poles and thick oars for a water-logged raft that has me sweating, guide us onto a barge to cross the Tennessee River to a place called Cuba Landing. A mink called Adam is chained to the seat of the man at the stern. Arena asks if she might pet him, but the man's head shakes sternly. The mink looks just as mean as the man, but the boatmen get us across that wide, deep river, and the folks in Cuba Landing fill our bellies with fried catfish, cornpone, and boiled peanuts. They call the latter goober peas. Arena says they taste like snot.

We ride to the Buffalo River, where there ain't no bridge, no rafts or barges, and no ferry to haul us across. An island rests in the middle of the river, which ain't as big as the Tennessee but looks deep and dangersome. Smoke drifts skyward from campfires on the island, where we can smell meat frying, and see horses being saddled and unsaddled. There are a couple of tents, and a red flag keeps popping in the breeze as the sun starts to sink.

"That's the next station," Arena says.

"Yeah." I look at my watch, then show it to Arena. Nine forty-one, she tells me. Meaning we got less than twenty minutes to swim to that island, else we'll have to camp on the bank.

I feel ashamed and sick. But, mostly, I'm feeling fear.

Horse-Horse moves close to me, and I make myself look into Arena's eyes.

"We can try to find some place a little shallower," she says.

"Not in this state," I say.

"You've swum rivers before."

"Not this big."

"Listen." She reaches over and pats Taos Lightning behind the saddle. "This boy, he can swim like a fish. Don't worry about a thing.

If you lose the saddle, grab hold to his tail. Or better yet . . ."—she points at the lariat strapped beneath the horn—"tie yourself on."

"Huh?"

"Tie one end around the horn. Wrap the other end around your middle. If you slide off, keep your head above water. Taos will keep swimming. You'll reach dry land. And I'll be right with you. Now this ain't gonna happen, but if Taos's head goes under, he'll drag you to the bottom. So you just slip out of that rope, and I'll pick you up."

"You're not going to drown trying to save my stupid hide," I tell her.

"Neither one of us will drown, Evan. And your horse won't neither."

I ain't convinced.

"Or," Arena tells me, "you can quit."

Nobody would've blamed Taos Lightning for losing me in the middle of the river. Not as bad as Pa done him. And I done him.

"All right," I tell him after I've followed Arena's advice and gotten myself hitched up tight. "It's up to you, boy." My spurs press against his side, and he jumps in.

I'm already holding my breath, even though the water ain't deep. What it is, though, is most certainly cold, and I get to shivering because I fear there might be cottonmouths underwater, waiting to bite me. Soon the water's up to my waist. Then I can tell Taos Lightning can't feel bottom no more.

Just ahead, Arena's yelling to encourage me.

I've kicked out of my stirrups, leaning low, feeling the water rush by me, soaking me, tugging at my boots. My hands grip the horn. I close my eyes. Even pray. Maybe I'm floating. I don't know. Can't hear Arena anymore, and then I feel something. I'm colder. The winds blowing, and water's running down my trousers, boots, hair, neck, arms. Taos Lightning snorts. His feet have found solid ground—muddy, but firm enough for him. Even firmer for me. He climbs the bank, and I see Arena right beside me, a few rods off to my left.

Once we reach the edge of the camp in the middle of this island, I rein up and spot a gent with spectacles and his sleeves rolled up. He has some papers in his hand, and he's looking at me and Arena, waving us over.

"Your names?" he asks.

We tell him.

"You two did well today," he says, and takes a pencil off his ear and makes some checkmarks on the papers. "But it was one of the ride's shortest distances. Five minutes to spare."

I slide out of the saddle and sit on a stump where I pull off my boots and empty them of water.

"What are you talking about?" I ask.

"Both of you left Parker's Crossroads at twelve after seven this morning. Had you ridden in here a few minutes later, you would've been disqualified for exceeding the ten-hour limit."

Arena takes off her hat and cocks her head. "How'd you know what time we left the last station?" she asks.

The man grins. "Telegraph."

I look around the island. No wires. In fact, I ain't seen any telegraph lines most days.

"There's no telegraph here," I say. "Don't remember seeing none at Parker's Crossroads, either."

Arena adds: "And I don't believe those new-fangled things called . . . tele- telephones have made it to this neck of the woods."

"There's a telegraph office in Clarksburg," the man says. "And one in Bakerville. Just about all there is in Bakerville." Sticking his papers under his left armpit, he holds out his right hand. "Your cards, please. I gotta punch them."

Which he does. Then he explains that every few hours—depending on how many riders are at the station at a given time—a telegraph is relayed to the next station, or the office nearest the station. There, the officials determine if the riders are within their allotted time.

"It's not foolproof," the man says. "Ask me, it's really only legitimate on a run like today. If this run had been longer, and you had had to rest somewhere overnight and then you arrived here sometime tomorrow . . . well, we really couldn't know if you rode ten hours after leaving Parker's Crossroads or twelve or fifteen. But this is one of the stations where we figure we can weed out the cheaters."

"Have you?" Arena asks.

He grins. "Alas, I am not allowed to say one way or the other. You must rest till twelve-oh-one. After that, you can leave any time you want. You'll find food over there. Hay, grain there." He points, before he goes on. "Most importantly, you'll get your next map from that tall kid with red hair and freckles sitting over at the camp desk."

Next morning, Taos Lightning swims me to the other side of the Buffalo River. I reckon a few of the fellows rode out right after midnight, and the rest before daybreak. Two that hadn't been at Parker's Crossroad when Arena and me got there, are just sitting underneath a tree, passing a jug of whiskey back and forth between them. I figure they got caught riding longer than ten hours. I should feel bad for them boys, but I don't. That means two more horses are out of this race.

It's a good morning for riding, and our horses enjoy long lopes. My legs ache, but not as much with these unmentionables under my britches.

And the ointment the doc gave me is helping, too, I suppose.

We reach the next station, another sawmill, in under ten hours. This camp seems even more crowded.

"We're catching up with people, Evan," Arena whispers as we wait for our cards to get punched.

I'm looking around, but not for other riders. When the fellow hands me my card and a map, I ask: "Ain't this one of those home stations?"

He pokes a finger at my map. "Next station. Mohawk Farms in Gallatin."

"Memphis was four stops back," I tell him.

"Yup, two hundred miles, give or take, ago," he agrees. "Fifty more will put you in Gallatin. And there will be your home station. Mandatory two-hour wait. Inspections of horses by animal doctors."

A man has walked up behind us. "If you get there," he says.

"Dindie!" Arena cries out, and starts to embrace the big man, but quickly stops herself. I don't stop myself, though, and I give him a big bear hug and pat him on the back.

"Figured you'd be in New England by this time," I say.

"Got lonesome," he says. "Thought I'd wait till y'all got here."

"Maybe you'd care to ride along with us in the morning," I offer.

"Which way y'all plan on riding?" he asks.

All three of us reach for our maps.

"The Natchez Trace," I read, and look at what appears to be the main road in these parts.

"You familiar with it?" Remo asks us.

Arena and me both shake our heads.

"About five hundred miles long. They made it a post road from Natchez . . . that's on the Mississippi River . . . to Nashville before I was born. But it's older than that. Been used by Choctaws and Chickasaws before that. Kaintucks used it, too. They'd use flatboats to haul whatever they wanted to sell in Natchez or New Orleans. Sell their goods. Sell what was left of their boat. Then they'd take the ankle express on the Trace to Nashville. From there, it was an easy trip home. 'Course, some folks did ride horses along it."

I'm still looking at that map.

"I wonder," Arena says, "how long it took those guys on horses to ride all that way from Natchez to Nashville."

"Longer than we've been riding," Remo said, "and we've covered close to twice what they did."

"There's three routes marked on this map," I say. "None of them is a main route."

Remo nods. "A choice to be made."

Three choices! Follow the Natchez Trace to the outskirts of Nashville, then take any one of a number of roads to Nashville, around Nashville, and on into Gallatin. Or take the Hillsboro Pike to Nashville and the Gallatin Pike to the next station. I'd already ruled out the third option because it crosses this big line of curving blue that's the Cumberland River far too many times for my liking.

"Trace is shorter," Arena says, after studying the map closely.

Remo nods. "A lot older, too. This one." He points to the Hillsboro Pike-Gallatin Pike markings. "Probably safer. Maybe a bit longer, but the Trace don't get much traffic these days. And it was mostly a footpath."

"Either way, it's a long ride for us," I say.

"Why didn't they mark one of these as the favored route?" I ask.

"To make you think. Or guess," Remo says, nodding as if he approves. "There's more to a race like this than just riding fast for a long, long way."

"I'm taking the Natchez Trace," Arena says.

That makes Remo look sad. I think I know why.

"Yeah," I say, even though to me the Hillsboro and Gallatin Pikes seem a lot better choice. "I'm with Arena." I'm lying, but it ain't like Dindie Remo can ride alongside Arena all that way. We've rode a lot of miles, and we still ain't that far from where that colored man got lynched.

"You sure, Evan?" Remo asks.

I bob my head. "Yeah. Besides, you done give me a history lesson. I'd like to be able to say I rid the same trail those Kaintucks walked."

"Then I'll see y'all in Gallatin," Remo says.

"Maybe you'll just see our dust," Arena says, and, laughing, we head off to find us some supper.

CHAPTER NINETEEN

The Trace is a winding road through dense forests, and I can't say it's wide. It's almost like we're riding through a cañon. Sometimes we can ride at a good lope, but not for long. Bugs are thick. The wind don't blow. For September, it's real hot and sticky.

Then we ain't riding nowhere. A bearded man wearing a straw hat stands in the center of the road, and he's aiming this long rifle right at us.

"Pay the toll, or pay the troll," he says. "Either way, you pay me." Then he laughs.

Crazy as a hatter, I think, but that long rifle is cocked, and the barrel and the front bead keep moving from Arena to me, back and forth.

The man wears overalls, only he ain't got no shirt underneath them. His boots don't match, and he's missing most of his teeth. His eyes is sunk deep in his head. He's lost most of the hair on his noggin, and he ain't shaved in months, maybe years.

"This is a public road," Arena tells him. "We have a right to pass."

"None shall pass except those who pay the toll or pay the troll." He seems to like that phrase. "Either way, you pay me. Five dollars."

"You're nothing but a highwayman," Arena says.

I wish she'd shut up. That long rifle might be a flintlock, but it's primed, and the cannon of a barrel can't be no smaller than .69-caliber. If I had my druthers, I'd be somewhere on the Hillsboro Pike about now.

"I'm the tollkeeper. I'm the troll. You must pay me . . . one way or the other." He licks his lips with the longest, ugliest, most disgusting tongue I've ever seen.

"Tell you what," he says, and swings the barrel of that flintlock at me.

It don't waiver no more. It's steady, and he's got a firm hold on that long gun, and the stock is tight against his shoulder. "You may pass. *She* will pay me."

The hairs on my neck rise and prickle. I feel my ears reddening.

"I don't have five dollars," I tell him, just to say something, but maybe that was the dumbest thing I could have said.

He licks his lips again. "The boys who rid through earlier, they said she'd be a-willin'. They say she's got plenty of experience. That she ain't all that particular. She looks fine. Real fine. You may pass, boy. She will pay the toll and the troll. And pay me good."

"You son-of-a- . . . ," Arena stops herself.

Don't matter, because now the old man's eyes

are flaming, and he's turning that long rifle back in Arena's direction.

Arena kicks her gelding into a lope. As the old coot's finger starts to tighten on the trigger, I'm spurring Taos Lightning, reaching for my lariat, kicking free of the stirrups, and diving out of the saddle.

The long rifle roars. My left side feels like I'm back in that burning warehouse. We land in a heap, me and that crazy jasper, the Kentucky rifle, and the lariat I've swung at that fellow's bearded face. We land hard. Air whooshes from my lungs. The smoking rifle clatters amongst pine cones and stones. I bring my knee straight up into the man's privates. He gasps. Then I find myself falling backward, clutching my side, and feeling the palm of my left hand burning like the hinges of Hades.

'Cause, I suddenly realize, my shirt—the practically brand new collarless shirt of pretty print—is afire. I start slapping the cotton. Thankfully, I don't feel any wetness, so no blood. But I'm too scared to look at my skin.

The road agent starts to rise, and reaches for his rifle, even though it's empty.

Blood's rushing all the way from my toes to my brain, and I'm madder than Pa used to get at Taos Lightning, or any other mustang he was breaking. My left side's scalded, my stallion is loping around the bend for parts unknown, Arena is maybe a hundred or two hundred yards closer to Gallatin than me, and that fool is raising his rifle.

I kick him in the face. Blood, maybe a few tooth stubs, spew out of his ugly face, and spatter the carpet of dead leaves and débris on the Natchez Trace. He goes down, flat on his stomach, and when he raises his head, I kick him in the base of the neck. I grab the rifle, and raise it by the hot barrel over my head. I'm about to bring it straight down on his head, when suddenly I realize what I'm about to do. So I turn, and bust that old relic across a hardwood tree.

The man don't move. Oh, he's breathing. Breathing right hard. I toss what's left of his rifle into the woods. And spitting, swearing, I stagger down the road. When I round the bend, all I see is another bend I've got to make my way around. I make it. And I don't see anything except trees and brambles and briars and a forest that goes on forever. Not my horse. Not Arena Lancaster's. And not Arena Lancaster.

Reckon I've walked a mile. In a pair of boots that still ain't formed proper to the shape of my feet. I'm feeling pretty forlorn. And just as I round yet another bend, there they are. Arena Lancaster, Horse-Horse, and Taos Lightning.

The horses are loose, grazing on green ferns and whatever else is growing in this dense jungle.

Arena's sitting on the side of the road, crying hard. When she looks up and sees me, she seems to freeze.

I go to her, sit down beside her. I want to put my arm around her, but I don't know what's proper, if she would want me to. I'm flummoxed about what a fifteen-year-old boy is supposed to do.

"I'm sorry," she sobs, and then she sees my shirt. "Oh, Evan," she says, and touches the reddened and oozing flesh.

I wince. It hurts. Hurts like blazes.

"It's not bleeding," she says.

I tell her: "I think it's just a powder burn."

This gets her crying again, and she buries her head, saying: "I'm sorry, Evan."

Trying to make her feel better, I come up with what I think to be a pretty good joke. "Maybe I can borrow your chemise," I say. "To go along with them bloomers."

It guess it wasn't as funny as I thought it would be, because she says: "I almost got you killed, Evan."

"Wasn't you," I tell her. "It was that danged old coot who belongs in some crazy house."

She presses her hand against my burning side, and now her touch feels cool. Other parts of my body ain't so cool though, so I think of something else.

Although we hadn't really had any dealing with

those two Texas cowboys, I wouldn't put it past them to have been the ones who had told the road agent that Arena might be coming down the trail. So I say to her: "It was them two Texans who left before we did. They must have give him the idea . . ." I feel the heat rising in my ears, matching the heat in my side. So I tell her: "I see those Texans, Arena, I'll kill them."

Don't know that I meant it, that I could do it. But I sure felt the urge.

Her hand comes away from my burned shirt and my blistering side, and she uses both of her hands to grab my face, so that I'm staring right at her, just inches away from her face.

"You're not killing anybody, Evan. What they told that old man . . . ," she says, but then stops and looks away. "They weren't lying."

I figure it to be about nine o'clock now. We could keep riding. We ain't seen nobody on this pike, and I don't reckon that tollkeeper I left unconscious in the middle of the road will be lighting out after us. We decide this place is as good a spot as any to spend the night.

"What are your parents like?" Arena asks.

Arena's question catches me by surprise.

"I don't know," I answer.

"Yes, you do," she says. "But I don't. Oh, I knew my mama. But my pa?" She spits. "Could've been anybody."

We have a little fire going. Our horses are picketed between some trees, about as close to a clearing as I've seen on the Natchez Trace. 'Course, we ain't got nothing to eat. It's too dark to forage. Nothing to drink but water.

I hear the sound of the cork being popped out of Arena's bottle. No, I reckon there's something other than water to drink.

I watch as she tilts the whiskey bottle up to her lips.

"Ma run off," I hear myself telling her. "I reckon she just couldn't deal with Pa's drinking no more."

So we talk. Till there ain't nothing left of the fire but coals and smoke.

I always figured my life has been as rough as a rock quarry, but maybe it ain't been so hard. Seems pretty easy, once I hear all poor Arena Lancaster has gone through.

"Why'd you enter this race?" I ask her.

"New England sounds like a nice place to be," she answers.

I think about something I heard one of the soldier boys talk about at Fort Union. One of his buddies had just got his discharge, and was bound for Tombstone down in Arizona Territory. The soldier staying had said: "Make sure you're running to something, and not away from something."

Sounded like sage advice to me, so I tell this to Arena.

She says: "Everybody's running away from something or someone, Evan. So are you."

Arena's right.

My side don't hurt so much now, but my legs is tormenting me again. Bloomers and ointment can only do so much good when you're spending ten hours a day in a saddle, riding hard and steady, and sleeping on the ground mostly, and fighting crazed old men who think they's trolls.

"Are you all right?" she asks.

"Yeah," I tell her.

"No, you're not." She sits up, and moves closer to me.

I've pulled off my boots.

"Roll up your pants legs," she tells me. "Bloomers, too."

"I won't," I tell her. When she glares, I tell her: "Well, I can't."

"Then take them off."

No way I'm doing any such thing.

"Evan," she tells me, "Doctor Jack will be at the next main station. You heard what he said. If he doesn't think your legs are healed properly, you won't be racing anywhere. You'll be going back to . . . wherever."

"You ain't no doctor," I tell her. "And you ain't got no special medicine."

Suddenly she gets this mischievous look in her

eyes, and she holds up the bottle of whiskey. It ain't the color of Taos Lightning, but it's dark, and the bottle's only half empty.

"That ain't medicine. . . ."

"It has been for . . ." The grin is gone, and she looks away, brushing her eyes with her fingers. Then she continues: "Alcohol . . . well, it purifies, they say." She takes a deep breath, and adds: "Evan . . . please."

If I do this, I'm thinking, *that means she won't be drinking it. I'll be doing it to help Arena. And . . . well . . . maybe it will help my legs.*

I reach for the bottle.

"You go back to your bedroll," I tell her. "And don't you look over here."

The twinkle's back in her eyes, but she obeys. I loosen my suspenders, unbutton my britches, and pull them off. Bloomers, too. Then I take off my bandanna and soak it with some of the whiskey.

Surely, I tell myself, *it can't hurt as bad as I think it can.*

But then I'm cussing like a Fort Union sergeant. Rolling this way and that, trying to put out the fire on my thighs. Tears are welling up in my eyes as I grind my teeth, turn this way and that, and cuss some more.

Arena rushes to me. She's got a stick and she tries to put it by my mouth. "Bite down. Bite down on this."

"You get away!" I shout at her.

"Bite down."

I do. Not that it helps.

She's got the bandanna and the bottle. I can barely make her out, but I see what she's doing. I want to spit out the stick and grab that rag out of her hand before . . .

Too late. My head falls back. Pain burns and burns and burns.

I'm embarrassed. I'm tormented.

She gently swabs the bandanna across the sores.

I just want to die. Not because of the pain, burning like that warehouse in Mississippi, but because Arena Lancaster is looking at my legs as she's using that whiskey-soaked bandanna. I'm so embarrassed. I hate myself.

When she's done, she shifts so that she can cradle my head in her arms. I spit out the stick, try to turn away, but she presses her body against my back.

"It's all right," she whispers. "It's all right, honey. I'm done. No more. Out of whiskey anyway. You're going to be fine. You will be fine. The pain won't last much longer."

It ain't the pain that torments me mostly. It's me.

"Cover my legs." I hate myself for even suggesting that. "Please."

"No, no, no. The air. The air will be good for those sores. Just go to sleep, Evan. Go to sleep."

I feel her lips press against my neck. A soft kiss.

She hums. Like I'm some baby or invalid. Maybe I'm both.

Sleep! Who can sleep when your legs are burning from rot-gut whiskey poured over open, festering wounds? When a pretty girl is hugging you, and wrapping her arms around you, and you ain't wearing no pants?

My breathing becomes shallower. Her left arm crosses over my chest. She grabs my left hand. Our fingers intertwine.

"Close your eyes, Evan," she says again. "It's all right. It's all right."

My eyes open to see the moon staring down at me.

Arena has moved over to her bedroll, and there she sleeps, snoring softly. I can barely see her face.

Then I stare at my legs, which ain't tormenting me.

Maybe the night air and the whiskey has helped some, but I figure that's enough air for now. So I pull up the bloomers, cussing softly because I'm still wearing these danged things. Maybe I can find some proper underclothes at the next stop. Gallatin's got to have a store.

My hands lock behind my head as I lean back against the saddle that serves as my pillow.

I stare at the sky till my eyes close again.

175

• • •

By the time Arena wakens, I've saddled Horse-Horse and Taos Lightning.

She ain't moving too good, and she hardly says a word as she throws off her blanket, manages to pull herself up, and stagger off into the thick woods. I have heard her gagging, vomiting, and coughing some nights, but last night most of the whiskey went on my legs, and not inside her belly. I wish I had coffee to make, but all either of us got now is tepid water in our canteens. She comes back, wipes her lips, and looks at the palomino.

"How are your . . . ?"

"Better," I say. I'm not sure that's the truth, but I'll know for certain sure once I'm in the saddle.

She stares at the sky. "It's late."

"We had a busy night," I tell her.

"You shouldn't have stayed with me," she says, with anger in her voice that I didn't expect. "You could've ridden out a long time ago. And you saddled my horse, too?"

"You were sleeping. I figured I ought to pay you back for your doctoring last night."

"Shut up." She moves to Horse-Horse, loosens the cinch I just tightened, then tightens it again.

"Plenty of race left," I said. "But we need to be in Gallatin today."

I fetch my Seth Thomas, and start winding it up. Set the hands to twelve o'clock high.

"You could've gone without me," Arena says again. "Yesterday. Before last night."

"You didn't have to do all the things you've done for me," I tell her.

"Evan," she says, "last night . . ."

"Nothing happened last night," I tell her. "Except you . . ."—how do I put it?—"you . . . helped me . . . made my legs better."

I can't figure out what's gotten into her, why she's mad at me all of a sudden. Horses I can savvy, sometimes. But girls?

She grabs the reins to her horse, and tries to climb into the saddle, but she can't. "I'm a . . ." I don't catch the last word, because she's buried her face into her bedroll that I've tied up behind the cantle. But I know what she just said. She's crying.

Wrapping Taos Lightning's reins around a clump of bush, I come up to her. Hesitantly, I put my arm around her shoulder and gently turn her around.

"You win this race," I say, "you got your whole life in front of you. You can start over."

"I'm scarred, Evan. Scarred for life."

"No, you ain't," I tell her. "Any scars you got ain't of your own doing. Like Taos Lightning. The scars on his hide, he didn't put them there. Pa did. Most of them. And I can't take them off, but I can make him forget them. And I'd like to . . ."

She don't let me finish. "Evan," she mouths.

"I win this race," I tell her, "and it's the same thing. You'll still have your whole life in front of you."

I put my hand back on her shoulder. I try to pull her to me, but she slips from my grasp, and presses herself against her gelding.

"Evan," she says as tears fill her eyes again. "Whatever you do, don't fall in love with me. You got to promise me that. Promise me."

My heart must've stopped beating. My tongue don't want to work. I sure don't want to cry, not in front of Arena Lancaster. I done enough of that last night, but that was mostly from the whiskey entering my raw wounds.

"I . . ."—my head shakes sadly—"I . . . can't," I tell her. "Can't make that promise."

For a moment, I spy that flash of anger in her pretty eyes. She turns away from me, grabs the horn, and pulls herself into the saddle. Once she's got her other boot in the stirrup, she gathers the reins. I fear she'll just spur Horse-Horse and gallop away. Maybe that would be for the best. Not for me, but for her.

I ask her: "Do you want to dissolve our partnership?"

"Shut up," she says, without looking at me. "Just get on that stallion and let's ride. We've got a lot of ground to cover today."

CHAPTER TWENTY

I try to figure out how many miles we've ridden together, me and Arena. Arithmetic ain't good for my brain, though I'm certain of one thing. No matter how much trail we've covered, how many hours we've ridden together, nothing feels as long as today.

A dead horse lies alongside the road. The saddle, blanket, and bridle have been removed. It's a zebra dun. Has to be one of the horses in this race, but I don't recognize it.

We swing wide of the carcass, and ride into Gallatin, past the railroad tracks, past a crossroads with one sign pointing to something called Long Hollow Pike, and past the sprawling boneyard on Water Avenue. It's one thriving city, I suspect, with its frame and brick buildings, lots of trees, plenty of dogs and cats. Children stop rolling hoops to watch us pass.

I point ahead at a rock formation, and Arena looks at it and shrugs. It's something like a butte that just sticks out of the ground, rising above the pastures and the hills. Basically, it ain't what we'd call a mountain or a mesa back home, but it's interesting enough. Grass and green things grow along the bottom, then there ain't much except gray rock, but trees grow along the top of the hill. The point of the hill, on the northwestern point, sort of looks like a face, with a nose and chin. Indeed, it looks like a Mohawk.

I see a wooden sign shaped like an arrow, pointing southeast:

Mohawk Farms
Robin T. Graham IV, Proprietor
1¼ miles

Mohawk Farms ain't like no farm I've ever seen. White fellows in blue jackets and black boots greet us. They take the reins to our horses, ask us to dismount, and even help us down. Stiff and aching as my legs are, I don't resist. They keep *sir*-ing and *ma'am*-ing us in soothing voices, and ask us to follow them into the stables.

Stables? I've seen pictures in storybooks and magazines of barns like this, but never knowed any actually existed. Painted red on the outside, this barn looks bigger than most of the warehouses I've seen in the South, and the corrals surrounding it look more impressive than the those back at Fort Union when that Army post was something to behold. You could fit a small New Mexico town inside this building.

Inside, we stop at a desk and give our names to a fellow, but he ain't decked out like the gents who greeted us outside. I figure this man, with his slippery mustache and spectacles, is being paid by Mr. Fox and Mr. Baldwin, while the ones in the blue jackets and black boots must be employed by Mohawk Farms and Mr. Robin T. Graham.

The fellow tells Arena where to go, and the nice man leading Horse-Horse shows her the way. The man glances at me and sends me and the man leading Taos Lightning deep into the bowels of this monster of a barn.

I spy the Arabian, even the French cross-country horse, but not the Spaniard, or those blow-hard Texans, who turn out to be brothers, Leonard and Billy Sale. I don't even see Dindie Remo, but it's a mighty big barn and he could be back yonder where they taken Arena.

Shortly, I spot Dr. Jack. My stomach starts to feel queasy, even when the tall Texan gives me a warm smile and pushes his chair away from the desk. He holds out his right hand. My legs start hurting, but I accept the handshake. Maybe he done forgot about my sores, though I doubt it. He nods at a guy sitting next to him in a green coat and black string tie. I figure him to be Mr. Robin T. Graham, owner of this fancy spread, but he ain't.

"Evan, I'd like you to meet Doctor Johann Hartwig of the American Society for the Prevention of Cruelty to Animals."

The man, whose head is bald but whose chin has a goatee, pops one of them monocles out of his left eye, and rises. He shakes my hand, too, using the hand that ain't holding that little eyepiece. It ain't much of a handshake, and he ain't much bigger than me. He sure don't look like no anarchist, whatever that is.

"I shall see to his horse," Dr. Hartwig says, as he grabs a black bag from under the desk and a pad of paper from the top, and follows the blue-coated dude who's taking Taos Lightning to one of about a hundred stalls in this barn mansion.

I want to follow, 'cause I don't trust nobody from that society, and I've never seen a man who has a monocle except in some illustrations in *Harper's Weekly*.

"How are your legs, Evan?"

I don't answer. I nod at the stall that this Hartwig cuss has disappeared into with my horse. "Can he be trusted?"

"I'd trust him better than I'd trust myself."

"Well, I've heard some mean things about this society."

"Such as?"

"They's anarchists," I let the doc know. "They even set fire to that warehouse in Mississippi."

Doc Jack sighs. He motions for me to sit in the chair in front of the desk. The last thing I want to do is sit, not after all the bouncing I've been doing for these past days, but I oblige the horse doctor.

"Do you know what an anarchist is, Evan?" he asks.

"They done what they done in Haymarket," I explain.

"I see. Well, I don't think Doctor Hartwig was at Haymarket Square in Chicago. And from what I've read and heard, I don't know if the police even know for sure who threw that dynamite bomb. Strikers? Anarchists? Some crazed fool?"

I've just learned something about this Haymarket thing. I didn't know nothing before.

"And," Doc Jack continues, "from the last report I received, the cause of that horrible fire you and others experienced has been confirmed. A fire broke out in the hotel's kitchen and spread rapidly. An accident, Evan, not anarchists. No matter, I know our good doctor was nowhere near Winona when that tragedy struck. Now, how are your legs?"

"Some better," I say. His question feels just like Arena's whiskey burning my thighs again.

His head nods, and he reaches under the desk. Next thing I know, he's pulling out his own black bag, which he opens. He pulls out a jar, which he slides toward me.

"This is a salve," Doc Jack says. "Probably better than that ointment I gave you." His hands disappear underneath the desk again and come up with a small package wrapped in brown paper tied with string. "These are bandages that you can wrap around your sores. That might get you through this race . . . if you don't mind the extra couple of ounces it might add to your meaty frame."

He's joshing. I look at the jar, but don't open it.

"It might burn a little," he says.

I think, but sure don't say: *Not as much as Arena Lancaster's rotgut.*

"How much I owe you?" I ask him.

He grins. "I'll put it on your tab. You can pay me back at the end of the race." He stands. "I believe Doctor Hartwig is probably done. Let's see what he has to say."

I ain't sure I want to hear what he has to say, but I make myself walk across the floor I reckon I could eat off of, it's so clean.

Dr. Hartwig of the American Society for the Prevention of Cruelty to Animals is putting things back in his black bag. Finally, he turns to me and the doc, and says: "His heart rate is exceptional, lungs healthy, legs and feet in fine order. But I dislike these scars on his back and sides." That eye with the monocle looks way bigger than his other eye, and meaner.

"Mustang," Doc Jack says in his Texas drawl. Then Doc pats my shoulder and says to me: "Isn't that right, Evan? You caught him in New Mexico Territory, correct?"

I blink before I answer, but it's the truth. Me and Pa caught him all right. That thought brings back mighty fine memories for a second. Pa hadn't brung no John Barleycorn on that trip.

"Mustang?" Dr. Hartwig says. "You mean a wild horse."

"Wild as a catamount," Doc Jack says. "Those scars are medals of honor for a wild horse like that. Bites from mustang stallions that challenged him for command of his herd of mares. In my younger days, I used to go mustanging in Texas. Risked losing my hair to Comanches or Kiowas. Have you ever seen a mustang running wild, Doctor Hartwig?"

Hartwig takes out his monocle, fishes a handkerchief from his vest pocket, and cleans the little lens. "Not in Boston," he answers. "Only in my dreams . . ." He stares at me with his eyes, both looking the same size now. "It must be something to see. Is it, young man?"

I shrug. "Yeah," I tell him. "I reckon so."

But thoughts are flooding my mind. Maybe I even smile as I say: "When me and Pa caught him . . . Taos Lightning, I mean . . . we were in desert country that butted up against the hills. Rough country. I remember him riding in. Me and Pa found this water hole, and had the fence and gate all built. But that mustang, he was smart. Real savvy. Maybe he smelled our scent. Or maybe he was just suspicious by nature. He stopped all his mares. Held his head real high. Me and Pa, we're hiding in the brush or behind some rocks, waiting, holding our breath. That mustang . . . Pa said he was real young to be heading a herd of this size . . . he come up, sniffing, snorting, pawing the earth." I pause as I watch the event play out in my mind.

"Finally, he walked right up to the entrance to the water hole. He stepped through, and all I had to do was slam the poles down. Then we'd have caught him certain sure. But that ain't what we wanted. Oh, he was fine, fine young stud. But we'd come for profit. We wanted as many of them mares and young horses as we could get.

"That horse, though, he didn't take the bait. He smelled something wrong, and just like that, he reared, turned, whinnied, and galloped off into the distance, with all the mares and colts and fillies following him. Left us with nothing but dust and a slew of horse apples. Pa, he started cussing, and stamping his foot just like that stallion had been doing."

I shake my head. I'm not thinking about my legs no more. I don't feel tired. I'm remembering Pa yelling and clamoring so, and then he's laughing, saying that stallion had just outsmarted him something good. And we went off to our camp to drink coffee and eat old tortillas and cold beans.

"But you caught him?" the vet from Boston asks.

"Yeah. Eventually. Three tries later. He was

probably mighty thirsty by then, and so was his brood mares. Maybe he cared more for them. It'd been one dry year. He led them in, and we slammed the door shut.

" 'Course, that was just the beginning. Then we had to break him. I mean . . . break him as much as he'd let us. He's still half wild. He's tossed me many a time when I wasn't paying attention. Sometimes I think he's teaching me. Making me smarter. Maybe my pa was right. Maybe he is the best horse we've ever had."

Suddenly embarrassed by how much I've been talking, I shove my hands in my pockets and stare at my boot tops.

Dr. Hartwig signs a paper, which he hands to Doc Jack. Finally, he comes up to me, wipes his monocle once more, and slips it back over his eye.

"I have seen many a wonderful horse, young man," he says. "But yours is truly magnificent. A horse like that, sir, will carry you anywhere you want to go. As long as you treat him right."

Seems to me I've heard that before. I shake the doc's hand. He ain't a bad sort, even if I still ain't certain that he's not some anarchist. I watch him walk out of the stall and head back for the desk.

The good feelings, the good memories, fade.

All business, Doc Jack says: "Evan, you may pick up your next map and card from the men at the table by the exit. But remember, you must stay here two hours and may not exceed your ten-hour limit for this day's riding."

I look up at this big man, and I tell him: "You know as good as I do that my pa put most of those scars on that stallion's hide. With whip. With quirt. With whatever he had handy."

"I know a lot of things, Evan Kendrick," the doc says. "I know that Doctor Johann Hartwig and all of these organizations fighting to stop the cruel treatment of animals have their hearts in the right place. I know that animals and people are often abused. Maybe most of that comes from ignorance. But education can cure ignorance. Have you thought about what a blessing it is to be participating in this race?"

I stare hard at him, thinking that getting my legs chaffed, almost getting burned to death in a warehouse, and getting a powder burn on my side by some old fool who meant to kill me, ain't what I call no blessing.

Doc Jack is still talking: "Boys your age, men my age, most people never see what's over the next hill. They are born, they marry, they die, in most cases, never straying forty or fifty miles . . . if that . . . from their home. What had you seen before you and your father left New Mexico Territory?"

I don't answer with nothing but a shrug, but I know, and I figure he does too. I'd seen Fort Union, mountains, high desert, Las Vegas, and

Santa Fe, which, I also know, is more than most of my neighbors ever saw.

"So far you've seen four states . . . Texas, Louisiana, Mississippi, and Tennessee," he says. "You'll see Kentucky tomorrow. You're riding not only with men from across this country, but from around the world. Irishmen. Frenchmen. An Arab. Mexicans. An earl from Liverpool. A squire from Dublin. Two Canadians."

"And far too many Texans," I quip.

He gives me that stern look, and says: "Watch it, Evan. I'm a Texan." Then he smiles, before going on. "You're also receiving an education, my good friend. Learn from it. Learn from those riders you meet. Dindie Remo has much experience. But you can learn from the Spaniard as well. Perhaps even the Arab. His horse is magnificent. There are cavalrymen, Californians. You are seeing how different, yet how alike, we are in our United States, too. Education is a good thing. Maybe you will learn how to speak proper English."

He laughs, puts his hand on my shoulder so I'll know he's joking, but I suspect he's serious about my English. Ma done what she could, I guess, and maybe one day I'll get a mite better at it.

"And remember what Doctor Hartwig told you," Patrick Jack drawls. "A horse like Taos Lightning can carry you wherever you want to go . . . if you treat him right."

I nod, take the paper, thank Doc Jack, then lead my horse out of the stall.

"Evan!" Doc Jack calls out.

I stop, turn.

"Go over to my desk before you leave. You'll find a pair of chaps under it. And, please, don't give me any guff about any additional weight."

CHAPTER TWENTY-ONE

Reckon I've got more than an hour before I can start breaking in these new leather chaps Doc Jack give me. Once I'm outside the massive barn, one of the blue-coated men walks me over to a table in the shade.

"Do you mind if *Monsieur* Kendrick joins you gentlemen?" he asks the four riders already sitting there.

"I can only speak for myself," the Spaniard says, his accent thick, "but I would be delighted to have this young *jinete* at our table."

Not only do the kind words this smooth-talking, smooth-riding *hombre* just loaded on me make me excited, but seeing him pleases me. I am not pleased by the fact that one of those two loud-mouthed Sale brothers from Texas is sitting at the table, too. Don't see the other one, though, but at least I've caught up with two of the best horses in the field.

"Is this the boy I've heard so much about . . . the youngest rider in the field, who replaced his injured father?" A quick glance at the speaker of these words, sitting on one side of the dark-haired Spaniard, tells me that this ain't no rider in the race. He's not wearing a blue coat, neither, but a white one. White britches, too, topped off with a checkered vest and black tie. His hat is flat-brimmed, low-crowned and of the finest straw I've ever seen. Don't even look like straw, but I bet it's comfortable on a warm day like this.

The man rises and shoots his hand across the table. "I am Robin T. Graham, owner of this farm."

He ain't what I expected. I figured Robin T. Graham would be an old, stout fellow, with white hair and beard. Can't put this slender man with long sandy-colored hair and a thin mustache and under-lip beard to be much older than thirty. His grip is firm, though. I sit down next to the Arab, who just nods at me. Sale just snorts.

Another blue coat pours me a glass of lemonade. He even asks what I want to eat: fried chicken, spare ribs, roast beef, or catfish. I don't know what to say.

"The ribs are divine," Mr. Graham says, so I nod, and the blue coat goes away.

"We were talking about the great races," Mr. Graham says. "El-Hashem has done many in the deserts overseas. What did you say the event is called, sir?"

The Arab looks up. His voice is thick, yet soft. He don't seem comfortable talking. "The Ocean of Fire."

"Remarkable," Mr. Graham says to me. "Three

thousand miles across the Arabian desert." Then to us all: "You gentleman might consider entering that race."

"They cannot," El-Hashem tells us. "Only pure Arabian horses may enter The Ocean of Fire. And the pedigree must be unblemished."

The Texan tosses a rib bone onto his plate. "What do you race, boy . . . camels?"

The Arab reaches for his glass of water. "Camels bring barley and water . . . for all there is to eat in the sand are *vatches*."

Sale snorts again.

"I wish that Frenchman had not left," Mr. Graham says, "for I would have enjoyed hearing his stories of racing cross-country in Europe."

I frown as I think: *The Frenchie's already left? I should look at the map, figure out where the next station is and the route I'm supposed to follow. Maybe I can catch up to that cross-country rider.* My thoughts are stopped when a plate filled with green beans, spare ribs, and biscuits is placed in front of me.

"Billy will catch that Frenchie," Leonard Sale says. "Probably already has."

So now I know the Billy Sale has left already and that this one is Leonard.

"Remarkable," Mr. Graham says, but I don't reckon he has been listening to the Texan. "Three thousand miles. We should do that. New York City to San Francisco. Wouldn't that be

193

something!" Then he asks: "Who's the best rider you've ever known?"

The Spaniard and the Texan immediately name themselves, but I think the Spaniard is joking. The Arab shrugs.

I say: "Well, I never met him, but my pa knowed a rider named Francis Aubry. Pa . . . he was maybe seventeen then . . . helped him win this race back in 'Forty-Eight, I think it was."

The Spaniard and the Arab, but especially Mr. Graham, seem interested. Leonard Sale finds a quid of tobacco and bites off a hunk.

"I've never heard of this Francis Aubry," Mr. Graham says. "Tell us."

So I tell them, getting most of it right, I think.

"Aubry was a little dude. He had been freighting supplies between Santa Fe and Missouri. Now caravans like that don't go fast, and Aubry liked speed. He had made some real fast runs between Independence and Santa Fe. One time he bet this gambler a thousand bucks that he can ride all the way from Santa Fe to Independence in six days. Eight hundred miles. 'Course, it wasn't on one horse. Aubry run it kind of like the Pony Express would all them years later. Relay stations. Not as fancy as the Pony Express, I hear, just setting mounts a hundred miles apart. Sort of like the way stations and home stations we've gone through on this race. Pa was at one of those stations, somewhere near the Rabbit Ear in New Mexico.

"At one station, Aubry found the horse herder dead and scalped and the fresh horse stole. He had to ride this little mustang on to the next stop. Anyway, the long and short of things is that Aubry rode into Independence, half dead, saddle covered with blood, and his hands roped to the horn of his saddle to keep them from letting go. Those Missourians had to cut him loose. But he done it. Five days, fifteen hours," I conclude. "He won the bet."

"Hogwash," Sale says.

"No. I have heard of this ride." It's the Arab who speaks. "It has been talked about in Zabid, where my brothers live."

"You calling me a liar, sheik?" the Texan shouts, and starts to rise, but the Spaniard beats him to it.

Only the Spaniard ain't looking at the Arab. He's removing his hat, and stepping away from the table. "It is an honor," I hear him say, "to have a woman of such beauty join us. *La patrona*, my name is Salvador Narciso de la Rosa. Your protector."

By then, I'm craning my neck, and what do I see, but Arena Lancaster being escorted to our table by that same blue coat who brung me here. My mouth falls open as that Spaniard takes Arena's right hand. He bows as he brings Arena's hand to his lips.

Arena looks plumb flabbergasted, but Mr.

Graham is standing, and Sale swears softly before taking out his chaw of tobacco.

Next, Salvador, the Spaniard, takes Arena by the arm and escorts her the rest of the way to the table. He pulls out a chair—the one next to him, of course—and slides her to the table.

Them ribs might have been the specialty of Mr. Graham's cooks in his kitchen, but they sure taste bitter to me as Salvador fawns over Arena.

Naturally, we begin the race as soon as we can. Leonard Sale goes first. The Spaniard a few minutes after him. Dindie Remo probably could have gone sooner, but he has waited for Arena and me, even though we hadn't seen him till our horses were fetched.

We three set out for Glasgow, Kentucky.

I can't tell you when we actually crossed into Kentucky, but at one point the terrain changed. Rolling hills are replaced by steep, high hills with rocky ledges, tan-colored, often covered with what looks like rust.

It's fifty miles to Glasgow. We cover it within that ten-hour limit.

We check in at what we're told used to be the Glasgow Normal School and Business College, but they moved that college to Bowling Green a couple of years back. Since we can't ride on right away, they tell us to spread our bedrolls out on the grass in front of one of them old college buildings once we've eaten.

I've just finished supper when this pockmarked fellow with spectacles and a notepad comes over. I know he's one of those reporters, and figure he wants to talk to Dindie Remo or Arena Lancaster, but when I get up to leave them, he says: "Mister Kendrick, you're just the person I wish to speak to."

"Huh?"

Arena laughs as Remo takes my plate and cup. Then he and Arena head over to the wreck pan to dump our dishes before checking on the horses.

Handing me a card, this little fellow tells me his name is Bob Nott and that he writes for the *Daily Courier*, which is out of Buffalo, New York.

"What you want to talk to me about?" I ask.

"I heard you told a story about a race from New Mexico to . . ."—he checks his notepad—"Independence?"

Oh, so he wants to hear about Francis Aubry, not me. "Independence, Missouri. Jumping-off point for the Santa Fe Trail." I chuckle. "I wasn't there . . . wasn't even born."

Mr. Nott tells me he wants to hear the tale. So I give it to him, same as I told the others. This Nott fellow must fill six or seven pages. Writes real fast.

I figure we're finished, when he asks: "Is Aubry your inspiration?"

When I don't say anything, he eggs me on: "You know . . . your inspiration. What motivates you. Or spurs you on. Get it? *Spurs?*"

I get it. And I know what *inspiration* means. I ain't all that stupid. I tell him so.

"No offense intended," he says. "I know you're not stupid, sir. You've made it from Galveston Island to southern Kentucky. Only twenty-six have done that. So far. But the officials don't expect more than one or two others to reach this station."

I wet my lips. I didn't know the number of horses still running. About half the number that started in Texas are out.

"You gonna use what I say in this article?" I ask.

"Of course."

"Will you make me sound smart?"

"I assure you, you're not stupid, Mister Kendrick. And your dialect and choice of words fit what our readers think of as true Westerners."

"Yeah, but I don't speak good English. And my writing is . . . well . . ."

He laughs. "I'll be doing the writing. As for your way with words . . . your verbs do not always match your subject, but you get your point across."

He don't know what I'm getting at. "I'd like to be smarter," I tell him.

He lowers his pad. "Wouldn't we all?"

"My schooling came well . . . not regular. My ma . . . she . . ." I don't want to bring up them stories, those memories.

He finds a card in his pocket and hands it to me. "If you make it to Buffalo, New York, I'll be there. That's where I work. And where my spinster sister teaches school."

My head shakes. "I ain't gonna . . ."

"You mean . . . *I will not*."

I try that out. "I . . . will . . . not have time for no school lesson."

"For *any* school lesson," he corrects me again.

I nod.

He pulls a newspaper out from the bag he carries, and says: "Maybe when you win this race, you shall settle in Buffalo. It's a fine city. And Niagara Falls is not far away. As I said, my sister is an excellent teacher. But the best education a man can get is by reading. Books. And newspapers." He hands me that copy of the *Daily Courier*, pointing to an article in the lower left-hand corner. "That's me."

Then he walks away, but he turns his head and says: "Good luck."

He's let me know something, though. We'll be passing through Buffalo, New York, on this ride to New England. Of course, I don't know where Buffalo is, other than it's not far from Niagara Falls, wherever that is.

• • •

The Spaniard, the Arab, the Frenchie, and the Sale brothers ain't around. I don't know how those boys, or the horses, can cover all that ground. We'd caught up with them in Gallatin, and you'd think they would be winded and worn down by now. Like I feel.

Tired as I am, when I look at one of those empty college buildings, I smile to myself and whisper: "Too bad, Doc Jack. I might have got more educated here, if they hadn't moved the school out of town."

"What'd you say?" Dindie asks as he studies his map.

"Nothing," I answer.

"You talking to yourself, Evan?"

"I was just thinking," I tell him, "out loud."

He looks back at his map. "Folks go crazy talking to themselves. Seen it happen. You might start talking to your horse. Better than talking to yourself."

"Do you talk to your blue roan, Dindie?" I ask.

"All the time," Dindie says. "My horse can carry on a good conversation."

They call this bluegrass country, but the grass ain't blue. It's green, not even bluish green. It's interesting, though. We don't pass many folks, just a couple of horse farms, not as fancy or as big as the one Mr. Robin T. Graham owned in

Gallatin. I'm getting that education Doc Jack said I was getting because all my life I thought that farms growed . . . *grew*, I mean . . . crops.

I'm trotting along with Arena when the rain hits, and I cuss myself because I ain't . . . *haven't* . . . been looking at the clouds. It's a good soaker, cold and hard, and about the time we've slowed our horses, the raindrops turn into hailstones. Little ones, but there must be a million of them, and they sting when they hit. Taos Lightning starts balking, and I can't blame him. By now, the path we're on is nothing but a sheet of ice. I swing down, and the stones start getting bigger and bigger.

"We got to find shelter!" I yell over the noise at Arena as she slides out of her saddle.

"Where?" she asks.

I point toward the woods on our left, where the trees are thick. As I glance at the trees, something catches my eye a short distance up the road among the trees. I'm not sure how I even see it, but a red flag is waving back and forth near a rock. No, it isn't a flag, but a bandanna.

Excitedly, I point. "I think it's Dindie!"

"Where?" Guess she can't see where I mean.

I pull Taos Lightning behind me and take her reins from her hand. "Stay low," I tell her. "As close to the horses as you can."

Horse-Horse doesn't care much for the idea, and it's all I can do to keep the stallion and gelding following me. My boots crunch the hailstones. Just about slip to my knees twice, and both horses lurch back, and it feels like my shoulders are ripping out of their sockets. That's about the time Dindie Remo reaches us.

He holds out his poncho. "Put this over your head," he orders Arena. She takes it, and he takes the reins to Horse-Horse from my aching hand.

"There's a cave up yonder," he says, and leads the way. Arena, huddled underneath that India rubber poncho already drooping from the weight of the hail, staggers off behind Remo and her horse.

Just as I figured, the hail—up to marble size by then—stops a few minutes after we squeeze through the cave entry. But because the rain keeps right on pounding down, Remo says we should let the storm pass.

"Moving fast," he says, leaning out of the cave, water rolling off the brim of his soaked hat. "Don't want to get caught in another storm. Besides, the rain might melt the hailstones."

Arena sits down on the ground, shivering. "We've only got about five more hours of riding. If we don't make it to the next station . . ."

"We'll make it tomorrow," Remo says firmly.

Which don't set well with Arena.

I look around the tiny cave, hoping to find some tinder and dry twigs, maybe pine cones, so I can get a fire going and warm us up.

The opening of the cave isn't deep, and we barely have room to stretch out comfortably. Of course, if we feel like exploring we can slide like snakes into some of the other openings. I suggest just that, in jest, and Arena gives me a mean look.

"Might be worth our while," I say. "This reporter give me . . . *gave* me a newspaper. He's been writing all about the places he's traveling to. Wanted to write about me."

"We were there, Evan," Arena says. "Remember?"

Boy, is she in one sour mood.

"Well, he wrote this story in this paper he gave me that's all about Jesse James in Kentucky. You know they say he robbed a stagecoach or something outside of Mammoth Cave. Which is right around these parts. And he robbed a bank in Russellville, wherever that is."

"That Jesse James," Remo says, "he sure got around. Over at Fort Concho, a man told me how Jesse James robbed him in Austin, Texas, when he was a passenger on a stagecoach some years back. Next day, he supposedly robbed a train way up in Kansas."

I say: "Maybe one of us should be riding Jesse's horse."

That does it. Dindie Remo breaks out in a belly laugh, and even Arena shakes her head as she giggles.

And the rain keeps coming down.

CHAPTER TWENTY-TWO

Louisville, Kentucky, bustles with folks and activity. After the rainstorms these past few days, this city's also muggy and miserable.

"Mighty hot for this time of year, too," says the man who punches my card and hands me a map.

It has been a short, easy ride to Louisville, forty-something miles, but that comes after a sixty-plus-mile ride from Glasgow to the wagon yard in Elizabethtown, which folks call E-town. It rained earlier in the day, but the sun started poking out around noon. We've dried out.

Evening's coming along, and I've rubbed down Taos Lightning good, cleaned his hoofs, and checked his legs. Once again, we've caught up with those arrogant Texans. I haven't spied the Arab, though, nor the Frenchman, nor their horses. The map I got says our next ride is even shorter than today's, and the station must be small because all it says is **Station, No facilities**.

Our station in Louisville is Randall Magee's Livery in the middle of town. Photographers are setting up their equipment and taking pictures. Men, women, and children crowd across the street to watch the excitement, while thick black smoke rises from the stacks of steamboats along the river a few blocks away. After I'm done checking on my stallion, I go to doctoring my legs, as far away from newspapermen, race officials, other riders, and curious citizens as I can get.

In the empty stall next to Taos Lightning's, I pull off my boots, pull down britches and bloomers and undo the wrappings. The salve stinks, but don't . . . *doesn't* burn, and I'm getting good at putting it on fast when nobody's looking. 'Course when it's crowded like it was in Glasgow and E-town, it's harder to find privacy.

As I'm finishing up, I hear Arena's voice. I start wrapping my legs as fast as I can manage, wipe the extra salve on the bloomers, and start pulling up my pants.

Her voice is fading, so I guess she's not coming this way. Then a voice calls out. Arena answers. She's talking to somebody, and she sounds excited.

'Course, it takes me forever to get the boots jammed on my feet, but then I'm standing, brushing the straw and hay off my clothes, running my salve-slicked hands over my hair, and pulling on my hat. I almost forget the jar of salve, and that wastes more time as I hurry back, fit it in the saddlebags, then pick up my chaps I accidentally knocked down, and toss them over my saddle and tack. Seems like an eternity later, I'm walking out of the barn and making myself smile.

"Evan!" Arena calls out. "Look who's here."

Salvador Narcisco de la Rosa looks about as happy to see me as I am glad to find him here. He bows slightly, releasing Arena's hand which he no doubt had brought to his lips again, and pulls on his black hat.

"*Buenos tardes*," he says.

"*Gracias*." He looks surprised, must have forgotten that I'm from New Mexico.

"*Señor* de la Rosa wants to take us to supper," Arena says, and the look on the Spaniard's face tells me he don't want all of us to go eat with him.

"Good," I hear myself saying, mainly for spite, but I also figure I need to protect Arena from her protector. "I'm half starved," I say too loudly.

Salvador tightens the stampede string on his hat. Something else tightening around this gent's throat would please me more.

Salvador Narcisco de la Rosa brung us . . . *takes* us to this fancy restaurant that has a balcony overlooking the river. They got candles in the center of the table, and the most comfortable chair I've ever sat in. The Spaniard orders something, and before you know it, the waiter brings over three tumblers of amber liquid with some green plant floating atop the ice.

Ice! In this hot city. They must have an ice plant somewhere.

Salvador lifts his glass to his lips and smiles after a taste. A quick nod sends the waiter off to another table, and the Spaniard gestures at our glasses. "My young American friends, there is no match for a fine Spanish wine. I have tried the wines in Missouri and New York. In Mississippi, someone poured a glass of muscadine wine. He swore it was the best in your United States. I wanted to spit it out. But this . . ." He holds the glass higher, and waits for me and Arena to pick up our drinks.

He sips again. "To taste this has made my journey across the Atlantic and most of your country worth it." He smiles over his glass at Arena. "That, and to have made your acquaintance, *la patrona*." He extends his glass, and Arena clinks hers against his. Hesitating, I follow suit.

We drink.

"Mint juleps!" Arena sings out. She takes a bigger swallow.

"You have had these before, *señorita*?"

She laughs in her drink. "Salvador, I've had practically everything before. Except muscadine wine, I reckon."

It ain't a bad drink. Sweet, with a little burn, like the green or red chiles we eat back home.

"What do you think, Evan?" Arena asks.

I look at her empty glass while Salvador snaps his fingers at the waiter, and points at the glass she holds. The waiter nods and heads for the bar of this fancy eating house.

As the Spaniard empties his own glass, I shoot down the mint julep. It's all right to be sipping this drink, but once I swallow most of my glass, my stomach catches fire. Somehow, I manage not to cough, and the snot don't drip out my nostrils. My heart starts pounding, and I draw in a deep breath. About the time I've let it out, the waiter's taking three more glasses off his tray.

Arena picks hers up. She's got that look in her eyes again, and she leans over at me and asks: "Evan, have you ever drunk liquor before?"

"Sure," I answer as I pick up the glass. What I say ain't no lie. Pa might've left some beer in a stein or bottle, and I gave them a taste. And once when this Mexican boy named Raul and me was helping Pa round up some stallions, he dared me to take a snootful of some of the old man's forty-rod. The beer didn't blind me, and, like I've done said, this mint julep has a bit of a sweet, refreshing taste to it. As long as I don't gulp it down.

"It's bourbon," Arena tells me. "Kentucky bourbon."

"And, my young friends, we are in Kentucky," Salvador says.

As soon as I wake up, I feel sorry for the stable boy who gets to muck out this stall next to Taos Lightning's. I roll over in my own vomit. The smell makes me gag, and I push myself up on my arms, and spray more vomit atop what I've already deposited. Straw and hay and who knows what are stuck on the side of my face, my clothes reek, and my head feels like there's an entire railroad crew laying track from one ear to the other, and from my nose to the back of my brains.

Not that I ever had no brains.

As my eyes open, those sledge-hammers inside my head start pounding harder. Takes a long while for things to come into focus, but all I really see is those mint juleps and whatever we ate for supper that's congealing in the muck inside the stall. The banging in my head don't quit, and I finally realize that it's Taos Lightning kicking the stall.

I try to stand, but can't. The stallion's moving around now, snorting, all fired up and mad about something. I bend my head, and try to throw up. 'Course, nothing's left in my stomach by this time, so it feels like what I'm trying to do is get my stomach and guts and throat out of my body.

I wish I was dead. No joke. Even burning in the fiery pit can't be as bad as this. Soon I tell God that I don't mean it

"Taos Lightning, what the devil's got into you?" I say.

A shout makes my head hurt a ton worse. Moaning, I put my hands over my ears.

The voice hollers even louder: "Arena! Miss Arena. I've found him! Hurry. He's in here!"

My face is clean. Well, it has been cleaned. My mouth tastes like the most awfullest stuff a body could think of.

"Evan . . . Evan . . . Evan . . . my poor, sweet knight. I'm . . . so . . . sorry."

Somebody has my head in a bear trap. I want to pull away, but I smell something sweet. And it ain't a mint julep.

"What the hell did you do to him, Miss Arena?" someone asks.

Then Arena's crying. I don't want her to cry. I just want to die. She's trying to explain, but I only catch a few words here and there: "Mint juleps." . . . "Salvador . . ." . . . "Marie-Ange's Bistro on the Ohio . . ."

Then there's a whole lot of blasphemy, and I recognize Dindie Remo's voice. He's yelling, pounding his fist in his palm, as he's shouting: "This kid ain't never had no liquor, Miss Arena. You fill him up with bourbon? Whose idea was that? Yours? That conniving Spanish son-of-a- . . . ?"

"Shut up," I hear myself saying, even though I feel like gagging again. "Just shut up, will you!"

"Evan . . ." Arena's talking again, and all I can think is: *Why don't God just strike me dead now?*

"I'm sorry," she's saying. "I didn't think."

"You never think." Remo's still blistering mad. "You just let that bottle do the thinking for you."

Now Arena's sobbing again. I want to punch that Negro-Seminole in the mouth. But I can't even stand up.

"Where's Salvador?" Arena asks.

"He rode out at daybreak," Remo answers. "Did he tell you he'd take you with him?"

"No! Please, Dindie . . . it wasn't . . ."

"You try to poison all your friends?" he asks Arena.

"Dindie!"

I start recollecting some of what happened last night, and I make myself speak. "It was . . . my . . . fault."

Which ain't a falsehood. I could've told the Spaniard and Arena that I couldn't join them for supper, and I sure didn't have to take all them drinks of sugar, mint, and bourbon.

"Let me get you some coffee," Remo says. "Drink it down. It'll be black, strong, and good for you."

I'm afraid to shake my head, so I manage to tell Remo: "I can't hold nothing down right now, Dindie." I squint and see the sun shining through the door of the barn. "What time is it?" I ask.

"Nine, nine-fifteen, something like that," he says.

Which makes me utter a couple of oaths.

"What are you two doing here?" I demand.

"We'll ride out together," Arena tells me.

"No, you ain't. You ain't . . ." I stop, take some deep breaths, make sure I ain't about to start heaving again. God, why was I so stupid last night? "You ain't losing this race on account of me, Arena. Go on. Just go on. I'll catch up."

They both protest.

"Get! Scat. Ride on, ride on," I tell them.

"You can't . . . ," Arena starts, but I've already pulled myself up. I look around for my hat. Arena figures out what I'm doing, looks around for my hat, and picks it up. She starts to try to put it on my head, but I stop her.

"Not yet," I say.

A bucket of water is sitting in the stall. I reckon they brung it to clean me up. It'll do. It'll have to do. I splash water on my face. It feels so good, I could keep right on doing this for hours, but there ain't that much water in the bucket.

"I'll saddle Taos Lightning," Dindie Remo says.

"I'll help," Arena adds.

"No," I tell them, but they don't listen.

Deep down, I'm glad they saddled my horse. I'd still be back in Louisville, most likely, if I had tried to put that rig on Taos Lightning's back.

The gent at the livery told me it was eleven-twenty when I started out. I've been in the saddle now for going on seven hours, which includes the two times I had to dismount and vomit coffee into some ditch.

Mosquitoes pester me as I sit in the saddle, sweating out that bad-smelling bourbon sweat, wondering if I'll live to see **Station, No Facilities**.

The troopers at Fort Union used to talk about

forty miles on beans and hay. I've been trying to do what they said they did. Twenty minutes at a trot. Walk. Lead. Gallop for a short while to give the horses a good stretch. Rest for five minutes.

"Six hours of that," I recollect a bowlegged trooper telling me, "and you've got twenty-five miles covered."

Now, I've been doing more loping for this race, but I figure that if a bunch of horse soldiers can do twenty-five miles in six hours, maybe I can do forty-one in ten.

Still, when you're sick as a dog with a head that feels like it got knocked wide open with a singletree, a trotting horse ain't comfortable. Ain't even humane.

Night has fallen. My stomach don't ache so much, but my buttocks sure does.

I've lost the map. Don't even know how, where, or when, but the station is supposed to be alongside this road. Finally I see lanterns glowing along the right-hand side.

The scent of coffee strikes me. It don't make me sick. I keep Taos Lightning at a trot, and don't rein up till I'm through the gate. Nobody's here. Maybe this ain't the right place, but why would someone leave a bunch of lanterns hanging on a corral post. The place sure smells of horse apples. And coffee. I see the fire, but know my manners. You don't dismount till you've been invited.

Some man in long-handle underwear steps out of a canvas tent.

"Yes?" he asks.

"This the race station?" I ask.

"Oh." He goes back into his shelter without answering. I don't know what to think. A few moments later, however, he emerges again. Having pulled on his gaiters and a duster, he walks toward me. He holds some papers.

I look around. I don't know if this is the third or fourth stop since leaving Gallatin, but this sure isn't one of the home stations. I'm not sure anybody's here, except this little fellow.

"Do you know what time it is?" he demands.

It strikes me then. I've ridden over the ten-hour limit. I just lost this race. I just lost our spread in New Mexico.

"What's your name?" he demands.

"Kendrick," I tell him. I feel like I'm about to throw up again.

"Kendrick. Kendrick." He's walking to the nearest lantern.

"Where's everybody else?" I ask.

At first, he don't seem to listen. Then he's pulls out a big gold watch from the pocket in his duster.

Absently, he says: "Most rode out after checking in. From here, it's a sixty-mile ride to Cincinnati, the next home station, and most of them . . ." He squints and leans closer to the paper. "Aha. Kendrick."

Here it comes. I try to steady myself for the kick I'm about to get.

"You left at eleven-twenty in the morning," he says. He brings his watch closer to his eyes. His mouth moves as he does ciphering in his head. His head shakes. I'm about to die.

"You're blessed, Kendrick. Came in with two minutes to spare."

This little fellow ain't . . . *isn't* a bad sort once you get a cup of coffee inside him. He has punched my card and handed me a map. He makes pretty good coffee, too, but he don't have any biscuits or crackers lying around for a body to eat. I think my stomach can hold solid food now. Hold anything, as long as it ain't Kentucky bourbon.

"Sixty miles to Cincinnati," I say, looking at the map as the man in the long-handles and duster throws more logs on the fire.

"The road should be good," he says, "but here's what you need to know."

I lower the cup of black coffee.

"The home station is directly across the river in Cincinnati. The ferryboat, named the *City of Fountains*, crosses the river."

Good, I'm thinking. *I don't have to swim the river, because it looked really wide back in Louisville.*

"You'll never make the first crossing. That's . . ."—he checks his gold watch—

"eight hours from now. The next departure is at one-eleven and arrives at one-thirty on the Cincinnati side."

So I have to be at the crossing by . . . Now I feel that kick.

"When's the next ferry after that one?" I ask.

"Seven-thirty." He goes on to explain why the ferry only crosses in the morning, afternoon, and evening. I don't rightly care about that. "But you can sleep in, get a start after sunrise, and be able to catch the evening ferry, and . . ."

"And," I interrupt him, "be behind all those riders who made the first couple of ferries."

I curse Kentucky bourbon, mint juleps, my own stupidity, and Salvador Narcisco de la Rosa.

"Well . . ."—the man refreshes my coffee— "you can always leave earlier."

I study him with suspicion.

"The rules say you must rest for one hour at this station. Since you're reached your maximum time limit for riding today, you must wait until tomorrow before you can continue." He brings the big watch up to his face.

"Tomorrow starts in . . . two hours and sixteen and a half minutes."

The wind blows hard against my face. My hat, to which I've added a stampede string, bounces on my back. I let Taos Lightning carry me toward Cincinnati.

Tired, I got a later start than I wanted. Told the jasper at the station to wake me up, but he was still asleep when I woke. But he did wish me luck as he wrote down the time when I rode out, and he yelled something else. "If you miss that ferry . . . !" But all I heard after that was Taos Lightning's hoof beats.

Now I ride. Nothing but a cup of coffee in my belly.

We lope down the Louisville-Cincinnati Pike. I wonder if I should slow Taos Lightning down, but there's nothing more comfortable than a good lope on this horse, and, well, there's a lot of ground to make up. My reins are long, and I realize the one on the left has gotten stuck between my leg and the saddle. Last thing I want to do is slow down, so I stand in the stirrups, and tug on the reins. It ain't . . . *it's not* an easy thing to do, to get reins out from underneath your leg that's scraping against the saddle when you're loping. I start to tell myself that what I'm doing is pure foolishness, and to rein in the stallion, get the reins where I want them, and kick this old boy into a trot for a while. We can lope later.

That's what I'm thinking.

Suddenly, I'm thinking: *Too late.*

I reckon a little yelp comes out of my mouth, followed by this moment when I know I'm flying through the air. This don't happen real slow. No, it's like *oh-bam-ouch-oomph.*

The pounding hoofs grow fainter and fainter. I'm seeing orange and red dots, but I'm breathing. My head hurts. My left arm throbs. This means one thing. "I'm alive," I say to myself.

The dots keep flashing, so I reckon my eyelids are screwed down tight. My left arm hurts the worstest, but I flex my fingers, and all of them move, not just on the right hand, but on the left, too. I tilt my head to the left, then right. This means my neck and back ain't broke. My left ankle turns my foot left, right. My right ankle turns that foot right, left. My eyes open, but quickly shut as I'm staring right into the sun, being flat on my back.

Finally, I sit up. Taos Lightning is still loping, rounding the bend about a quarter mile down the pike.

I cuss, sigh, and roll up the sleeve on the left arm. The skin's already turning purple, but now I watch as I wiggle my fingers. That's a boost of confidence, and I push myself to my feet.

Which hurts, but I don't fall.

I've had worse horse wrecks. But never at a worse time.

Staring down the pike, all I see is a long walk to loneliness. To defeat. I figure I'm closer to Cincinnati than that lonely way station, and there's nothing for me back there except coffee and one lonesome race official.

I start walking.

Once I make the first turn, I see another turn about five hundred yards away. That's my goal. Make that turn. Then I'll set another goal, figuring if I just do that, give myself little goals, just a bit of ground to walk, I'll be in Cincinnati before I know it. Like tomorrow. Or the next day.

When I make the next turn, I stop, blink, and stare in wonder.

Taos Lightning is just standing there, snorting and stamping his right forefoot.

This ain't . . . *isn't* the horse I've known. The old chuckle-headed liver chestnut would've been hightailing it for the high country till his heart burst. He swings his head this way and that. I expect him to gallop away, and give me a sideways glance as he snorts and neighs and keeps on toward the next bend in the road. But he just stands there, waiting.

Cautiously, I move closer. I get close enough to pick up the reins dragging on the ground. My left arm's really throbbing now, but I swing the reins over the stallion's head, and move to the horse's side. I straighten the saddle with a couple tugs, tighten the cinch, and whisper some endearments at this old widow-maker.

"You want to run, boy?" I ask, as I swing into the saddle.

CHAPTER TWENTY-THREE

Trot. Walk. Lope. Rest. Trot. Lope. Rest. Trot. Walk. Lope. Trot. Walk. Gallop. Lead. Rest. Lope.

The road swings north. I can see the town sitting on a bunch of hills. Can see smoke from the factories and from steamboats on the river. We gallop now. And I feel like throwing up again.

A ship, thick smoke belching from the twin stacks and the side-wheels churning up water, makes way from the Kentucky side for the city of Cincinnati.

Some stevedores, or whatever they are called, are walking away from the wooden pier.

I point, trying to keep Taos Lightning under control. This old boy still wants to run.

"Is that the *City of Fountains*?" I yell.

"Yes, sir," says one of the men.

"Is it the one- . . . ?" Only I can't recollect the exact time the ship was supposed to steam away.

The fellow knows. His head bobs. "Yes, sir. Next one don't leave here till seven-thirty. But if you . . ."

I don't hear the rest of what he's saying as I put the spurs to Taos Lightning. We charge out onto the bank, onto the wooden pier, and Taos Lightning don't even slow down. He leaps, and we make a massive wave and spray of water as we land in the Ohio River.

It don't take me no time at all to understand that I've just made the biggest mistake I've ever made in my life. Worse than drinking mint juleps. Worser than anything.

Horses ain't meant for this kind of swimming. The current's strong. My horse and me are being carried downstream, out of the wake of the *City of Fountains*. Taos Lightning ain't found bottom, and he won't. Water must be between ten and twenty feet deep around here. Folks in the back of the *City of Fountains* are gathering at the stern, pointing at me. Some wave hats. Some are probably making bets. The smart ones would be betting that me and my horse both drown.

I can feel Taos Lightning's legs churning. He's trying to gallop in this deep, cold, hard-flowing water. Pa once told me that some horses cotton to water. Some don't. Some are like fish. Most are like me. I'm wishing I had thought to lash my lariat to the saddle horn and around my waist, but it's too late to make that happen now. Both of my hands clutch the stallion's mane. I swallow mouthfuls of water. Try to spit them out. Feel like I'm choking. Suck in deep breaths whenever I can.

The captain of the ship keeps tooting his horn. Maybe he's sounding a warning for some fishermen to come help pull this crazy young fool and his horse out of the depths.

I start wondering how far it is across to the Ohio side. Has to be more than a hundred and fifty yards. Maybe closer to one-seventy-five. Or farther.

Taos Lightning takes short breaths into his lungs, lets the air out a lot longer. His back seems to want to invert itself, and he's using his chest and neck more for this long swim. I'm just turning my head this way and that, not about to let go of the chestnut's mane. I can't see the *City of Fountains* no more.

As I said, most horses I've known don't care much for water. A few I've rid have stepped into a creek river and had an urge to roll. I've crossed the Pecos when it's flooded a few times, but the Pecos is nothing compared to the Ohio.

Taos Lightning keeps snorting. Sometimes he almost sounds like he's happy. Other times he sounds like he's drowning. I just keep bouncing in the saddle or bobbing like a cork.

I kick my stirrups loose, bend my knees, pull my feet up out of the water. Might not be what I should've done, I quickly think, because if Taos Lightning's hoofs get tangled in the stirrups, then we're in big trouble. I know one thing about horses and water. Horses can't hold their breath. If their heads go under the surface, they drown.

The horn on the steamboat blows loud and

long. I cringe. Taos Lightning ain't one for noise, and I fear that we're both a long, long way from Ohio. I look to my right, don't see the steamboat. On my left, I see nothing but brown water.

Taos Lightning has gumption, I'll say that for him. He's not slowing down. He's snorting like crazy, but still swimming, or loping under water, trying to find bottom, and I'm losing my grip on the mane. I feel my body sliding off the stallion's back.

The wind whips my face. Water washes over my back. The motion of Taos Lightning's movements has changed, and I realize that he has found bottom. We are climbing out of the Ohio River. I start to slide back into the saddle, and my feet feel for the stirrups, but I give up.

My boots and legs splash into the river, and, clutching the reins, me and Taos Lightning walk up on the bank. I don't know where we are, how far we are from the landing for the *City of Fountains*, but I know my boots are on solid ground. I'm out of the water. So's Taos Lightning. We're both alive.

Shouts, curses, and cheers greet me. I'm on my knees now, sucking in deep breaths, wondering if I can ever fill my lungs to satisfaction. Taos Lightning's breathing is labored, too, but as water rolls down my face, I see what looks like an entire army racing down the bank. Far behind them, I spot the smokestacks of that side-wheeler.

I'm not sure how far we drifted downstream. I'm wondering what time it is as I can't remember when we left the station on the pike. I pat my vest pocket, and cuss. The Seth Thomas must be somewhere at the bottom of the Ohio River. So's the map.

I know I don't really need the map, but a chill travels up my backbone. I rise, hurry over to Taos Lightning, and my heart pounds as I open the nearest saddlebag. I let out the longest breath when I see the card that needs to be punched and recorded at this main station. I mutter a short prayer, and, hearing voices, I turn.

A hard shove sends me sprawling.

"Are you crazy?"

I sit up in the sand, my head pounding, and when my vision clears, I realize that it ain't . . . *isn't* Arena or Dindie Remo who just knocked me on my hindquarters.

"You swim a horse across that river?" Doc Jack says, looking pale. "Can you even swim yourself?"

Dindie Remo and Arena Lancaster aren't far behind the doc. The Spaniard is, too, and he's holding the reins to Taos Lightning. A couple of reporters keep scribbling, and an artist furiously sketches in his pad.

Staring at me, Dr. Patrick Jack keeps on yelling. "That was the most foolish stunt I've seen in this whole race, Evan. You could've killed yourself and your horse. What were you thinking?"

I'm cold from the water. My arm is throbbing from when I fell off my horse. I'm aching something fierce all over, and this tall, old Texan is yelling like a fire-and-brimstone preacher.

"I wasn't about to wait six hours or more for the next ferryboat to get me across the river," I bark right back. "That's what I was thinking! That if I want any chance at winning this race, I had to get across."

"Six hours?" Doc blinks back his astonishment. He manages to get his breathing under control as he stands over me. I flinch, expecting to get another good shove, but he's trying to calm hisself down now. He bites his lip, sighs.

Dindie Remo and Arena Lancaster lift me up off the bank of the Ohio.

"Evan . . . ," begins Doc Jack, his voice quieter now. It seems he still has trouble getting his lungs to work regular, but he steps aside and points at the river. "You didn't have to wait six hours to take the next ferry. Do you see that?" He points.

I look. Then I remember that stevedore trying to tell me something, but I hadn't listened, just raked Taos Lightning's sides with my spurs. Maybe the fellow in the union suit back at the way station had tried to tell me the same thing. Or maybe he was getting back at me by not mentioning that there was a bridge over the river.

Maybe that was his idea of a joke since I woke him up in the middle of the night.

"It's the suspension bridge," Doc Jack says. "It's been up for . . . oh, pushing twenty years, I suspect. Called the Cincinnati-Covington Bridge."

There it was, clear as day. I don't know how I didn't see it. The sandstone and limestone towers resemble woodcuts of the big bridges in Europe I've seen in magazines. Even from where I'm standing, I can make out men and horses and buggies, crossing from Kentucky to Cincinnati.

"Ten cents," Doc Jack said, "for horse and rider."

"Quite frugal of you, Evan," Dindie Remo says. "You saved a dime."

We check in with the race officials after a long walk. Taos Lightning's bleeding from both nostrils, but another horse doctor says that's normal after a horse swims. The vet promises he'll keep an eye on him. All the commotion causes a bit of a stir, though, because they can't quite figure out when I actually arrived at the station to be checked in. But the judges look at all the notes they have and figure that I'm within the ten-hour time limit. So I get a new card and a new map.

Jokes start popping up here and there about me and my "seahorse". As we start to eat supper, some newspaper and magazine reporters come up to talk to me about my latest feat. Dindie Remo and the other riders, including the Sale brothers, roll their eyes at the questions, so I don't tell those newspaper boys much.

Doc Jack still ain't laughing, so I ignore him. But he ought to've believed me when I said I didn't do that swim on purpose, that, had I seen that bridge and knowed the rules, I would've paid the dime to cross the suspension bridge.

While the racers and reporters at the table keep right on making their jokes, Doc Jack walks over to where we're having us a fine old time.

"Come here," he says. "I want to show you something."

"Who?" I ask.

"All of you."

The sun's starting to sink by this time, but everyone, including the reporters, follow Dr. Jack away from the camp on the bank of the Ohio and across a couple of streets.

We've been laughing most of the time, both at Remo's jokes and the stories that Spaniard keeps telling. I hate to admit it, but Salvador can be funny when he's not wooing Arena Lancaster or getting me roostered on mint juleps.

The smiles and the laughter stop, though, as Doc takes us up to a door marked: **Morgue**. My stomach's turning sickly again as Doc holds it open.

He takes us into a room, where he nods at a man wearing a coat that's not as white as his face. "You're not the only one to have missed the ferry, Evan," Doc says as he walks over to a table with a blanket drawn over it with something underneath. "It was last night," Doc continues. "He tried to swim the Ohio, too." Then Doc nods.

The white-faced man pulls the covering over the bloated man lying on a table.

"Oh . . ."

I feel for Arena Lancaster as she gasps and turns away. I don't turn, though. Can't take my eyes off the body. Can't figure out who it rightly is.

"This ain't funny, Doc!" Remo bellows.

Doc Jack don't back down, not one whit. "No, it's not funny, Remo. You've covered a thousand miles or more. You have less than eight hundred to go. Fifteen horses are dead. Do you think any one of those horses wanted to win this race? Two riders are dead. Is three thousand dollars worth dying for?"

Nobody says a word.

The body gets covered back up, and the pale fellow just stands there, waiting for us to leave.

We're all quiet for a time, until Remo asks Doc Jack: "Who was the other fellow who died, Doc?"

Doc shrugs. "A man from Louisiana. Struck by lightning. I don't recall his name. I guess that's the way of things in our country. We'll remember the winner. No one recalls the name of the losers." He lets out a strange laugh.

"I would like to know the name of *this* man, Doctor," the Spaniard says, nodding his head in the direction of the table. "I will ask my priest to remember him at Mass."

"His name?" Doc's voice sounds old now. Shaking his head, Doc answers: "His name was Aristide Voclain. He came from the Bouches-du-Rhône to ride a thousand miles from Galveston to Cincinnati, only to drown in the Ohio River in the dark of night."

The little Frenchman, I think. I should have recognized his jodhpurs right away.

"The Frenchie?" says Leonard Sale from where they stand in the back of the group. Then he snorts and says: "That's too bad, ain't it, Billy?"

I watch as Billy tries not to giggle.

Those two belong stretched out on that table, not that Frenchman.

"What became of the horse this man rode?" the Arab asks.

Doc shakes his head as I picture that cross-country runner. It don't seem right.

"At the bottom of the river," Doc says. "A long, long way from Salon-de-Provence."

It ain't . . . it's *not* easy to put a thing like that out of your mind, but Dindie Remo tells me and

Arena something once we're back in the camp. He says we can't do a thing about the horses that have died or the men who got killed. We just got to keep pushing on. It wasn't us who caused the lightning to strike that poor man and his horse, and we didn't send the little Frenchman and his cross-country horse diving into the river at night.

So we break out the map and study it.

"Sixty miles," Arena says. She pokes Dindie's map, which he has placed on the ground. "To Shawnee Farms."

"Three choices again," Remo says. "Not a one looks straight."

"This one crosses a lot of rivers and creeks," Arena says.

"This one seems to take the long way to get there," Remo says.

"What about this one?" I run a finger over a route I've been considering.

"Evan," Arena says, "that's a railroad track."

Remo laughs. "I don't know, Miss Arena, maybe Evan has a point. Be nice to sleep in a Pullman and maybe find a faro layout in the smoking car."

Arena sees something else, though. "You're serious, aren't you?"

"It's a straight line," I tell them.

"You ever try getting a horse to cross a bridge built for trains?" Arena asks.

"I don't think we'll have to," I say. "None of

those rivers look big on this map. I heard those Sale brothers ask a man outside the . . . that building"—I can't bring myself to say *morgue*—"about the country north and east of here."

Dindie Remo had been eavesdropping, too. He says: "Farm country. Some hills. Mostly flat or gently rolling. That's something railroad folks . . . those laying the tracks . . . would want."

We study the map closer. It looks like if we follow the railroad tracks, we'll have to cross something called the Little Miami River. There might be some creeks and small streams they left off the map, but the next big body of water we'll come to is the Rattlesnake, just before Shawnee Farms. We could cross that, head downstream from the railroad tracks, and ride into the next station. Maybe even ahead of the Sale brothers.

"Do you think anyone else will try that route?" Arena asks.

"We'll see if anyone lopes off to the northeast when they ride out in the morning," Remo says.

We don't know which way the two Texans go, because they leave shortly after midnight. The others, who leave before us, seem to be opting for the route with the fewest curves and rivers. We ride for the railroad tracks, putting our horses into a trot alongside the iron rails. We don't see any horse tracks. Don't even see a train or handcart. It's another good day for riding.

"Speak up more often, Evan," Remo says. "You ain't as dumb as I thought you were."

But Dindie Remo ain't saying that when we come to the Little Miami River, though. He's cussing me up and down and hisself for listening to a fool kid.

I can't see the Little Miami below, not down this steep ravine that's blanketed by scrub and timber and brambles that look sharper than Dindie Remo's Bowie knife.

Oh, the railroad tracks go straight across the cañon, but even if we could get our horses to walk over cross-ties between iron rails, we'd have a hard, hard time getting them to climb over the Baldwin locomotive that's sitting in the middle of the bridge, with a tender and a caboose behind it. Nobody's aboard, not in the engine or the caboose, and even if one of us knew how to get that thing moving, well, we'd still have to figure out how to get the horses across.

"Any ideas?" Remo barks.

"Let's just go south and pick up the first road," Arena says.

"We'd waste half the day," Remo says. "Wouldn't get to the station till tomorrow at best." He kicks dirt and rocks down toward the river.

"Well, the map ends with these tracks," Arena snaps right back. "So you want to gamble on finding something up there, and go around this . . . jungle?"

Remo stares at the green abyss, but we can't rightly see where it ends or what's beyond it. Besides, Remo points out: "North just takes us farther from where we need to go."

He glares at me again. "What about you, Kendrick? Got any other brilliant ideas?"

I point. "Down," I tell him. "Then up."

CHAPTER TWENTY-FOUR

You go mustanging in New Mexico Territory, you learn to ride down some trails—if you'd even call them trails—that are slick, steep, dangersome. Looking back on some of those trips, I'm not rightly sure Pa and me ever rode down, or up, anything quite like this.

The cañon cut by the Little Miami isn't wide at all, and it's not like we're jumping off the top of one of those buildings we saw in cities like Memphis, Cincinnati, or Louisville, but there's certainly nothing resembling a trail to the bottom. Plus, plenty of trees grow along the edges, and rocks cover the slopes on both sides.

We tighten our cinches, and I swing into the saddle first.

"Maybe . . . ," Arena begins, looking paler than I've ever seen her. "Should we . . . would . . . maybe we ought to lead the horses down."

Remo's saddle creaks as he hauls his lean frame onto the back of his blue roan. "Horses have better footing than we do. Better eyes, too."

"Just lean back in your saddle," I tell her, "and give Horse-Horse plenty of rein."

"I know how to ride," she snaps as she finds the stirrup and mounts.

I kick Taos Lightning a bit, and he moves to the edge of the big hole in the ground. He snorts, shakes his head. I don't blame him.

"What do you think?" I say, waiting for somebody smarter than me to call off this crazy idea.

Remo's pulling on his gauntlets. He takes a deep breath, and without glancing at me or Arena, says: "Been nice knowing you folks."

The blue roan starts down.

I wait about a minute. He's maybe thirty feet to my left before I jump Taos Lightning into the gorge. Arena's about twenty, twenty-five feet to my right. I don't know if she's coming or not, and I'm not about to glance behind me to find out.

Pebbles, rocks, and dust start cascading down to the river. I'm leaning as far back as I can, shifting my balance as Taos Lightning goes one way or the other. No longer can I see Dindie Remo because of all the dust our horses are kicking up, but I can see the fallen tree in front of me. I hold my breath. We're moving down too fast to stop, and I get ready to kick free of my stirrups and jump in case Taos Lightning starts to roll. Somehow, though, he manages to step over the tree with his forehoofs—it's not that big— and then brings his hind legs over.

I'm still in the saddle.

We reach a level spot, and this time I chance a

look over my shoulder. As the dust drifts toward the clear sky, I spot Arena and Horse-Horse. They're coming down. She's a good rider, and the palomino's a fine horse.

We're not on level ground anymore, but back to twisting and turning. I had hoped the descent would become less steep the deeper we got, but it's the other way around. We slide faster. I barely manage to push away a branch that almost whacks me in the throat, duck underneath another one, when I feel something cut through my shirt sleeve. I start to cuss, but a branch cuts off the oath by popping me in the mouth.

I spit blood, feel the salty taste on my tongue, but there's nothing I can do about the bleeding. All my effort is aimed on staying in my saddle. The Little Miami's just ahead of me now, and before I know it, Taos Lightning is standing in the water to his knees.

Looking back, I see Horse-Horse jumping the last four feet, almost spilling Arena from her seat, but she rights herself as the palomino slides on his haunches into the river, where he stops and stands.

Dindie Remo is a few yards over. He's gripping the saddle horn tightly, head bowed. I don't know if Negro-Seminole scouts pray, or if he's about to throw up. I feel like both praying and vomiting. I'm drenched in sweat, and dust on my face and hands begins to cake into mud.

"Nice view!" Remo calls out.

You can't see a thing except trees, dust, and the sky above us.

"They'll never find our bodies here." Arena's voice sounds a bit shaky. She's joking, I think.

I swing out of the saddle, my boots splashing in the Little Miami, and rub my stallion's neck. "You're a great horse, boy," I whisper. "Best I've ever rode. Now I just want you to get me back up on top. We make it, I'll give you a sugar cube and a carrot." I'd swiped a few cubes and a carrot at our last way station.

Bending down, I lift Taos Lightning's legs, checking the shoes, his hoofs. Wouldn't want a stone bruise on the trip up. His legs look good, aren't cut up too much.

"He all right?" Dindie Remo hollers. I nod, and watch as Remo and Arena check their horses.

"Yeah. Yours?"

"Fit as a fiddle," Remo says.

"Better than me!" Arena calls out.

There's no sense in putting off the climb up. We don't say anything, just step back into the saddles, and kick our horses into the river, then through the brush along the bank—I'm thanking Doc Jack for giving me chaps—and then we spread out again to start our climb up, Remo to my left, Arena to my right.

Never really considered myself lucky. I don't

play faro or poker or anything like that. But luck's with me this day.

Somehow, I pick the easiest way out of the cañon. I guess it's really Taos Lightning that picks the way. But *easiest* likely is not the right word to describe it. Taos Lightning doesn't struggle or stumble as much as Remo's gelding, or Arena's palomino.

I keep my weight forward, leaning toward the stallion's neck, still giving him plenty of rein and letting him choose his own path up the steep ridge. Rocks and dirt cascade down the hill toward the river as we climb. We've made it past the trees, so rocks and dirt are all we have to deal with now before reaching solid, level ground.

Then Arena screams. I turn, almost losing my seat. Could have tumbled right back down toward the Little Miami. I can see they're in trouble, Arena and Horse-Horse. The animal has stumbled, and Arena has been thrown. For a second, I fear the gelding will roll right over that feisty girl.

A quick glance tells me Dindie Remo has his hands full just trying to get out of this place alive, and I don't know if he even heard Arena above the sound of the falling stones and rocks sliding down.

I'm practically to the top, so I leap out of the saddle, yelling: "Go on, Taos! Go on!" Without looking back, I start to make my way to Horse-Horse and Arena, slipping and sliding as I go.

Like I said, I'm lucky today. Real lucky. I can't explain how this all happened, but I come sliding down toward Horse-Horse's left, reach out, and snag the reins. I bite down on my lip right where the branch clipped me and taste blood again. When I come to my knees, I wrap the reins around my right hand, wishing I had Dindie Remo's gauntlets. Pulling hard on the reins, I try to stand. Horse-Horse jerks me back down, but I lean back hard. Seems like the palomino's about to give up and go toppling down with the rocks and dirt to the bottom of the cañon.

When he stops, comes to his knees, and tries to stand, I have enough time to leap to my feet, too, and I start moving up and back toward the trail Taos Lightning had used, if you can even call it that.

"Grab his tail!" I shout at Arena as I continue to lead him. "Grab his tail! Let him pull you!"

Slip. Slide. Stagger. Keep moving. Up and over. Up and over. A few times I fall, but I don't stay down. Have to keep moving, pulling. Horse-Horse snorts, fights me all the time, till he figures out that he's moving out of this nightmare. The rising dust is blinding and choking me. I ain't sure where I am. Just know that I'm heading up.

Up.

Up.

Then I catch movement just ahead and to my left. As I squint, I see that it's Remo. He and his blue roan must've made it to the top, and now our pard is coming back down to help. As he raises his hands, I slowly understand that he's slipping the loop of his lariat over Horse-Horse's neck. Feeling the tug of the reins as the lariat slides over the palomino, I get pulled back. Horse-Horse starts to stagger again, but Dindie Remo's already lunging forward and up, the lariat digging into his shoulder as he moves. I tug harder on the reins. We pull, cussing and groaning.

Till Horse-Horse finds surer footing. Just a few feet more, I tell myself, and then Dindie Remo has reached the top. Horse-Horse explodes with a sudden leap and bursts forward. I lose my grip on the reins, land on rocks and dirt. Arena yells.

I roll over, trying to get up, to save Arena from tumbling all the way back down to the river, but she's beside me. My hand grasps her arm, and, gaining ground, I pull her toward the top as Remo comes down and reaches to me. We slip, slide, step again. Again. Up. Only to slide back ten or twelve feet, kicking more rocks down. I cough. I even laugh. And we try again. Again.

Move, I tell myself over and over.

My left hand latches onto a big root. I tug, and feel myself leaping up, landing on something that's not sliding down. I catch a glimpse of the three horses, breathing heavily, reins dragging the ground.

Then we're on solid ground, Arena and me. Level ground. I feel like kissing it with my bloody lip.

CHAPTER TWENTY-FIVE

We lead our horses into Shawnee Farms. A man in duck trousers and a porkpie hat greets us, welcomes us to his farm. It's a real farm. I see grain bins and fields that grow corn—acres and acres of it—during the summer. I smell coffee and cornbread. He tells us his name. I can't tell you what it is, though.

Another man asks for my card. I nod at the saddlebag, and stagger off toward the bench set up in front of a cellar that's probably filled with vegetables. There's two pots of coffee sitting over a fire. I find a keg of water. I drink the water that stings my busted lip. I let it run down my chin. I douse my head. I drink again, and then just stretch out my legs in front of me, leaning against the seat of the bench.

"Evan . . . ," Arena says as she kneels down beside me. "Did you hear what that man said?"

I don't know which man she means, and it doesn't matter right now.

"We're the first to arrive," she says.

My chest heaves. My legs and arms feel like every muscle and bone wants to pop out and run away. I don't answer her. Don't know what to say, or even if my voice box still works.

Dindie comes over and stretches out next to me. He offers me a cup of coffee.

Maybe my head shakes. I'm not rightly certain.

"Kendrick," he says, "we're leading the race. The Texans. The Spaniard. The Arab. They're all behind us."

I could care less right now.

"We've checked in, but we have to wait an hour. Maybe forty minutes now. But you can see forever in this country. There's no dust. We can ride another hour and seventeen minutes."

Arena bounces with excitement. "Put that much more distance between us and them," she says, a huge smile on her face.

I know what they're telling me. My mouth opens.

"Go on," I tell them both.

Arena freezes like a statue. "I'm not leaving you," she says in a whisper. "You got us here. *You*."

"Just sit here, Kendrick," Remo says. "Rest. I'll get your stallion ready. I'll come back in half an hour, then we'll put some food and coffee in our bellies before we put more ground behind us."

My head shakes again. "Go on," I tell them, a bit louder this time.

"Evan," Arena says, "we're ahead of everybody. We can stretch that lead."

Nope. They don't understand. I shake my head

again. I find enough energy to put some bark in my voice. "I'm not killing my horse," I say.

Remo gives Arena a look. He tries again. "We won't push them hard. Just . . ."

I don't let him finish. "I'm not riding my horse no more today. Not after all he did."

Anger comes into Dindie Remo's face. He stares at Arena, but then he shakes his head and smiles.

"You've growed some, Kendrick," he says as he pats my leg, a little too hard for my liking, but the sores aren't bothering me that much anymore. "Got smarter, too," he adds as he rises and draws in a deep breath, lets it out. "You're right. Those horses need to rest. We'll lick those Texans and that Spaniard tomorrow. Good and proper."

Arena starts to say something, but I don't know what it is because I drift off into sleep before I can ask her.

"Good morning, Evan."

My eyes shoot open. It's my father's voice I just heard, and I see Pa squatting over me, grinning, holding a steaming cup of coffee near my nose.

Maybe I've been dreaming. Maybe this whole race ain't nothing but a dream.

"Ready to ride?" a voice says.

But it's not Pa's voice.

I didn't really open my eyes before, I just thought I did, so I do now, and when they open, I don't see Pa, but Dindie Remo squatting in front of me. My hands must work without my brains knowing it, 'cause I'm holding the hot cup of coffee.

"Texans rode out about two, three in the morning," Remo says as he stands. "Rest of us are getting ready to go now. I've saddled that stallion of yours. You up for it?"

Another day in the saddle. My butt hurts just thinking about it.

Still, I let Dindie Remo pull me to my feet, and I don't spill much of the coffee. I see the Arab, the Spaniard, and a couple others. Arena's adjusting the cinch on Horse-Horse. I finish the coffee in about five or six swallows, leave the cup on the edge of the bench where I slept all night. Stiffly, I move to Taos Lightning, pat my vest to find the map and card in the bottom pocket that used to hold the watch till I lost it. I leave the map. The card I stick inside the saddlebag. Then I'm grabbing the reins and the horn, and I let out the heaviest sigh in the world.

How long have I been pulling myself into this saddle? My knees and legs ought to know what to do, but they don't want to co-operate. I think about grabbing hold of my left leg and lifting it to the stirrup, but my arms and shoulders revolt against that idea. And Taos Lightning's not a big horse. Not like I'm riding the Spaniard's Andalusian. That thing must stand sixteen hands.

I know I gotta find a stump or rock or anything that I can use to help me mount. Shorten the distance I have to pull myself up. I also know that I can't let Remo, Arena, and especially the other riders see me doing it. They'd give me grief the rest of the race. I'd be run all the way back to Mora County . . . in shame.

Letting out a breath, I look over the saddle. Arena has stepped onto a keg of nails the farmer brought over to her. Even standing on the keg, the farmer helps her into the saddle. Well, I think, I could use that keg. But Arena's a girl, I tell myself, and then hate myself for even thinking such a thing. This girl has ridden as far as any of us guys still in the race. She's showed her worth and saved my hide plenty of times. Still, I wish I had a keg and a farmer to boost me into the saddle.

Then I see the Spaniard. By thunder, that smooth-talking, dark-skinned *hombre* is stepping on piled-up sacks of potatoes to reach the stirrups of his big Andalusian. And Dindie Remo has walked his blue roan over to a little dip. He moves the horse so that the horse is standing in this little depression, but even he groans as he slowly climbs atop his gelding's back.

I see a stump, and take Taos Lightning over to it. Even with the stump, it's a struggle to get into the saddle, but I'm there. I've found my stirrups. The race official, with his suspenders hanging

CHAPTER TWENTY-SIX

We ride through a thunderstorm in Columbus, where our host at the station serves us something he calls a hamburger. Only it ain't ham or any part of a pig. It's like a fried beef cake, with onions, and served stuck between two slices of bread. It don't . . . *doesn't* taste half bad. Dindie Remo gulps down four. The Spaniard looks at his burger as if he's been handed a plate full of turnip greens. I hate turnip greens.

We ride through fields and farms, towns and cities, across forks and branches of creeks and rivers whose names I forget, as soon as we are past them. Over hills, past apple orchards. We wave at farmers and their families as they pull off alongside the road, or trail, or pike, on their way to town or church or wherever.

We swim our horses across the Chippewa Creek and ride ourselves dry. I am too tired to be scared.

We ride into a city called Akron, where we are treated like we are President Grover Cleveland. Reporters from newspapers swarm amongst us like bees. A man named Dyke gives us sacks of clay marbles that he says he makes at his toy company. Not wanting the extra weight, I hand mine to a little boy. He grins his few-teeth smile and runs off without thanking me. None of the newspaper or magazine reporters talk to me, but a bunch of women practically box in Arena. They treat her like she's a hero, and I reckon she is. They tell her that she's the best champion for women's suffrage—whatever that is—to hit this city since Sojourner Truth was here back in 'Fifty-One for the Women's Convention asking: "Ain't I a woman?"

I tell myself to learn what *suffrage* means and who Sojourner Truth is.

Doc Jack isn't here, so I get this rail-boned vet to look over Taos Lightning. Another horse doctor is giving Billy Sale a hard time about his quarter horse's health. They yell at each other, and I hear the doc tell him: "You touch the butt of that pistol one more time, young man, and I'll see you in jail. This isn't the West. This is Ohio. And we have laws."

Too bad Billy listens to him. I'd love to see him in jail.

"Lungs seem healthy. Heart beat is not abnormal."

I realize the old vet with the bushy Dundreary whiskers is talking to me.

"Minor abrasions on his legs, but that's to be expected. Overall, I'd say he's in remarkable condition." He sticks his doctoring stuff in his black satchel, signs a piece of paper, and hands it to me. "You wouldn't want to sell him, would you?"

Taking the paper I have to give to another official before he will give me my next map and new card, I just smile. "Not even for three thousand dollars, Doc."

We ride across the Grand River Valley, where the air turns cooler and the leaves have begun showing yellow. It strikes me that October must be approaching. Maybe it's already here—I should check the date penciled in on my race card when I have the chance—and that we are north. North. Almost to Canada. That this race will soon be over. But then what?

We ride to a town called Conneaut, where our way station is in front of the town meeting house, where the mayor gives us all a lengthy speech, saying how fitting it is that we should ride through this town on our historic race, because history has been made here before. Indians used the trail before the town was ever founded.

"Our ancestors used this trail on their march west. The only difference," he says, "is that you are going east. And you are riding horses."

He grins. Which means I guess that it's time to start clapping. The townfolk do, so we join them.

We walk. Yes, we walk, and climb into buckboards that haul us down Conneaut Creek to Lake Erie. We've been grumbling about this part of the race for some time, but we're pretty much all together so it's not like the Sale brothers or the Arab or the Spaniard, or even me, Arena, and Remo will get a jump ahead of anyone. We are told we have about an hour to rest before we can ride out toward Erie, Pennsylvania.

We aren't complaining once we arrive at Lake Erie.

We're amazed.

"Is this . . . the ocean?" I ask stupidly.

"*Lake* Erie," the Spaniard says, but he don't say it like I'm ignorant, though I am.

"You saw the ocean . . . at least the Gulf of Mexico, when this race started, boy," Leonard Sale says, and he makes me feel ignorant. Which I am.

"I didn't see anything in Galveston," I say, "except rain and clouds."

Remo comments: "Ain't that the truth."

"Canada's on the other side." Arena points across this biggest patch of water I've ever seen. Geese honk. Gulls—that's what Remo calls them—swoop across the water and settle on piers.

It's a wonderful thing to behold, and there's the artist from *Frank Leslie's Illustrated Newspaper* sketching us as we stare at this wonderful lake.

The chilling wind feels refreshing as it comes off the lake. Some women bring us lemon cookies and milk to eat and drink, which we do, and then we are loaded back in the wagons and returned to the meeting house.

We saddle our horses. The two Texans are the first to gallop out. We walk our horses a bit, before we climb out of the saddle and retighten the cinch, then somehow manage to pull ourselves back in the saddle. Our departing time is noted, and we leave Ohio for the Pennsylvania border just up the road.

We ride to Erie, Pennsylvania, where the old, wooden buildings need a fresh coat of paint. I imagine how cold this country must get this far north, how harsh the wind must feel around February.

Trains—must be at least a dozen—send up clouds of smoke over the city. Boats and barges rock in the lake. People don't pay us any mind, except the policemen, who yell at us to get off the tracks before we get killed, and to get to wherever we're going in a hurry.

We ride to Fredonia, New York, which also butts against Lake Erie, but is smaller than Erie. These buildings, too, are in need of fresh paint.

We ride. Feels like we've been riding forever.

CHAPTER TWENTY-SEVEN

Buffalo, New York, is big.

Weaving around buggies and carts and street cars, we find Cabell's Stables and slide off our horses.

Three German fellows with carts wave us over, each saying in a strong accent that his dachshund sausage is the best in the city. The sausages sure smell good, but anything would smell good right about now. Ignoring them, I lead Taos Lightning inside the brick building, looking for Doc Jack.

I don't see him. I end up getting the same vet who checked my horse back in Akron. He ain't a bad fellow. It's just that I would really like to find Doc Jack. It's important.

"Unsaddle the horse, Mister . . ."—the vet says as he looks at the card I've handed him— "Evans."

Evans? That ain't my name. He doesn't remember me. Still, I do what I'm told, heave the heavy saddle and blanket over the side of the stall. I'm about to ask the horse doctor something when my prayers are answered.

"Doctor Craig," says a familiar voice, "I'll take care of this one." It's Doc Jack and he adds: "There's a handsome young woman four stalls over. If you could see to her."

The old man starts smoothing his long whiskers, and says: "You're a man after my own heart, Patrick. I'd be delighted."

Doc Jack seems strange. A bit pale, he doesn't even look at me, just watches Dr. Craig leave the stall and head for Arena's. When his stunningly blue eyes look at me, I'm pretty nervous. His mouth opens, closes.

"Doc, you gotta check on Taos Lightning for me. Quick," I tell him.

I'm already moving toward the stallion, letting the liver chestnut smell my hand, then I'm rubbing him till my hand stops at the underside of Taos's belly. I wait for Doc to come over. He kneels, and sees where I'm pointing.

There's a sore that's kind of bloody, but it don't seem to be infected. He likely got it when we went up and down that cañon at the Little Miami River. I reckon I was so tired I didn't notice it till it got worse.

Frowning, Doc touches it with his finger, leans closer. "How long has this been here?" he asks.

I tell him I just noticed it this morning, but add when I figure it got started.

His eyes widen, and he turns. "You went down that cañon?"

I nod, adding: "With Arena and Dindie Remo."

He smiles only briefly. "They put that on the map to see if anyone would try it. I hear they parked a steam engine on the bridge. You could've been killed. . . ." He stops short, and studies the wound again.

I don't reply to that because I could've been killed swimming Taos Lightning across the Ohio. Or in that fire in Mississippi. Or when I got thrown. I could have been struck by lightning like that fellow from Louisiana.

"You still have some of that salve I gave you for your legs?" Doc asks as he stands, his knees popping.

"I'm about out, but I have a little left."

"I'll have another jar for you come morn. . . ." He smiles, but I know something's bothering him. "Loosen the cinch a notch," he tells me. "It's just a little cut. Nothing really to worry about, as long as it doesn't become infected. Use the salve before you saddle him and when you unsaddle."

I start to thank him, but then I'm aware of something. "You can put human medicine on a horse?"

Now his smile is genuine. "I don't know. I'm a veterinarian, Evan. But I've given horse medicine to a fifteen-year-old boy with leg issues." He reaches out and puts his hand on my shoulder. "Evan . . ." Taos Lightning snorts, interrupting him, and we both look at the little mustang. "You've grown up, Evan," Doc says. "The boy I first met in Galveston wouldn't have pointed out that little sore to a race official. He wouldn't have cared. What's another horse? Just something you

257

ride into the ground, and then you get another."

I feel like crying, so I don't say anything, just turn to rub Taos Lightning on the nose. The mustang's head rises quickly and bumps my chin, causing me to laugh.

"Maybe I'm smarter now," I say as I rub Taos's neck.

"I'm glad to hear that. Some people grow up without learning a thing. You've learned to respect that horse. And Taos Lightning knows you're worthy of his respect. Maybe you've both grown up."

I smile at the compliment, then I look again at Doc Jack. His face is tight, and his eyes are sad.

"You're going to have to grow up some more, son," he says slowly. "It's your father." He reaches inside his black coat and pulls out one of those yellow telegraph papers.

"Evan . . . he died."

It sounds crazy, but suddenly it's like I'm looking down at the two of us from above. It's like I'm outside myself, like I'm floating.

"Evan?" Doc Jack says.

Now I'm looking straight on at the vet, not looking down on him. I feel numb all over.

"How?" I hear myself ask.

The horse doctor sighs, shrugs. "He was . . . worn out, I guess."

I study Doc, then I say: "Why don't you tell me the truth?"

He frowns. "Does it matter?"

"I'd like to know."

Doc Jack sighs heavily as he backs up and leans against the stall, as if he needs support. He wets his lips a few times, starts but stops, and starts again, maybe considering what words to use.

"The telegraph . . ." Doc Jack's shakes his head, and then he just blurts it out. "He left the hospital. Found a saloon. Got drunk again, and fell down some steps." He pauses, but not for long. "A policeman found him the next morning. He was taken back to the hospital, but pneumonia had set in. There was nothing the doctors could do."

Well, what should I have expected? That he'd die like one of those martyred heroes of the Alamo?

"I've said this before, Evan, but it's worth saying again," Doc Jack tells me. "My wife used to tell me that a man who can't handle his liquor just lacks strong morals. My wife was smart in many ways . . . God rest her soul . . . but I have to disagree with her on this particular item. I know I'm in the minority here, but men who drink like your father have . . . well . . . I guess addiction is the proper term. Do you know what it means?"

I nod. "Pa said he was addicted to horses." Recalling him say that makes me smile.

"It's like a disease, this addiction," Doc Jack says after a bit of quiet. "Like a cancer, or an ulcer. They drink because they cannot stop, because like cancer, it grows . . . that need. And like a cancer, it can kill you. It wasn't that your father lacked proper morals, he was just like most people who drink and drink and drink. He was sick."

I know what he'll say next, so I say it for him.

"So now he's . . . well . . . he ain't suffering."

Doc only shrugs. "I don't know, Evan. I'd like to think so, but, truthfully, I just don't know."

I start thinking I've got to give Taos Lightning a good brushing, and put some of that salve on his cut. I have to remember to loosen my cinch a notch or so in the morning. I have to study this map. I've got so much to do. And this race is winding down.

Doc clears his throat before saying: "Evan."

I'm at the saddlebags, my back to the horse doctor. I let my shoulders sag. *Why don't you just leave me alone?* I think to myself.

He says my name again.

Slowly, I turn to face him.

"Mister Fox and Mister Baldwin have agreed to pay your way home. Taos Lightning will go with you."

It happens again. I see myself and Doc and my horse in this stall from above. I'm hearing his words, but I'm just not understanding what this tall Texan is telling me.

"You'll have to take a number of trains to

get to Galveston, where you can pick up your father's remains. This, too, has been taken care of by Misters Fox and Baldwin. They'll pay for transportation back to Las Vegas, New Mexico, and from there to your home. If that is where you wish for your father to rest."

I snap out of it, and I look at Doc, hard. "You're kicking me out of the race?" I say much too loudly.

"No . . . it's just . . . Evan, your father is dead," he answers.

"Race rules say once you're out, you're on your own," I remind him.

"Richard Fox said these were extraordinary circumstances."

"You talk him into this, Doc?" I look deep into his eyes, and add: "I thought you were a friend."

"Listen to me . . . ," he starts to say—

But I won't let him finish. "No!" I yell so loud Taos Lightning does a bit of a stutter step. I'm mad now. Mad as I've ever been. I step up real close to Dr. Patrick Jack. "You know why I'm running this race, Doc. If I don't win it, I ain't got no home to go back to."

But Doc's as fired up as me now. "What chance to you have at winning, Evan? That rider from the Arabian desert . . . that Spaniard and his Andalusian? Those are professional riders, son. They do this for a living, for the sport, because they have what it takes. You're still a boy. And those Sale brothers, they've been out in front almost all the way from Galveston. You finish this race, and, yes, you will be on your own. Richard Fox's generosity has its limits, especially when his bankers tell him how much this has cost him."

I lower my voice. "What chance do I have of winning? None, Doc. Nary a chance . . . if I don't try. If I quit."

Right then I see that reporter fellow whose sister is the schoolteacher outside the stall across from us. He's talking to a Kentuckian who rides a dun thoroughbred, but they're both looking in our direction. So is everybody else because we're shouting so loud at each other.

"You're leaving, Evan," Doc says as if it's final. "You're grieving now, and you don't know what you're saying. I'll see you and your stallion onto the train tomorrow."

"If you toss me out . . ."

"We're not tossing you out!" Doc shouts, then turns away from me. He pauses as he becomes aware of the people staring our way.

I get an idea in a flash, and I tell it to Dr. Patrick Jack as firmly as I can. "You make me leave, I'm telling that reporter over yonder. He writes for the *Daily Courier* here in Buffalo. He's always looking for a good story."

"You're going to blackmail us, Evan?" Doc says angrily as he turns back to me.

"I'm going to finish this race," I answer.

Neither of us says anything more as the reporter from the *Daily Courier* starts walking over. I don't blink. Doc suddenly looks about twenty years older.

"All right, Evan. It's your . . ." He stops. Was he going to say the word . . . *funeral?* The newsman from Buffalo stops at the gate to the stall.

"Doctor Jack, Evan . . . Bob Nott." He nods at me as he reintroduces hisself. "Might I have a few minutes of your time? I know this isn't an ideal time, considering your father's unfortunate . . ." He doesn't get the chance to finish his sentence.

"How did you know about Evan's father?" Doc yells.

The reporter backs away from the fire in Doc Jack's eyes. "Why, Mister Fox told me . . ."

"Fox," Doc says, and spits. "I thought he was showing that he had some generosity, some humanity in his belly. He's just after publicity. That conniving . . ." He pauses briefly before stating forcefully: "Put that in the paper, Nott, and you'll rue the day. Talk to Evan Kendrick. He's the story. He's who you want to interview. Not me. He's the kid who isn't quitting this race."

"What did you tell that fellow with the paper?" Dindie Remo asks.

We're sitting outside, me and Arena and Remo,

sipping lemonade and eating those dachshund sausages that look as funny as they sound, but make pretty good eating. We stare at the horses moving around the corral. New York horses aren't much to look at.

I sigh. "Nothing. Just that I was going to keep riding. He said he understood, and gave me a couple more newspaper articles about the race to read." I don't tell them that his sister couldn't come see me, and that Nott hisself wouldn't be following us to the finish line. He also told me that if I win, and I happened by Buffalo on the way back home, I should look him up.

I go back to my dachshund sausage.

"You want to talk, Evan?" Arena asks as I'm finishing it up.

I just shrug, then finally say: "I don't know."

"My father's still alive," Dindie Remo says, "but I know how you feel."

"How?" I snap.

"Because my two sons are dead," he answers very quietly.

I don't know what to say.

"Here's what I know," says Dindie Remo. "You grieve. You mourn. And at some point, you remember the good. Not the bad. That keeps you whole. Keeps you sane. Brings peace to you and . . ."—he looks away before going on—"the ones who have taken that journey."

"You didn't know my pa." Bitterness ain't

hidden in my voice. "There ain't much good to remember."

"I never knew my pa," Arena says, and curses under her breath. "Ma didn't know him, neither."

Dindie Remo lights his pipe. "My mother never knew her father," he says. "Her father was sold when she was but a baby. They were slaves. In one of the Carolinas, can't remember which one. Her brother, though, took her when she was maybe five, six years old, ran off. All the way to Florida. Joined up with the Seminoles. So here I am."

"My mother left me," I tell them. Can't figure why I'm telling my friends this, but mostly I'm wondering out loud why Ma could have done such a thing. "She didn't say one word, leave a note, nothing," I add. "She just ran off. Ran away. Now Pa's dead. I ain't got nobody."

"That's not true," Arena says.

I stare at her.

Remo says: "You got a good horse. I used to think that's all I ever needed. But I got wise in my old age."

"You have us," Arena says. Turning away, she rips off her bandanna and uses it to dab her eyes. Then she cusses some, and leans back against the corral. "I . . . want you . . . to know . . . something."

I move closer as she turns to face me.

"I ain't had . . . ain't touched a . . . bottle.

265

Not one drop. Since . . . since . . . that night in Louisville. It ain't easy . . . ain't easy at all. But . . . I'm so sorry, Evan."

I pull her close, and she buries her head against my shoulder. What do I do now? I want Remo to help me with her. But all Remo does is squeeze my shoulder. I smell the smoke from his pipe.

"Did y'all see the write-up in the New York *Clipper*?" he asks after some minutes have passed.

I've never even heard of the New York *Clipper*, and right now I have my hands full trying to figure out what I'm supposed to say to Arena to make her stop crying.

"Sporting journal," Remo says. "The write-up was mostly about the Sale brothers. A porter at one of those carts showed it to me this afternoon."

Arena finally pulls away. She blinks and sniffs and says: "Cart?"

Remo grins. "I've et about twenty of them dachshund sausages today. They's some tasty."

This makes Arena smile.

"What about the *Clipper*?" I ask.

Remo has managed to get Arena's attention off her crying.

"Well, I had to give the paper back to the porter," Remo says. "He just let me read it. And like I said, it's mostly about those two Texans. But there was one part I really liked, and wish I could show it to you. But it said . . . 'Three surprise contestants, still among the fourteen remaining, are Arena Lancaster, a wild young Texas girl, a veritable Helen of Troy who spurs a palomino gelding that runs like Kentucky Derby winner Ben Ali; Ian Kendrick . . .' Sorry, Evan, they got your name wrong. 'Ian Kendrick, the race's youngest entrant whose mustang stallion has shown amazing endurance and fortitude, equaled only by its master; and a half-breed Seminole Indian who won honors and glory fighting with our brave soldiers on the Western frontier.' "

"You remembered all that?" Arena says, then sniffs and dabs her nose.

"Got a good memory for things I read." He laughs and shakes his head. "I think I got most of it right. Maybe not. So I'm a half-breed Seminole? They left out the Negro part. Left out my name, too." He pulls his hand off my shoulder. "I wish that *Clipper* reporter had talked to me. I would've told him that I wouldn't still be in this race if it wasn't for my pards." He nods at us both. "I don't think all three of us would still be racing if we weren't . . . well . . . pards. Friends."

Arena smiles, then nods and asks me: "What are you thinking about?"

I guess she sees the way my eyes are moving. I'm stuck on something Dindie Remo just said that he read in that *Clipper*.

CHAPTER TWENTY-EIGHT

The next two days blur together. Pa's death hasn't really hit me yet. I wonder if it ever will.

I ride alone. Arena reined in a few miles back. She told us Horse-Horse was having trouble breathing. She wanted to rest him a while. She told us to keep going, that she'd catch up at the station in Rochester.

When she said that, Remo and I looked at each other, and said at the same time: "I'll stay."

"Neither one of you are staying," Arena said.

We didn't listen. We flipped a coin. Remo called it right, so he remained behind. I have to pity him. Arena was giving him an earful when I rode off.

Actually, I wish I'd called heads. Then I'd be back there. Instead, I ride alone.

Fifty-six had started. Twelve riders are left. I'm one of them. So are Arena Lancaster and Dindie Remo.

I think about the other nine. Billy Sale has fallen behind. I passed him about an hour ago. His brother Leonard is somewhere in front of me. The Arab. He's tough, and he's proud, and he knows what he's doing. I mean, both the rider and the stallion. Salvador Narcisco de la Rosa. That Spaniard might rile me with all his fancy talking and how he stares at Arena, but that Andalusian is always calm and proud.

The Kentuckian. I hadn't given that brown stallion much notice, but he has a deep chest, and at seventeen hands is the biggest horse left in the field. And the Kentuckian is shorter than I am. Don't weigh much more than a dried-out cholla.

And there's this funny little New Yorker who's riding this trotter. I'm not making this up. The horse, a bay about fifteen-and-a-half hands, is this new line of horses called Standardbreds and is said to have been sired by Hambletonian 10's great-grandson. Which I guess is pretty important stuff. I heard Doc Jack and another fellow saying that Standardbreds are meant to race little carts around. Harness racing is what it's called. They call these carts sulkies. But this fellow is riding his Standardbred. Trotting. How in blazes can a man tolerate a trot for maybe two thousand miles?

He's somewhere behind me, too.

There's a cowpuncher from western Montana who rides an Appaloosa mare. That's the only girl horse still in the race. The Californian is on a bay Tennessee Walking Horse. That roan has a gait that looks like the Californian is riding on a cloud, and I've never seen a horse that can keep running so fast, so long. The Californian, I fear, has been holding that roan back.

'Course, I've been doing the same with Taos Lightning.

Then there's the Irishman, but his horse, an Arab-thoroughbred cross, was suffering at our station last night, and I'm not sure that bay stud is going to be able to run anymore. Which I'd hate to see, because the Irishman's a real funny fellow. On the other hand, that would reduce the field to eleven.

I've made good time. I find the station at the base of a tree-lined hill. There's so many people around there, I get confused, and wonder if this might be a main station. No, that's not it. They punch my card and give me a map. They say after I rest an hour, I can continue on for one hour and fifty-four minutes. I'm told that Leonard Sale, the Arab, and the Spaniard have already left. The Californian is saddling his mount. Looks like he's about to leave.

"Why don't you go introduce yourself to Buffalo Bill," says the fellow who gives me the map.

"Huh?"

"Bill Cody. Buffalo Bill. Are you daft, boy? You don't know who Buffalo Bill is?"

Sure, I know. Everybody knows about Buffalo Bill. Next to Kit Carson and George Washington, he's about as famous as a body can get.

"Cody's promising that the winner of this race will get a contract with his Wild West show," the man says.

I can see Cody now, his long hair blowing in the wind, one enormous hat in his hand, dressed in a buckskin jacket and the tallest boots I've ever seen on a man, not to mention the biggest danged belt buckle. That thing must weigh fifty pounds. But it does keep Cody's belly flat.

"He just closed his run at Erastina on Staten Island," the race official goes on. "My sister saw him there. Cody plans to open a new show, including the *Drama of Civilization*, at Madison Square Garden this winter. You ought to go talk to him. You win the race, you could have a job with Buffalo Bill."

From the corner of my eye, I see the man wink at his partner. Just joshing me. He doesn't think I have a chance at winning. He doesn't know me at all. Or the mustang I ride.

Suddenly, I think about Pa. We were chasing horses on Glorieta Mesa, pretty far south for us, and he had this half-dime novel. Don't know where Pa found it, bought it, or stole it, but he handed it to me. It was a story about Buffalo Bill, all blood and thunder, and a lot of fun to read. I know, because that night, we sat around the campfire, and, since Pa didn't have any whiskey with him, he gave me that penny dreadful and said: "Evan, read this to me."

I have to walk away. My legs are stiff from riding, and when one of the race officials asks where I'm going, I just say I need to limber up my legs. I don't look back. I walk to the Erie Canal, sit down, put my boots in the water. I don't cry none. I just remember.

Dindie Remo was right. He said that I'd remember the good. And I do. Another memory comes to mind. Pa . . . and Ma . . . on my birthday. Gosh, I must've been only five or six years old. Ma had made a cake, but it turned out to be more like a mushy pancake. Pa had that gleam in his eye, and he spooned some of that soupy mixture into my mouth, another into Ma's, and finally one into his. And we all got to laughing and eating and Pa just kept shoveling that awful-looking, bad-tasting cake into our mouths till it was all gone.

Criminy. How long have I been sitting here?

Some city folks are walking along the side of the canal, and I jump up and hurry back to the station in my wet boots. There's Buffalo Bill Cody, surrounded by four newspapermen, one Indian, and two cowboys.

The man who gave me the map points to me and says: "We wondered where you got off to. You can ride out of here in five minutes."

"Bounce," Cody calls out, "saddle that mustang for this young *hombre*! It'll give me time to get acquainted with him." Then he holds out his hand to me. The gloves he wears are bright with beads, and his grip is firm. He's pumping my arm, saying stuff I don't make out because I'm trying to find that race fellow.

"Did Arena Lancaster and Dindie Remo check in yet?" I ask. Then, with Cody still working my arm, I turn and yell at the fellow he just sent to saddle Taos Lightning. "Not too tight on that cinch, mister!"

"I've read much about you, sonny," Cody says. "Heard a lot of grand stories about your daring, your spunk, and that brave-hearted mustang you ride. Yes, sir. You win this race, I'm sure we can reach an agreement that will satisfy you, me, and the millions who will flock to our show at Madison Square Garden."

I get my head back in line with the race man. "Did they?"

"No," he says. "No one has arrived since you came in."

Cody says something. A reporter asks a few questions. The Indian grunts. And here comes the fellow named Bounce, leading Taos Lightning.

"You ready?" the race official asks, and he finds his pencil to record the exact time I ride out.

I think: *I haven't even studied the map yet. I don't know where we're going.*

But first I check the cinch. Bounce is a fair hand, and he listens. The cinch is fine. I start to swing into the saddle, but then turn back toward the table where the official stands.

"I've got something like an hour and fifty minutes to ride today?"

"If you leave now, you'll have one hour, fifty-three." He looks impatient. Guess he really wants to mark that time down and get it over with and get me out of his hair.

"Can I ride back?" I ask.

The fellow lowers the pocket watch in his left hand. "Back?" he asks.

"Toward Batavia," I tell him. "I need to find Arena and Dindie. Make sure they're both all right."

"What in tarnation?" Buffalo Bill Cody asks.

The man sets the pocket watch on the table. He's got a disgusted look on his face like maybe he ate too many of them hamburgers or dachshund sausages.

"Well . . . I . . . well . . . yes, I suppose so. Sure. I mean, you can ride anywhere you want. But no longer than one hour and fifty-odd minutes. But I . . . I don't know if that means you have to rest another hour when you . . . ?"

I'm in the saddle now. I thank Buffalo Bill Cody. I thank Bounce. I thank the man I just befuddled, and I spur Taos Lightning on the road. I ride . . . west.

"He didn't want to eat much today," Arena tells me. "Didn't eat yesterday. But Horse-Horse . . . he's always been . . . finicky."

We're back at the Rochester station. Buffalo Bill and his performers are gone. So are most of the reporters. The good news is that I found Arena and Dindie Remo only a couple of miles from Rochester. The bad news is that the Kentuckian, the Montanan, and Billy Sale, who arrived after I rode back to find my friends, have already left for Port Byron, the next station on the way to wherever we're to finish this race.

Horse-Horse coughs. The race official frowns.

"He's still having trouble breathing," I observe.

"Yeah," Remo says. He looks at the race official. "Is there a horse doctor in this town?" He answers his own question. "Got to be. This is a big city. Can you get us a horse doctor?"

"Sir," the man says, "the next examination of the horses is . . . well . . . I'm not at liberty to say."

Remo grabs the fellow by the lapels of his vest, and practically jerks him over the table.

"Just tell me this, and you'll not give away any of your race's secrets . . . how many stops till we get to a horse doctor?"

"Three," he answers meekly.

"Three." Remo releases the man who staggers back and overturns the table, scattering his papers and pencils, and his pocket watch. The man quickly starts collecting his stuff before the wind scatters it.

"So we've got a hundred and fifty miles or so

before this girl's horse can get somebody to look at it?" Remo says to the official, who pales at the question.

"Actually, it's closer to two hundred miles," he finally answers. It's . . . the last . . . main station before the . . . finish."

Remo lets forth more cussing than I've ever heard.

"Dindie." Arena's soft voice seems out of place now. Me and Remo turn toward her. So does the race official, who is joined by other race officials who busy themselves collecting the scattered papers. "Do you know what's wrong with Horse-Horse?"

Remo sighs. "Not for certain, Miss Arena."

"But . . . ?" She's bracing herself.

"It's a lung sickness, maybe. We need a horse doc to tell us for sure."

I know what it is. "Strangles," I say.

Arena sinks to her knees, and buries her face in her hands.

I sit down by her, saying that it's not as bad as it sounds, that strangles hardly ever kill a horse.

"But," one of the race fellows adds, "it's very contagious."

I wish that man hadn't said that.

Then the man who started all this, who Remo wanted to rip apart, says: "Oh, dear. That man named Sale . . ."

"Who?" Remo demands. "What are you babbling about?"

"William T. Sale. Billy Sale. The fellow from Texas on the quarter-horse named Butch. His horse appeared to have difficulty breathing, too, before he rode out. And his horse had this awful . . . well . . . disgusting yellow pus running out of its nose."

Remo and I stare at each other. That's another symptom of strangles.

"Listen to me . . . ," I say as I stand up and move to the race fellows, who stare at me as though I've got a pistol aimed at them. "You need to send a telegraph to Port Byron. And where's the next home station?"

"I c-can't . . . ," sputters one of the men.

"I've never been in this state before," I tell him. "I don't know where anything is, and right now I don't care. But this is important."

"It would give you an unfair advantage," he says. "If you win the race and Mister Fox learned that I . . ."

I cut him off. "If you don't get Doctor Patrick Jack and the race promoters alerted, there might not be a horse left to win the race. You got any notion how contagious strangles can be?"

"Amsterdam," he says.

"Huh?"

"Amsterdam. It's the last home station. That's all I can say."

278

I point a finger at the official who looks the calmest, and tell him: "You send a telegraph to Port Byron. Make sure it gets to Doctor Patrick Jack as well as the race promoters. Tell them that Billy Sale's horse has strangles. That the horse needs to be kept away from other horses." I pause and look around, before I point to another of the checkpoint staff. "You find the best vet this burg's got. Not just any horse doctor. You get the best one. And you get him here. Now. *Pronto*. Or else."

"How do you feel, Miss Lancaster?"

The Rochester vet, Dr. Jackson, who doesn't look that many years older than me, is packing up his satchel, which is a colorful carpetbag. I thought all docs carry black bags.

"Oh . . ." Her voice sounds distant.

"I ask," Doc Jackson says, "because strangles can be passed from horse to human. Rare. But it has happened. Any fever? Congestion? Discharge?"

"I'm all right. Will Horse-Horse . . . ?" She can't finish.

"He's young and he's strong. He's just sick. He'll recover." The doctor closes his bag. "But I'm afraid his race is over."

"You sure, Doctor Jackson?" asks Buffalo Bill Cody, who has returned.

"You know strangles, Mister Cody," the young doctor says.

"I know a certain Texan that I'd like to strangle," Cody says. "Even if he wins, Billy Sale will not be appearing in my Wild West show. I promise you that."

"If that horse has strangles," Doc Jackson says, "he won't win. He might not make it to Port Byron. He certainly won't be racing on to Amsterdam."

Other racers have arrived, too, but not all will be moving on, including the Irishman.

"Gentlemen," a newly arrived race official says, "you realize that the ten-hour limit has expired. None of you may . . ." He shuts up when he realizes we already know what time it is.

"I guess I'll be going home now," Arena says. She makes herself smile at Remo and me. "You think you two can find your way without me?"

I can't even look at her. Feel like Taos Lightning just kicked me in the gut.

"You take care of yourself, Miss Arena," Remo says. He's patting his pockets for his pipe. His pipe is on the rock right in front of him. That's how lost Remo feels.

"Wish I . . . ," Arena starts to say, then sniffs before she can go on. "I wish I could see you two cross that finish line together."

"Don't you worry about that, little lady," Buffalo Bill says as he steps closer to us. "You will be in Rutland. This I promise you. I will get you there myself. Most definitely, you will witness the end of this race."

The race folks are all grimacing now. Bill Cody just told us that long-held secret to save us all from anarchists. Too bad they couldn't have saved Arena Lancaster and Horse-Horse from Billy Sale.

Rutland. Where in blazes is Rutland?

CHAPTER TWENTY-NINE

Feels like part of me is missing as I ride. I grieve. For Pa. For Arena Lancaster. Even for Horse-Horse.

We gallop past Billy Sale, who waves to us frantically over the horse he has ridden to death, shouting that we have to help him get his horse back up. Even that doesn't feel good, or like justice. Remo and I do not stop. We say nothing. We don't run our horses over that idiot, even though we'd like to.

We ride into a country of high hills and thick forests. We ride past black rocks and rough country and farms that are bigger than the ones we saw in Ohio and Tennessee. We ride toward a town called Amsterdam and, eventually, another burg named Rutland. We ride, Dindie Remo and me, without Arena Lancaster.

As we ride along the Erie Canal, I suddenly recall a song Pa used to sing. There's another good memory. As Remo and I lope along, I start to hum the music. Somehow the words form, and I see my father smiling, and I seem to hear him singing along with me.

> It seemed as if the Devil
> had his work in hand that night,

For all our oil was gone,
and our lamps they gave no light.
The clouds began to gather
and the rain began to fall,
And I wished myself off of that raging
    canal.

All of a sudden a skunk bolts out of the woods. Just like that, our horses are raging.

Four jumps. My backbone feels like it has cracked in thirty places, but my feet remain in the stirrups, and I'm gripping the reins for dear life. My teeth slam together. My jaw aches. My hands burn from the leather reins. I see the flash of black and white that must be the skunk, and I'm just praying that that varmint doesn't let go with his stinky spray. He doesn't, and he's soon gone. Taos Lightning is calming down when I hear the splash.

Somehow, I know what I need to do. What I have to do. Grabbing the lariat, I kick free of the stirrups and leap out of the saddle. Maybe Taos Lightning will bolt for parts unknown. Maybe he'll stay nearby—like he did when he tossed me that time. But, right now, I don't think about the horse. I just want to make sure Dindie Remo's all right.

He ain't.

Remo and his blue roan have plunged into the canal.

"Dindie!" I shout.

I see him come up, splashing and snorting, his face a mask of fear, his mouth spitting out brown water. Then he's gone again.

I see the blue roan come up pretty far downstream from Dindie Remo, and then he goes under again. My gut tightens.

I want to jump in to save Dindie, even though I know that would just get us both drowned. So I throw the rope at Dindie.

"Grab it!" I shout, but he can't hear me.

He's up, then under again. I haul up the wet rope. I make a loop, start swinging, and when Dindie Remo pops above the surface again, I let the lariat sail. The loop lands just over his head and outstretched arms. He starts to sink. I pull tight.

Folks will say this is brag, but it's not. It was nothing but luck. Or maybe . . . maybe it was Pa. Pa taught me how to rope before I could hardly walk.

I'm backing up, but Dindie, even dry, is too big for me. And soaked through now, he's too plumb scared and he's fighting me. I feel myself being dragged toward the edge. Remo's going to pull me into the Erie Canal, too, which means I'll drown just like he's going to.

Let go of the rope, my brain tells me.

But I can't. Either I'll save him, or we'll both die. I can't save him alone, though.

Suddenly, as if in answer to my prayer, I'm not alone. The Californian and the New Yorker are next to me, helping me save Remo. The Californian has wrapped his arms around me, and the New Yorker is bracing hisself on the edge of the bank, letting oaths fly as he tugs on that rope.

There's another splash. Someone who happened by has jumped into the canal to try to help Remo. Then more folks are rushing over to us. One helps with the rope. Another jumps into the canal. I'm hoping that those two are good swimmers, when I see a man running toward us. He's shouting that a boat drifting down the canal has changed course and is heading over toward the ruction in the water.

I thank God for putting so many people in the East.

"Come on," I tell Dindie, who is standing at the canal's edge, just staring down into the dark water. We can't see his horse. I can't say exactly where he went under the last time I saw him. "Come on. This isn't doing you any good, Dindie. He's . . . gone," I say.

"Ain't doing you no good, neither," he says. "Ride on to the station, kid. I'll be along directly."

"I'll take you in."

"No you won't. I'm not weighing you down. You ain't gonna lose this race because of me. Me and . . . that . . . *skunk!*" He laughs, though it's not funny.

"I won't leave you here, Dindie," I tell him.

"You will, even if I have to knock you out and lash you to the saddle, you're riding. I didn't come all this way, teaching you what you need to know, to let you turn fool white boy and lose this race. Get out of here. I'll see you at the end." He smiles, pats my shoulder, then nudges me over to Taos Lightning. "Rutland, Vermont. I promise you, I'll be there. Please, Evan. Ride on. You got to. For Miss Arena. For me. For your ownself."

A sickness almost overpowers me as I leave Dindie Remo.

As Taos Lightning moves faster, I remember more words to the song. This time, the lyrics put gall in my mouth. Maybe I jinxed my good friend by remembering that tune.

> But sad was the fate of our poor
>   devoted bark,
> For the rain kept on pouring and the
>   night it grew dark.
> The horses gave a stumble and the
>   driver gave squall,
> And they tumbled head over heels into
>   the raging canal.
> The Captain came on deck, with a voice
>   so clear and sound,

Saying, "Cut the horses loose, my boys,
  or else we'll all be drowned."
The driver swam to shore, although he
  was but small,
While the horses sank to rise no more in
  the raging canal.

I can't remember how I got where I am. Where I stopped. What the maps I received suggested I do. What I ate. If I ate.

Arena's bloomers are gone. With nothing hardly left but shredding patches of cloth, I wadded them up and left them in a trash dump in Syracuse. I ache all over. Taos Lightning is laboring as we cross this bridge. Some band starts making music. For one brief moment, I think I've won the race, that I'm riding into Rutland, Vermont, but I'm not. Hung with flags and bunting, this pretty little town of hills and trees and a baseball field greets me with a sign that says:

Welcome, Riders & Horses, to Amsterdam, New York

I find the baseball field that has been designated our last home station. I reckon they don't play baseball this time of year. Leaves are falling. It's cold. Haven't seen frost yet, but the other morning I did see my breath as I saddled Taos Lightning.

There are six of us left. That's it. No Dindie Remo. No Arena Lancaster.

The nasty Texan—Billy Sale's brother, Leonard—has the lead. The Arab. The Spaniard. The Montanan on the Appaloosa. The Kentuckian and his thoroughbred. And me.

No, it's not me. It's the mustang stallion I ride. He does all the work.

I hand in my card, and a black man takes Taos Lightning to see a vet while I'm given the final list of rules. If my horse passes the examination, we will start tomorrow morning with a long ride along the road to Saratoga Springs and then to Whitehall, New York. From there, we will proceed the next day to Rutland, Vermont. The first horse and rider to cross the finish line will win eternal glory and three thousand dollars.

Two photographers want to take my picture. Twice that many ink-slingers ask to talk to me. A saint of a woman hands me a cup of hot coffee. But I just walk away from the throng to the outfield, where, I'm told, the vets are examining the final six horses.

Those six horses hardly resemble the horses I saw back in Galveston. They've lost weight. Not a one without cuts and scars. Their coats look rough, but that could be due to the cooling temperatures. It's October, after all, and we're practically in Canada, or near about.

The sight of Doc Jack scribbling on a pad as he steps back from my liver chestnut does me a world of good. He sees me, and smiles.

The doc looks different, too. Thinner like all of us, and his hair looks grayer, his eyes are bloodshot, and he's sporting a couple of days' worth of hair growth on his chin. He hands a slip of paper from his pad to the Negro steward, who leads Taos Lightning away. Then Doc Jack makes a beeline for me.

The first words out of his mouth are: "Before you say it, I'll say it. I was wrong. You were right. Evan, I don't know how you managed to get this far, but here you are."

"How's Taos Lightning?" I ask.

That makes his eyes beam. "No sign of strangles. He's tired, but aren't we all? He could use a good watering and lots of grain, but I guess he can get that over the winter. The important question is . . . how are you?"

It hurts when I shrug.

"Two days and it's all over," Doc Jack reminds me.

Yeah, I think, *but they'll be the longest two days of my whole life.*

"You heard anything from Dindie or Arena?" I ask.

"Arena's horse will recover. So will the other two that had to pull out thanks to one stupid veterinarian who could have prevented this whole tragedy. Mister Baldwin fired that idiot on the spot. I would have shot him. But he's not to blame as much as that Billy Sale from Texas, who has no business even owning a horse."

"And Dindie?"

Doc puts his arm on my shoulder. "Why don't you ask him yourself? In two days in Rutland."

I straighten, and my eyes brighten. "You mean . . . ?"

"Richard Fox is bringing all the riders who made it as far as Rochester to watch the finish. You'll see him there."

"Yeah," I say, not feeling very sure that I'll make it, so I add: "If I make it that far. I don't know if Taos Lightning has any more speed left in him."

"Speed won't win the race now, my young friend. It's endurance. It's savvy." He looks over his shoulder. "The road from Whitehall to Rutland is horrible. It's been raining in that country. The rivers are swollen. And it was a wet spring and summer. The woods are thick. So, nobody will be galloping for long under those conditions. You'll wind around and up and down from here to Whitehall. You'll want to give your horse plenty of rein, let him run, feel the wind on his face. Like I say . . . you'll want to, but don't. Save him for the final twenty or thirty miles. You'll need every ounce of energy you both can muster."

"Are you supposed to be telling me stuff like that, Doc?"

He walks away. "I didn't tell you anything, Mister Kendrick, except that your horse has passed my inspection."

CHAPTER THIRTY

The air turns so cool it burns my lungs. Autumn has always made Taos Lightning a little spunky, and he wants to run, but I keep Doc Jack's words in my mind, and maintain a tight grip on the reins. We ride through Saratoga Springs, where even a cold, drizzling rain does not stop throngs from coming out and cheering us as we pass through. At least I ride through. I have to figure the Spaniard, Texan, and Arab came in before I did. As for the Kentuckian, I haven't seen him since this morning, when we pulled out of Amsterdam.

The roads begin to thin. The forests become thicker.

The hills turn steeper.

The wind blows colder.

I pull on my new yellow slicker that I got back in Amsterdam, tug my hat down lower, and wonder if this rain might turn to sleet.

It comes down harder.

No longer can I see the sun, hidden by towering trees and darkening clouds. This isn't the rain that greeted us in Galveston, or the thunderstorms that pounded us with hail in Tennessee. Or was that Kentucky?

I wonder if I've ridden longer than ten hours. I keep telling Taos Lightning that Whitehall has to be just around the bend. And when it's not, I nod my water-logged hat at the next curve. And the next. And the one after that.

This is the main road. And it's the only road. And in the mud, I make out the tracks of other horses. Two of those horses, by the looks of the prints, are loping. The other is walking.

No blaring brass bands, no flag-waving hordes of men, women, and children greet us in Whitehall. It's a fair-to-middling town compared to those big cities we've been passing through of late, but I guess Whitehall goes to sleep early. Or folks here don't like to stand in the rain.

Swinging out of the saddle at the railroad depot, I wonder if I'll be able to climb up again on the horse's back. I lug the saddlebags into the building, and hand my card to the man sitting by the fireplace. He punches it, and hands me the last map.

"This being the last leg," he says, "you all leave based on your arrival time. Ten minutes apart. Four of you so far. You go fourth."

I'm looking at the map. One road, but it winds, goes this way and that, crosses a few rivers or creeks. Other paths are marked away from the main road, but I don't see how we can get to those places. Looks like you have to go through some hills and, from the hills I saw before it grew too dark, that will take a lot of doing.

"Twenty-five miles?" I ask.

"Something like that," the man says, and yawns. "Some say it's a few miles longer."

I think about that horse soldier at Union. Trot twenty minutes, followed by a walk, then lead the horse a while. Gallop. Rest every hour for five minutes. Six hours, and you can cover twenty-five miles.

But if three fellows—Leonard Sale, the Spaniard, and the Arab—are ahead of me, they can do the same thing. And they'll have a ten-, twenty-, and thirty-minute head start on me. Which leaves me needing a miracle to catch up with those hard riders before Rutland.

"You can bunk by the fire with the others."

I turn and see at least one fellow in his soogan. "No sense in you men sleeping in the rain," the race clerk says.

"But my horse has to sleep in the rain?" I ask. I didn't see that quarter-horse, Arabian, or Andalusian hitched to the post in front of this old building.

"The livery's two blocks down," he says. "Just be here at daybreak."

My boots are soaked, my socks wet, and my feet freezing by the time I lead Taos Lightning into the livery. An old man with white hair to his shoulders takes the reins to my stallion. I can't make out what he says, but he leads my liver-chestnut mustang to a stall, while pointing out the coffee on a stove in his little office to me.

I'm too tired to drink. God bless that old man—he unsaddles Taos Lightning and starts to rub him down.

"I can do that," I tell him.

He stops to stare at me. "What you can do, boy, is sleep."

Turns out that Salvador Narcisco de la Rosa is *my* protector. He's kicking my bare feet, and calling out my name.

Rolling over, I stare at that Spaniard, who's tightening the hat's stampede string against his throat.

"*Buenos días, amigo.*" He grins at me. "It is time. To ride to glory."

I sit up quickly. The Spaniard's grin turns into a laugh, and he strides out into the dim light of early morning. It looks like it has stopped raining.

My socks are still wet, but I pull them on, or what's left of them, and somehow manage to get my boots on. I find my hat, but Taos Lightning and all my tack are gone. I step outside, smell coffee, and see five horses in front of the depot, saddled and ready.

Five! I blink. One's the Appaloosa. That

means the Montana cowhand got here sometime after I went to sleep, but there's no sign of the Kentuckian and his thoroughbred.

"The first rider, Leonard J. Sale of Texas, will leave in five minutes," a race official is saying as the horses paw. "All riders are to mount up now," he announces. "Wait your turn. Also, the ten-hour limit is off. You are to ride till you reach the finish. Good luck to you all."

No time for coffee. No time for hardly anything, though I do find a privy and empty my bladder. Then I'm putting a foot in the stirrup. Groaning and aching and just plain miserable, I settle my backside into the saddle.

Taos Lightning bucks.

I think maybe it's the weather. Then I have no time to think. My feet keep the stirrups, my butt comes out of the saddle and slams back onto it.

"Ride 'em, bub!" Leonard Sale yells, and laughs.

I pull the reins, try to keep Taos Lightning from ramming against another horse, causing some terrible wreck before the last day of the race can get started. He keeps bucking. Two. Three. Four. Five. Six times.

Then he does something he seldom does. He starts to roll.

There's no time to think. He's rolling to his left. I'm shun of those stirrups and diving to my right. Air whooshes out of my lungs as I land hard on the woodpile meant for either the locomotives that come through this burg or for the fireplaces during those long, long winters. The wood's wet, but that doesn't mean the wood's soft.

Hoofs pound the wet earth. People are shouting. The Montanan and the Spaniard come to me. I feel like maybe I can lay here for . . . well . . . forever.

"You all right, boy?" the Montanan asks.

My ribs hurt. Hurt bad on my right side. Breathing is becoming an agony.

"Got him!" somebody yells. I make myself roll over. The old man from the livery has lassoed Taos Lightning, who fights the lariat for a few minutes before finally settling down.

The Spaniard's hands reach under my shirt. His touch is cold, and I flinch. Somehow, I sit up. The Texan, Leonard Sale, shakes his head. He's still on his horse. The Arab has not turned around. He sits in his saddle.

"Rules are rules," the race executive says. "Mount up."

"You rode a good race, boy," the Montanan says. "Think those ribs are busted?" he asks Salvador.

"I cannot tell," the Spaniard says as he rises. "*Adiós*."

I make myself stand. I find my hat, but I can't bend over to grab it. This little tyke comes out of nowhere, runs across the street—his mother or sister screaming at him—and he picks up my hat and brings it to me.

God bless him.

When I get to Taos Lightning, I let him smell my hands, get my scent again, and I rub his neck. I'm not thinking about my ribs even though my breathing is ragged. If I can get one foot in the stirrup, I know I'll be fine. At least, I tell myself that.

My hands hold the horn, and that's as far as I'm getting. But that long-haired old codger from the livery is boosting me into the saddle. I get my leg over Taos Lightning's back, straighten, catch my breath, and spit off to the side.

"That ain't blood, boy, is it?" the old man asks.

Maybe he's joking, but maybe he ain't, so I wipe my lips, but don't see no red. Turning my head, I want to shake the fellow's hand, but I'm not sure I can bring my arm around that far. He holds something up toward me, between his thumb and pointer finger.

My eyes harden. It's a cocklebur.

"There's a sidewinder in this bunch, boy," he says. "Watch yourself."

"Go!" the race man yells, and I have to pull hard on the reins. It hurts to look, but there's Leonard Sale and his quarter-horse, loping down the road. The Arab walks his proud horse to the next spot in line. The Spaniard circles his Andalusian and bows at some of Whitehall's womenfolk on the boardwalk.

I sit, try to find a way breathing won't cause me to double over, all the while seething with rage.

I'm in trouble.

When I put Taos Lightning into a little lope, I feel all right for a while. My ribs start hurting, but I can't lope on this road anymore. Not only is it a quagmire, but rocks and timbers have rolled down across its path. Taos Lightning has to step over the débris, which makes my side torment me.

If I dismount, I know this for certain sure: I'll never be able to climb back into the saddle.

We stop. I turn the stallion so I can look back down the road. That Montanan ought to have caught up with me by now. Did he run into trouble? Did he try to cut across the hills and forests to one of those other roads?

Don't worry about who's behind you, I tell myself. *Focus on who's ahead of you. Or don't focus on anything but staying atop your horse and getting to Rutland.*

By thunder, what can I do?

It looks like half the mountain came down across the road. No way I can climb over it, and Taos Lightning's balking at the wreckage. I back the horse up and look for sign. Seems that two horses must've made it before the slide happened. Or maybe one or both got buried under that ton of rocks and brush and mud. Another left the trail here, and headed north. I study that hill, shaking my head. If Taos Lightning slips, I'm done for. So I take the reins and give him a little kick. There's enough clearance, maybe, for Taos Lightning to get around the slide. As long as he doesn't slip into the ditch, and I get knocked out of the saddle by a limb, maybe we can get around it—if the slide doesn't go on forever.

Again I'm thanking Doc Jack for the chaps as my legs scrape against the shards of black rocks and the broken branches on my left. I lean as far as I can to my right, ducking underneath tree branches on the side of the road. Then I see the end of the slide. A clear road, or as clear as it can be after all this rain. We come out onto it. I let Taos Lightning rest, lean over, despite the throbbing in my right side, and pat him.

"Thank you, boy," I whisper as again I notice the tracks of two horses. Those would have to be to the Arab and the Texan. I don't think that big Andalusian the Spaniard rides could have gotten through. So he must've tried to climb out to the north.

The Montanan? His horse might be able to squeeze through, but I don't think he can. Man must stand six-foot-four. Then again, he might not be traveling on this road. Don't reckon I have to worry about the Kentuckian, who still hadn't reached Whitehall by the time we all rode out this morning.

I laugh. That sends a bolt of lightning through my whole body. I don't have to worry about anyone right now. I'd best focus on getting out of this mess alive.

I let Taos Lightning walk along the road, which is narrow, with thick woods and towering hills on my right, and a sharp drop-off on the left where a river runs sharp and high. On the other side of the river are more hills, and I wonder if maybe I should just ride down that embankment, follow the river, hoping that it flows all the way to Rutland. Getting down that grade, though, might kill my mustang and me.

I dismiss that crazy idea and try to make out the signs. These tracks don't make sense.

Two horses were running, but it seems that, well . . . they're running real close to each other. Mud's dug up everywhere. Like they were . . .

Then I understand, draw a deep breath, which I immediately regret as spasms of pain cause me to groan. Then I hear something. Edging Taos Lightning closer to where the side of the road drops steeply toward the river, I see them both. I rein in Taos Lightning, who certainly doesn't want to get any closer.

Bringing my left hand to my lips, I call out: "Are

you all right?" Which again causes a lot of pain.

Maybe the roar of the stream prevents the Arab from hearing me. He just sits on the bank, cradling the head of that fine Arabian horse in his lap, stroking its forehead.

"Do you need a hand?" I yell.

This time, he looks up. His nose is bleeding. The wrappings around his head have come off. His robes are soaked, and he's just sitting there, with that wonderful, beautiful horse. Even with its busted legs and broken neck, that horse looks so marvelous. It should have won this race. Or, at least, made it to Rutland.

"Go," he says. "Go!"

I shake my head. "I can toss down the end of a lariat. I can pull you up."

Maybe I could. Maybe not. But I ought to try.

I don't know much about this man, or his kind, but he's proud. And he has done races like this one, even longer, so I know he's tough.

"Go. You might catch him," he says.

I can't just leave a man like that.

He must know what I'm thinking. "I will follow this." He motions at the water. "It will take me to . . ."—he struggles with the word—"Whitehall."

That's still a dangersome trip afoot.

"Go!" he barks now, angry, defiant, and even above the sound of the water, the shout causes Taos Lightning to stutter step.

"I'll tell them what happened!" I yell. "When I get there." Thinking: *If I get there.*

I start to follow the tracks made by the Texan— after he ran that great stallion and fine rider off the side of this cliff. Now I know who put that cocklebur under my saddle. The Arab calls out: "*Siddiq!*"

I don't rightly know what *siddiq* means, but it must be a compliment because the Arab's smiling. He looks practically human.

"Good . . . luck!" he shouts.

"Same to you," I say, as I tip my hat in salute, and ride off.

Well, now it's over. There's supposed to be a bridge across the river where it bends, but it's gone, washed out, leaving me with a thirty-foot plunge straight down, or climbing a hill with trees as thick as marble. Which is what the rocks on the base of the hill look like.

The Texan took the other side. That tells me that the Texan didn't destroy the bridge, which I had considered before I saw his tracks. He rode north. Can I make it that way, too? It looks real steep.

Then Taos Lightning starts snorting. He bucks. My ribs feel like they're tearing through my innards, and I grab the reins, pull tighter, and glimpse this giant bear charging out of the woods on the other side.

The animal slides to a stop. It seems to be just as scared of me and my horse as we are of it. But . . . it's not a bear. Although Taos Lightning is bucking, snorting, and kicking back, somehow I stay in the saddle. When I look back at the animal, I realize it is a giant moose. As I try to study the creature, never having seen one before, it turns and bolts right back into the wooded hills. It takes me a couple of minutes to get the stallion under control. My ribs are throbbing, my butt's aching, and I'm sore all over. I lean over, almost spray everything in my stomach over Taos Lightning's withers. I reach for the canteen, but lack the strength to lift it.

After several minutes, I give Taos Lightning, still a mite skittish, a little kick, and we ease our way over to where the moose disappeared.

I wet my lips.

The Texan went north. But if a moose with a rack of antlers that spread five feet or more can get through that thicket, then certainly a wiry little kid, who weighs less than a feather, and a puny mustang can get through, too.

Leaning as low in the saddle as I can, we start to follow what animal trail there is.

Taos Lightning has to leap over rocks. I duck underneath limbs. One knocks off my hat, but I don't care. I should dismount, but once I'm out of the saddle, I'm afoot forever. We climb, duck, scratch, bull our way through, and start going

CHAPTER THIRTY-ONE

Don't have any notion what day it is, where I am, hardly even who I am. I lean low in the saddle, my left hand wrapped around my body, clutching my ribs, my right hand gripping the reins loosely. I'm sweating and freezing at the same time. Half asleep. Feel more dead than alive.

The hoofs' soft sound turns harder. I hear the angels singing. No, it's a band.

My eyes open, and, though my vision's blurry, I make out buildings of dark granite, and red brick, and painted wood. Men, women, and children are lined up along the street as far as the eye can see. Flags are waving. I think I'm back in Saratoga Springs.

I try to straighten as much as I can, but the pain almost knocks me out of the saddle. My throat's so parched it hurts, and there's no spit in me to swallow. As I ride past people on the boardwalks, or even before I get to them, they fall silent.

Me and Taos Lightning must look a fright.

The band stops playing. I think: *Where's the Texan? Where's the Spaniard? Even the Montanan? They must be here already. Is this Rutland? Is this heaven?*

Ahead of me, I think I see Mr. Fox and Mr.

Baldwin holding a string of ribbons—red, white, and blue—that stretch across the street.

The finish line?

It can't be. Glancing behind me, I suck in a breath and that almost sends me onto the cobblestone street. A rider just appeared around the corner.

"Hurry, Evan!"

I look back. Is that Arena?

Then I see Pa. He's leaping down from the bandstand behind the finish line, where a bunch of photographers and newspaper people and all sorts of folks have gathered. He runs and ducks underneath the ribbons those two race organizers are holding.

My eyes blink. It ain't Pa. It's Dr. Patrick Jack.

Taos Lightning keeps staggering along.

Somebody else steps out of the crowd, off to my left. I can hardly make him out, but that hat I remember. A big Texas sombrero that dwarfs the fellow's head.

It's Billy Sale.

He shouts something. He pulls something out of his coat pocket. The woman next to him screams. People near Sale scatter, ducking and diving.

Sale is holding a revolver.

"That mustang ain't winnin' this race, pard!" That's what he's saying as he cocks that pistol. He points the barrel at Taos Lightning.

Although fear envelopes me, it doesn't paralyze me.

I dive. Taos Lightning turns away, scared, at the crowd, at the movement of that wild, horse-killing Texan. My body slams against Billy Sale, as his revolver roars. We crash to the ground, and now I'm really hurting. Billy Sale spins away. My side with the busted ribs feels like it's afire. I roll over, face up, try to sit up, but pain slams me back onto the cobblestones. My left hand clutches my side, and I can feel blood oozing through my fingers.

"Taos . . ." I try to sit up, but can't. Someone's holding me down.

"Lie still," Doc Jack is saying. "Lie still."

"Taos . . . ," I mumble.

Now, it seems like everybody's talking. People are moving all around me. I can't see my horse. Can't see if he's dead or alive.

"Evan! Evan! Evan!"

That's Arena's voice. She must have fought her way through all these people circling me, because suddenly she's at my side. She grips my hand that Doc Jack must've pulled away from my ribs, where I'm bleeding badly. She doesn't even care about the blood that's staining the sleeves of her pretty new dress.

"Taos?" I ask. My voice is quieter now.

"He's all right," Doc Jack says. "Dindie's got him."

I breathe easier, but even that hurts like blazes.

"Can you folks clear out?" Doc says. "Give this boy some room, some air. Just move back. Move. And somebody get a doctor. I'm a horse doctor. Get a doctor. The kid's been shot." He presses his hands against my side.

"It's a crease, Evan," Doc says. "We'll get you stitched up. You'll have a scar, though."

To match the powder burn on my side that fool on the Natchez Trace gave me, I want to say, but I can't get my mouth to work.

"But," the horse doctor says, "you busted your ribs up real good."

I smile, and whisper: "Done that earlier." Did *that, I mean,* I think to myself.

As I turn my head, I glimpse some men in dark suits and pith helmets as they drag Billy Sale across the street, him sobbing, his knees scraping against the cobblestones. I see Taos Lightning. Dindie Remo's holding him close, rubbing his free hand along his neck—just how Taos Lightning likes.

I look at Arena. She's biting her lip, tears are rolling down her cheeks, and she's looking at the street, too, but not at Dindie and my mustang.

The Spaniard rides into view. He looks about as tuckered out as I am. His horse doesn't look any better than Taos Lightning. Both rider and the Andalusian drag their way down this street

310

in Vermont. When they come up alongside me, Salvador pauses, and, for a second, I picture him getting off, leaving his big horse, and taking Taos Lightning across the finish line.

But that wouldn't fall under Mr. Fox's rules.

He doesn't say anything, doesn't nod or smile or shake his head. He just shoots me and Arena and Doc Jack a glance and nudges the stallion on.

Can't blame him. Like as not, he has people depending on him, betting on him, and he came from a lot farther away than I did for a chance at that three thousand dollars.

I wonder what became of that Montanan and the Kentuckian. They didn't win, neither. I hope the Arab makes it back to Whitehall. Hope Billy Sale rots in jail and that his brother remains lost in these Vermont woods forever.

The photographers take pictures. The crowd cheers, but it's not as loud as it had been earlier. The band's not playing. Then folks start coming closer to me, crowding me again, and Doc Jack can't do anything to stop them.

Well, it ain't every day that folks in Rutland, Vermont, get to see a half-dead wrangler from New Mexico lying on the street, bleeding from a gunshot wound, and a pretty girl holding his hand. This ought to please Mr. Fox for all the publicity he's going to get—and all kinds of wild stories and illustrations he'll be printing in his pink-paged publications.

"Will you people please give us some room?" Doc tries again. "And where's that doctor?"

I smile at Arena. I squeeze her hand.

Well, here I am. With busted ribs and my side plowed by a revolver's bullet. Got no three thousand dollars. No glory. No folks. And once word of this race's finish gets back to Mora County, New Mexico Territory, I won't even have a home.

None of that matters. Because I've got two mighty good friends in Arena Lancaster and Dindie Remo. Three, if you count Doc Jack—and I sure do.

I hear a whinny that I recognize. My eyes close, and I smile because I also have a horse, a wiry mustang stallion the color of trader's whiskey. A horse that can take me anywhere . . . as long as I treat him right.

AUTHOR'S NOTE

This novel is based on a horse race from Galveston, Texas, to Rutland, Vermont, reputedly held in 1886.

Frank T. Hopkins left accounts of the race, which he said he won on a seven-year-old dun stallion after thirty-one days in the saddle—and then waited roughly two more weeks before the second- and third-place winners arrived. No one else finished the race; fifty-six had started. Hopkins averaged fifty-eight miles a day.

The problem is that no one else left any account of that race. I first discovered that fact years ago when I began researching a possible magazine article about the Galveston-Rutland race. An archivist in Galveston responded to my query by saying that she just finished looking into that event for another journalist—and found absolutely nothing.

Allegedly sponsored by Richard K. Fox of the *National Police Gazette* and California investor "Lucky" Baldwin, the race was never documented in contemporary sources—not the Galveston or Rutland newspapers, not in sporting journals, not even in the *National Police Gazette*. No corroborating evidence has been found. Detractors say the lack of sources proves

Hopkins a fraud. Defenders argue that the race had to be kept on the hush-hush to keep animal-rights activists at bay.

Hopkins also claimed to have won a three-thousand-mile race, this one against a hundred other riders, in 1909 on another mustang in what today is Yemen. That story, or lie, was turned into *Hildago*, a 2004 movie starring Viggo Mortensen and Omar Sharif.

There's no corroborating documentation about Hopkins's victory in the Yemen desert, either.

Endurance races were held. The story my fictional Evan Kendrick tells about Francis X. Aubry is based on history. In 1848, Aubry bet $1,000 that he could ride from Santa Fe, New Mexico, to Independence, Missouri, in six days. He did it—all eight hundred miles—in five days, sixteen hours. Not on one horse, however. He arranged for relay stations roughly every hundred miles, but that's still quite a feat.

Also, in *The Great Endurance Horse Race* (Stagecoach Press, 1963), Jack Schaefer documented a six-hundred-mile race from Evanston, Wyoming, to Denver, Colorado, held in 1908.

Hopkins, as far as historians have found, never left a detailed route of the alleged 1886 race. Mississippi mud and Gallatin, Tennessee, were mentioned, so I included both in the novel. Most routes and stops I guessed at by studying maps—and cities I wanted to visit or revisit. I made that happen in the summer of 2017 when my son and I took our annual baseball trip, combining baseball with horse-race research. Buffalo Bill Cody came to mind while passing through Rochester, New York, where Cody lived for a while and where some Cody family members are buried. Putting "dachshund sausage" vendors in Buffalo hit me while dining at Ted's Hot Dogs, an institution in that New York city. The hamburgers came about after a lunch stop in Columbus, Ohio, at the Thurman Café. Several ideas popped into my head while heading from one ballpark to the next.

Hopkins claimed few of the incidents that appear in this novel, and the fire that destroyed much of Winona, Mississippi, actually happened in April 1888, not September 1886.

The Patrick Jack family history dates to the Texas revolution, but Patrick Jack, the veterinarian who appears in this novel, is fictional. Another Patrick Jack, a descendant of the famous Jack family, won an auction for the New Mexico Children's Foundation, which helps fund nonprofit children's organizations across the state. Mr. Jack bid a lot of money to have his name used in one of my novels, so I thank him for his generosity and patience.

Sources for this novel include Schaefer's aforementioned book; *The Mustangs* by J. Frank Dobie; *The Blood of the Arab* by Albert Wadsworth Harris; *Horse Facts* by Susan

ABOUT THE AUTHOR

Johnny D. Boggs has worked cattle, shot rapids in a canoe, hiked across mountains and deserts, traipsed around ghost towns, and spent hours poring over microfilm in library archives—all in the name of finding a good story. He's also one of two Western writers to have won seven Spur Awards from Western Writers of America (for his novels, *Camp Ford*, in 2006, *Doubtful Cañon*, in 2008, and *Hard Winter* in 2010, *Legacy of a Lawman*, *West Texas Kill*, both in 2012, *Return to Red River* in 2017, and his short story, "A Piano at Dead Man's Crossing", in 2002) as well as the Western Heritage Wrangler Award from the National Cowboy and Western Heritage Museum (for his novel, *Spark on the Prairie: The Trial of the Kiowa Chiefs*, in 2004). A native of South Carolina, Boggs spent almost fifteen years in Texas as a journalist at the Dallas *Times Herald* and Fort Worth *Star-Telegram* before moving to New Mexico in 1998 to concentrate full time on his novels. Author of dozens of published short stories, he has also written for more than fifty newspapers and magazines, and is a frequent contributor to *Boys' Life* and *True West*. His Western novels cover a wide range. *The Lonesome Chisholm Trail* (2000) is an authentic cattle-drive story, while *Lonely Trumpet* (2002) is an historical novel about the first black graduate of West Point. *The Despoilers* (2002) and *Ghost Legion* (2005) are set in the Carolina backcountry during the Revolutionary War. *The Big Fifty* (2003) chronicles the slaughter of buffalo on the southern plains in the 1870s, while *East of the Border* (2004) is a comedy about the theatrical offerings of Buffalo Bill Cody, Wild Bill Hickok, and Texas Jack Omohundro, and *Camp Ford* (2005) tells about a Civil War baseball game between Union prisoners of war and Confederate guards. "Boggs's narrative voice captures the old-fashioned style of the past," *Publishers Weekly* said, and *Booklist* called him "among the best Western writers at work today." Boggs lives with his wife Lisa and son Jack in Santa Fe. His website is www.johnnydboggs.com.

Center Point Large Print
600 Brooks Road / PO Box 1
Thorndike, ME 04986-0001 USA

(207) 568-3717

US & Canada:
1 800 929-9108
www.centerpointlargeprint.com